ABOUT THE SERIES

GEMS OF AMERICAN JEWISH LITERATURE is a new series devoted to books by Jewish writers that have made a significant contribution to Jewish culture. These works were highly praised and warmly received at the time of publication. The Jewish Publication Society is proud to republish them now with introductions by contemporary writers so that a new audience may have an opportunity to discover and enjoy these timeless books.

Other titles in the series:
Wasteland by Jo Sinclair
Allegra Maud Goldman by Edith Konecky
Leah by Seymour Epstein

Coat Upon A Stick

NORMAN FRUCHTER

INTRODUCTION BY GRACE PALEY

THE JEWISH PUBLICATION SOCIETY
Philadelphia • New York • Jerusalem   5747 • 1987

Coat Upon a Stick was originally published by Simon and Schuster, Inc., in 1962.

Library of Congress Cataloging in Publication Data

Fruchter, Norm, 1937–
   Coat upon a stick.
   (JPS gems of American Jewish literature)
   Originally published: New York : Simon and Schuster, 1963.
   I. Title.   II. Series.
PS3556.R77C6   1987   813'.54   87-3147
ISBN 0–8276–0291–X

Designed by Bill Donnelly

Introduction

Coat Upon a Stick is about an old man, a Jew living and praying in one of the last synagogues of the Lower East Side. His old body suffers pain; his soul, a thin little prayer-soaked soul, is starved by deceit and fear. It is terrified of memory. Throughout this book he is actually unable *not* to steal, cheat, or proudly outwit any adversary he may meet—at the newspaper stand or the supermarket. But these are only the little, ten-cent crimes of late, bitter poverty. (With the same furtiveness—as though ashamed—he secretly gives away his only coat to a friend in a wheelchair.) When young, he betrayed a young woman, robbed the man who helped him get to the United States from Russia, deceived his coworkers, chiseled his customers. He has never forgiven his son, Carl, who grew up with a burden of Orthodoxy too heavy for the second-generation boy. Carl has a sensible son of his own, about to be Bar Mitzvah. He tries to visit from time to guilty time, to make peace with his father's insulted love. The old man's rage against Carl for leaving home, the secure house of Jewish law, is a terrible sound in this book, an unforgiving cry torn out of the old man's throat again and again.

The other old men—and the rabbi too, in his cynical, hopeless way, are not much better, only a couple of dollars richer. Then, out of this narrow mean world that Norman Fruchter has shown us with relentless unsentimentality, Zitomer, one of their own, suddenly rises, ablaze with revelation. This congregation, he shouts, does not live by the Ten Commandments. They probably don't even know them. Do they understand that the commandments were given to Moses to guide the moral life of the people of Israel for the next thousands and thousands of years—to define them among barbarians—that the commandments are the basic law written by God's own hand in stone? Zitomer interrupts the services, stops to harangue the men at work in their stores, even in front of customers. Zitomer's voice is the scream of Amos, or maybe Micah, crying out against landlords and profiteers. Zitomer's name carries in its Russian parts the possible meanings "Jew," "to live," "peace," and "world." This may be accidental, but I hear it.

And so the central dialogues of the book are created. The Law of Moses and the prophets' dreams are set in opposition to the laws and strictures of the priests. Still, we may wonder—the book wonders—was it the moral law or was it the law of the priests that gathered the Jews up into a net, a net that kept most of them from falling into Rome and Christianity. During the hundreds of years of European Jew-hatred, that net must have seemed to be woven of the very fabric of God's love. The people turned inward, turned their backs to the oppressor and became fistfuls of men and women in a great dispersion, a people who for almost two millennia created communities that did not engage in and had little to do with aggressive war.

I said dialogues. And there *are* dialogues. *Coat Upon a Stick* is a very Jewish work, constantly talking. It believes that what happens inside a person's head is dialogue, not stream-of-consciousness or third-person reporting. Free association is just right for psychology, but these Jews are made of history, and they talk in long, hard sentences, especially to themselves. They *are* the tradition of argument and discussion learned in yeshivas and shuls. In the midst of ritual obedience they somehow keep the adversarial conversation going with themselves, with each other, or with the God who has always been pressed to answer questions, to be responsive. What *were* the final plans for Sodom? Should Israel or should Israel *not* have a king? The prophets themselves often felt unequal to their moral tasks, which occasionally included too much traveling. "Why me?" asked Jonah, and he went in the opposite direction.

But somewhere in Jewish consciousness, sour and sad, is God's recorded answer to Moses. After so much work and talk on the mountain, Moses longed only to see His face at least once. The answer: "No man shall see me and live." But finally God gives in a little (as usual). He offers, ". . . while my glory passes by . . . thou shalt see my back parts but my face shall not be seen. . . ." Thinking of that small, impoverished congregation in *Coat Upon a Stick*, I remembered that passage. Of course He may have said to Himself, "This is probably not the first Jewish joke, but it's a good one and should last this disobedient, argumentative people a couple of thousand years at least."

Coat Upon a Stick seems to happen on the famous Lower East Side, where once-dense populations of immigrants ate, slept, peddled, worked in small shops, picketed bosses, organized unions, made poems for newspapers. A world, in other words. That population has disappeared into the suburbs, into the massive buildings of the Upper West Side. The community is abandoned. Here and there blacks, poorer than these remnants of Jews, appear, house-cleaners of slums, or customers in the pathetic Jewish shops.

But where are the women in this book? A couple of land-ladies, a grumpy wife. There are no women in the synagogue's balcony, no old wives behind the *mechitsa*. The patriarchal law of the synagogue, the separation of the sexes, has turned to iron. No women come at all to the daily stitching and restitching of the law.

Also, where is Germany, the putrefaction of the Holocaust that has touched our Western bodies, slaughterer and slaughtered? Where is its taint? This book was written in the earliest '60s. The Holocaust, it's true, had not yet become that last call by aging survivors whose stories their children tear from them even when they don't, can't, won't, talk. "Tell us, tell us," the young beg. What was it like to be a Jew in those days in that place? Tell us before you die so we, the third and fourth generation, can be Jews again. The work of research and publication was not yet complete. Perhaps it—the word *Holocaust*—had not yet become its own definition. Still, Carl, the son, is a TV repairman, a job that was born in the post–World War II world—and he travels to his father's decimated community from the working-class suburbs of Queens.

The absence of the Holocaust, like the absence of women, works to throw the shul and its congregation up . . . up into the timeless air where true magic happens. True magic is always direct, which reminds me of the way in which Fruchter brings the figures of the old man's past to haunt him. "Haunt" is probably the wrong word, for they come not as dreams out of mist but by true magic. As a meaty rabbit leaps out of a real hat, the wife of the cheated friend (both long dead) visits, sits at his table, drinks tea, jumps youthfully to his kitchen counter, and refuses to leave until he screams, "Go! Go!" These scenes, together with the long internal conversations, give the book a certain rudeness, a forthright clarity.

Near the end, the old man visits Zitomer and his talking friends in their converted storefront. They too are old Jews—union organizers, Communists, bringing unfortunate memory of worker betrayal to the old man. They are no doubt prophets, too, who play chess and offer one another little illuminations of truth and utopian prophecies.

Somehow, the old man wants to know, has he been a good Jew? How *is* one to be a good Jew, a good person? Surely one can be both at the same time. The argument between the prophets and the priests isn't resolved. For those of us who came after or out of the generation that accepted the Enlightenment, who want to remain Jews in the Diaspora—it's important to know that these questions are still asked—probably more so now than when Fruchter's book was written.

The last time I saw Norman Fruchter was at a meeting of Brooklyn Parents for Peace, called to inform neighbors of the dangers of allowing nuclear naval carriers into New York harbors. He came late because he's a member of the local school board.

The first time I met Norman Fruchter we were in North Vietnam. It was 1969. We were traveling the length of North Vietnam on a dirt road called National Highway One. He, with a couple of others, was making a film about this journey, the lives of the Vietnamese people and the life of the devastated earth under American bombing. This is what impressed me: brains, anger, wit, kindness.

This extraordinary book had already been written—though I didn't know it at the time. If I *had* read it I would have seen Fruchter more clearly—a kind of American-born Zitomer, a Jew who, by definition, had a traditional obligation to be one of the creators of a just world.

The amazing final fact is that, having read this *Coat Upon a Stick* twice, I find myself talking to it. And every now and then, because it is a work that cannot do without dialogue, it answers me.

Grace Paley

Coat Upon A Stick

For my grandfather

An aged man is but a paltry thing,
A tattered coat upon a stick, unless
Soul clap its hands and sing, and louder sing
For every tatter in its mortal dress.

W. B. Yeats: SAILING TO BYZANTIUM

One

The old man stirred at the same time each morning. Somehow, in those thirty minutes between five-thirty and six, the old man began to sense the lumps and hollows of the cracking straw mattress arcing beneath his back, began to hear the creaking of the rusting bedsprings accompanying his breathing. The old man pushed his nose above the ridge of pillow and ran his tongue along the dry caked line of his lips. Dawn had already lightened his walls; cheerless gray light filtered through his window. The old man turned onto his right side, moaned, and opened his eyes. He had time left, more than a half-hour to huddle beneath the blanket and quilt and turn back toward sleep. But he knew that no matter how much he turned on the narrow bed, no matter how deeply he dug his face into the darkness of the pillow, he would not sleep. He stared into the half-light and listened to the steady wheeze of his breathing. All the other morning sounds escaped him. A milkman scraped the bottom of a metal milk carton against the top of another, an early morning delivery truck's roll of tires drifted up from the waterfront. The old man did not hear. Someone with heavy boots, home early from night shift or just starting out to work, sent up a whistling tune in time to the clip-clop of his foot-steps. A bird screeched, then twittered angrily. The old man did not hear. He had long ago taught himself to register only those sounds necessary to his daily routine: the voices of his acquaintances, the members of the congregation, and Rabbi Davis; the hum of approaching cars; the synagogue's telephone. From one of the third-floor windows across the street, a morning quarrel shrilled into threats and curses. The old man sighed, pulled the blanket above his forehead, squirmed onto his stomach, and screwed his eyes more tightly shut against the gray light.

His hands scratched at the wrinkled sheet. He tried to breathe slowly, deeply; whispered to himself to relax, to rest. But his breath rasped out of him in short bubbling shallows, and each time he inhaled he triggered fresh morning pains. His back was waking to its usual throbbing aches; his legs twitched and prickled beneath the blanket. The old man moaned again and turned back onto his side. A finger of pain poked along his right rib line. He held his breath. The aches across his back began to echo the pounding of his heart. His right leg, curled beneath him, twinged at the knee. The old man sensed a cramp but was afraid to straighten his leg for fear the shift would lock the cramp into place. The side of his nose itched. He rubbed his nose and chin against his shoulder and smelled the stale cloth of his pajama shirt. The blanket made a tent above his head, trapped his night breath and sweat and staleness from the sheet and pajamas he rarely changed, and sent the smells against his nose.

He dug his face into the clammy softness of the pillow. His right knee was still not cramped, but his back was alive with all its usual aches, and periodic fingers of pain moved across his ribs. He eased onto his back, drew the blanket down and tucked it underneath his chin. He opened his eyes. Another morning.

He pushed himself off the bed and padded across the floor to the stove. The bare floorboards curled his toes against the cold wood. He glanced out the window as he passed, but the shade was drawn over the window that belonged to the woman who wound the red *shmatta* around her hair. The old man fumbled the teakettle from the stove, ran cold water into its grimy top, then replaced the lid and set the kettle on the stove. He shook the matchbox. A few matches rattled. He slid the box open and struggled to force his fingers around one of the matches. The box shook in his hands. He slid the box farther out of its lid. A corner of his pajama sleeve brushed the box as his hands shook the match loose; the box fell to the floor, scattering the matches across the boards.

The old man rested his hand on the stove and stared down at the matches. Then he bent down very slowly, until he was almost squatting next to the stove, and wedged one of the matches between his fingers. He groped for the box with the other hand, found it, and slowly straightened. He struck the match very carefully, so that it lit the first time, and forced the burner on. The gas caught flame, hesitated, then circled the burner and glowed a steady blue-yellow. He moved the tea-kettle so that it covered the flame.

The water boiled swiftly. The old man took down the box of tea bags, set one in the cracked glass that stood on the drain-board, and put the glass on the porcelain-topped kitchen table. The sugar and the spoons sat on the shelf above the sink. The boiling water whistled in the teakettle's spout. The old man turned off the burner, lifted the kettle from the sink, and poured the water into the glass. He half filled the glass, stirred, and watched the water turn delicately to orange, then deep orange-brown. He filled the glass, shuffled back to the stove, and replaced the kettle.

He sat in his kitchen chair, feeling the rough wood where the paint had peeled through the thin cloth of his pajamas. He stared into the steam rising from the glass as he moved the spoon in its endless circle around the glass's rim. The dull scraping sound of the spoon against the cracked glass echoed the heartbeats he counted thundering against his ears. The steam rose in a fragile wavering column, up past the old man's nose toward the ceiling.

"It's still too hot to drink."

The old man stopped scraping the spoon against the side of the glass. Shmuel Yaakov stood against the stove, his arms spread downward, his hands propped against the charred porcelain.

The old man shook his head. "Go away. Go away."

Shmuel Yaakov chuckled. "Funny thing about tea. Takes such a short time to make, and such a long time to cool."

"Go away," the old man said. "Who asked you to come? And before breakfast yet? I can't even get up like a *mensch*, you have to come before I've even had my tea?"

Shmuel Yaakov straightened, took one step, then another, toward the table. "Of course, in the old country, we didn't have tea bags. I never saw a tea bag until I started coming to you. But they're very sensible, tea bags. Very practical. Very American."

The old man shut his eyes. He shut them very tightly and counted to ten. When he opened them, Shmuel Yaakov was so close to the table he felt he could reach out and touch the heavy, manure-stained sleeve of Shmuel Yaakov's coat.

"Go away!" the old man screamed. "For God's sake, go away!"

Shmuel Yaakov's coat began to fade. The old man shut his eyes again and counted very slowly, trying to seal his ears against all words and all laughter. "Go away," he murmured. "Go away. Three. Four. Five. Six. Go away. Seven. Eight. Nine. Go away. Ten!" He took a deep breath and listened. The room was quiet. "Go away," he whispered again, and opened his eyes.

Shmuel Yaakov was gone. The old man sniffed the stale air and thought that he could still smell the manure on Shmuel Yaakov's coat. "So. He's gone." He picked up the spoon and began to scrape once again around the sides of the glass. The steam still rose past his nose to the ceiling. Before breakfast yet, he thought. God knows how long they will keep going away when I tell them to. What will I do when they don't listen to me any more? What will I do then?

He shifted his leg against the bottom rung of the chair. They don't bother to listen to me now, he thought. They come whenever they want. Once upon a time, I was the boss. If I wanted to talk to one of them after dinner, Shmuel Yaakov or Smetyanov or Naomi, I just settled myself in the chair with a cup of tea and thought about them until they came. But now— now they just come whenever they feel like it. Thank God I can still get them to go.

He bent his face toward the tea until his nose was almost over the rim of the glass. Maybe it's cool enough. He set the spoon on the table and lifted the glass to his lips. He sipped. The hot liquid burned his lips and the tip of his tongue.

"Pffaugh!" He let the few drops dribble down his chin, and wiped his mouth with his pajama sleeve. "Too hot." He picked up the spoon and began to scrape it around the sides of the glass.

"Like I said," Shmuel Yaakov chuckled. "It takes such a short time to make, and such a long time to cool."

"No," the old man said. "No."

"Sometimes," a voice laughed from behind him, "sometimes I think they should invent lukewarm tea, for old men who have so much to do they don't have time to sit and wait for their tea to cool."

Shmuel Yaakov leaned against the stove, grinning down at the old man. "No," the old man said. He would not turn in his kitchen chair to look at the window, where the voice laughed. He did not have to turn. He could see, in the space behind his forehead, Naomi perched on the narrow ledge, swinging her stockinged feet back and forth against the radiator.

"I think that an old man is very lucky he has something important to do," Naomi said to Shmuel Yaakov. "Instead of rotting away in a dirty old room, like so many old men that got nothing important to do."

The old man tried to stare at the column of steam, rising more feebly now from the glass.

"Certainly. An old man is lucky to be a *shamos* at a synagogue. More than lucky. Honored." Shmuel Yaakov scratched at his head. "So many old men rot away their lives, but an old man who is a *shamos* at a synagogue is an honored and respected man."

"My father always wanted to be honored and respected. Well, maybe not honored," Naomi said, "but respected. Always he wanted to be respected. So I'm a butcher, so what? he used to say. A butcher's job is as important as any other job."

"Certainly a butcher's job is important. But not so important as a *shamos*. Without a *shamos*, how could you have a synagogue?"

"Go away," the old man mumbled. "Go away and don't come back until I want you to come back. Go away and leave me alone."

"My father always said that people would respect him because they knew he was an honest butcher. After all, he'd say, how many honest butchers are there? He said people would respect him because they knew he was honest."

"Go away," the old man said, a little louder. "Go away, both of you. Get out of my room. Leave me alone."

"But surely, surely," Shmuel Yaakov said, "no one imagines that a *shamos* isn't honest? How could a man become a *shamos* unless the rabbi and the whole congregation knew he was honest? A man who is a *shamos* is respected. He has to be respected. No one ever even wonders whether or not he's honest."

"Go away! Get out! Now! Right now!"

The old man lifted the spoon from the glass and threw it at Shmuel Yaakov. The spoon clattered off the wall, and the old man's hand slipped down to the table and knocked the tea glass. The glass seemed to teeter for a moment, then tumbled onto its side and sent the tea spilling across the table. The old man jerked away an instant before the tea poured off the ledge of the table down onto his chair, but he jerked backward, and the chair tipped, swayed, and crashed sideways to the floor. The old man screamed as the chair seat slammed into his legs, and screamed again as the floor thudded into his back. The tea was dripping over the side of the table. The old man scrambled over the chair and crawled along the floor until he bumped softly into the side board of the bed. He pulled himself up to his knees, eased his chest and shoulders onto the bed, and rolled so that his legs came up off the floor, grazed along the side board, and finally twisted until they rested on the bed. He lay on his side, one arm folded beneath him, breathing slowly and deeply. His legs ached where the chair seat had pinned them against the floor. His back throbbed. He moaned softly and opened his eyes. The stove and the table wavered as if the glass were still sending its column of steam curving toward the ceiling. But Shmuel Yaakov's stubby figure no longer stretched itself against the stove. The old man turned his head slowly, until he could see the window ledge. Naomi was gone.

The old man wriggled his arm out from underneath him and closed his eyes. So. At least they still go when I tell them to. But what will I do when they don't even go? He moaned again, softly. He closed his eyes, then opened them, and stared up at the ceiling.

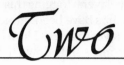

Two

Carl opens his eyes and the sun streams through the three-quarter closed Venetian blinds. Almost all the houses on Belmont Avenue now sport Venetian blinds, but Carl was among the first to get them. Actually, Carl thinks, Millie got the blinds. I never cared about the goddamn blinds. Carl glances sleepily along the pillow and there is Millie's humpy body, her head predictably shoved underneath the pillow. Carl watches her back's slow rise and fall, decides it's too early to get up, and turns toward the wall and the electric clock that hums a decibel or two above threshold level. When Millie first bought the clock to replace the old chipped wind-up that had ticked by Carl's night table for fifteen years and jangled him awake at six-thirty every morning except Sunday, Carl had missed its harsh metallic ticking. The alarm bell of the new electric clock burred like the bell of a diesel pulling out of a station way on the other side of town. Carl's mornings would begin at a station, the train burring softly as it pulled away, Carl in dream-flight skimming along the concrete ramp of the station platform, dream-shouting noiselessly, Wait for me. Wait for meeeeeeee!

But this Sunday morning Carl can sleep as late as he wants, and he murmurs smugly as he snuggles deeper beneath the covers. A whisper of uneasiness, a momentary fever of doubt, stirs under the warm layers fogging his brain; he has been dreaming, and his dreams have been unpleasant. But the whisper is too faint; the fever passes. He feels his mind sliding down, down, feathery-moss slide down to the spongy gray clay of his stomach. He sleeps.

The dream comes almost at once. The same dream, and Carl stirs; a pinpoint of consciousness commanding as many nerve connections as it can. But he is too deeply drawn into sleep to throw off the dream. He moves slowly above a waterfront, and in his dream's eye he sees the streets and alleys of the East Side that he played in as a boy. He drifts across the docks and the cobblestone streets that wind up from the riverfront and the afternoon shades quickly into evening. The street lamps flicker on and he can no longer see the littered surface of the streets. He hears the shouts and splashes from the docks and slips and bulkheads, and smells the garbage, garlic, dogshit, dirty laundry, man sweat and woman sweat and clogged sewers and rotting warehouses and rats and cockroaches that announce a summer evening. He listens to the hand bells of the ice-cream trucks, the quarrels in Italian, Polish, Yiddish, and German ringing off the tenement walls, and then he hears his own name shouted across the black oily surface of the water. He swoops down to find himself poised on the edge of a dock, his arms stretched awkwardly forward to touch trembling at fingertip. The water gurgles four feet beneath him.

"Carl is a scaredy! Carl is a scaredy!"

"Whatsa matter, Carl? You yellow?"

Dickie's white face bobs in the water.

"You're chicken, Carl. You're a scaredy."

"I'm comin'," Carl hears himself shout. "I'm comin'." His voice is weak and squeaky with fear, and from his dream-perch far above himself shaking on the dock, he wonders if he will dive. Then he feels his toes leaving the dock, and his dream-self wonders whether he is diving or jumping. But before he can decide, he is inside himself, falling, his stomach is whooshing toward his toes. His head jerks backward toward the dock, stretches in a bulging arc of a neck that grows and grows and grows. His stomach touches his toes and then shoots through the soles of his feet, thwopping into the water with a grinding splash that turns Carl onto his side in his sleep and forces a shallow moan through his lips. But he is far too deeply inside his dream to wake, and he rides himself down, down, deeper into the sticky darkness of the water. As it rolls over his head like some ponderous velvet curtain, he flails out with his feet and pushes himself to the surface.

"Hi! 'Bout time you came in."

Carl whooshes water out of his mouth, rubs the goop out of his eyes, and slicks his hair backward off his forehead. He grins at Dickie.

"Hi," he says.

"Let's race out to where Joey is. He's by the buoy."

"Okay."

The buoy is thirty feet away, across a shallow stretch that only the flat-bottomed barges can use, the bottom so silty and high you can walk on tiptoe all the way. Neither Joey nor Carl can swim; they dog-paddle toward the buoy, keeping their eyes and noses out of water, saving themselves for the last few flailing strokes when the race is won. The buoy bell clangs.

"C'mon, you slowpokes!" Joey yells.

Carl glances up to check his direction, sees the red glow of the buoy's tip about eight yards ahead and a touch to his left, and then feels the splashes as Dickie's arms and feet begin to pound at the water. He half dives, half pushes himself forward, beats at the black water with flailing windmill strokes, holding his breath and blindly tearing at the water until the buoy's metal side scrapes against his hand. He grabs at the bar and hoists himself up, sucking in air in huge hoarse gulps. Dickie splashes in the water behind him, and Carl turns to watch Dickie's head bob up, a good five feet to the left of the buoy.

"Hey, slowpoke," Joey yells. "You can come up now. The race is over. Carl won."

"I couldn't find the buoy. I got water in my eyes and I couldn't find the buoy."

"No excuses. Not fair to make excuses. Carl beat you fair and square."

"Not making excuses. I couldn't see the buoy, that's all."

Carl rubs more of the oily water out of his eyes, and as Dickie and Joey's voices fade, his dream-eyed watcher slips away from his boy's body perched on the buoy's side. Pools of reflected light from neon billboards atop the warehouses lining the river shine on the slick surface of the water. Fewer kids cluster on the docks and Carl hears less shouting from the streets that run west from the breakwaters. A cooler wind drifts across his face. Soon it will be time to go home.

"It's getting late," Dickie says.

"Yeah," Carl answers, from his dream-self far above the buoy.

"Hey, Carl. Carl! Ain't that your father?"

All Carl can see is the giant pointing finger of Joey's hand.

"Where?" he mumbles.

"Over there. On the dock, see. By the high wall near the warehouse. Standin' near the corner and lookin' out at us."

Carl's dream-glance soars across the water. Underneath the yellow light from a street lamp on the corner, his shoulders hunched and his head bent forward, Carl's father waits.

"Oh, shit!" Carl says.

"He's lookin' for you."

"Guess you'll hafta go in."

"No," Joey says. "Maybe you don't. Lookit, Carl, his eyes ain't very good. Get down quick. Into the water. Then move around here, back of the buoy. Away from the light. He can't see you there."

"Yeah. Hurry, Carl. Me'n Joey'll block the front of the buoy."

Carl's dream-eyes watch himself slip into the water and glide with a few strokes to the back of the buoy, where he crouches low in the water, hanging onto the buoy's side, with the bulk of the buoy's bottom between himself and the dock.

"You really think he can't see me?"

"He's not Superman, he ain't got X-ray vision. How's he s'posed to see through a stupid buoy?"

Catcalls and laughter from the shore. Carl hears whistles and jeers, but stays low in the water. "Carl," he hears his father call. "Carl."

"Caw-rhill," kids' voices mimic across the water, mocking his father's accent. "Caw-rill. Carill. Carole. Yoo-hoo, Carole. Beddie-bye, Carole."

"Carl," his father calls again. "Carl."

"Yoo-hoo, Carole honey. Carole."

Carl fights the anger and the shame that rise inside him until he can feel the pressure of the hot tears behind his eyes, and then soars out of himself crouched behind the buoy, sweeps over the water to his father on the dock. His father is staring out toward the buoy and the lights dotting the Brooklyn shore, and as Carl approaches he sighs and turns to stumble up the cobblestones.

Wait, Carl tries to say. Wait, Dad, wait!

But no sound moves past his lips. His father climbs the steps to the street and stops to stare back into the blackness of the river, shakes his head, and begins his shuffle home. Carl edges downward to stop his father, to touch him on the shoulder, to look into his face, but his fingers move through the cloth of his father's jacket and the flesh of his father's shoulder, and his father's face is set toward home, away from the river.

Carl feels the movement of his dream-self upward from the river and the docks and the tenements sweating in the nighttime summer heat, and as he begins the long spiral to wakefulness he makes a final grab for his father's figure. Wait, oh please, wait, he pleads, but he can hear nothing, not even the laughter from the kids lining the breakwater, and the inky lamplight-puddled black of the night turns cloudy-gray, yellow, and finally white as sunlight, and Carl is awake.

He stares at the sunlight filtering through the blinds. He is still himself as a child, and for a moment pain and sadness well so deeply in him that he whispers, "Wait!" to the dream-ghost of his father's stooping figure. Millie mumbles from the pillow beside him, and he sighs and thinks that his father is only thirty miles away, and yet, how long has it been? Two months? More, maybe. Carl sighs again. What good does it do to go see him, he thinks, and the sharp pain and ache of his little-boy sadness begin to ebb. It does any good to go see him? If it was a simple wrong that I did, long ago I could have said, Listen, I'm sorry, and that would've been the end of it. But it wasn't anything simple that I did. He was him, so he did his share, and I was me, so I did mine. And today my car sits in its garage here in Highland Park, and he sits in his little room with the dirty window, and we could be strangers, that's how close we are to each other. And who's to blame? Is it his fault? Is it my fault? But a splinter of sadness still sticks to a corner of his brain, and he wonders if he is afraid that maybe it is all his fault.

He turns onto his side and screws a glance up at the clock.

Nine-thirty. David is up by now, probably washed and dressed and downstairs setting the table as a surprise for us. Or maybe he's halfway down the street to Phil's, to buy the paper so he can read the comics. And the sports page. Carl turns again, this time to stare at Millie, curled into a curving lump with her hands tucked under her elbows. Let her sleep, he thinks. She's sleeping so soundly, what's the point to wake her? She's got nothing to do today; she can afford to sleep late.

Carl closes his eyes and tries to remember when the twisted angry quarrels with his father began. When I was thirteen. No, maybe even fourteen. He forces his eyes open as he feels himself drifting back into sleep. The taste of the dream is still strong inside him, and he thinks that he doesn't want to dream again. But his body is slipping backward, he has already lost touch with his toes and calves and his knees are easing away. He thinks to make a last attempt to fight off the drowsiness that is creeping over him, and decides to turn toward Millie, to jostle her so that she wakes and mumbles sleepily to him. But his sleep-will is too rooted, and before he can transform the impulse into a command that will go racing through all the arcs and connections down to the muscles of his arms and legs, sleep has numbed the nerves and blocked the channels of the brain, and Carl can only twist his head against the pillow as he drifts dreamward once again.

His dream-eye floats downward toward the same littered, cobbled streets, slows to a stop in daylight and watches a group of men shuffle toward a steaming metal pot on the back of a truck. He waits, dreading what Marcus's voice must surely say.

"Carl!" Marcus shouts, "Ain't that your father?"

And Carl stares at his father, slouched near the head of a shabby column of men, and tries to turn and race away down the street. But his feet, as always, refuse to move, are sunk into the pavement. His father turns from the steaming pot and the dirty-jacketed man with the huge ladle to stare first at Marcus and then at him.

"Carl," his father says.

Always, Carl's dream-self thinks. Always Carl. Why doesn't he let me alone? Did I tell him to go stand in a lousy soup line? Then he is blinking tears out of his eyes, and his father stretches his arm and then shuffles out of the line, toward him. Carl's feet jerk free of the sidewalk and send him pounding down the street to bury his face in Mrs. Rosenthal's starch-smelling sheets.

Then he was downstairs in the dining room, staring at Mrs. Rosenthal's seamy face with the fat cheek pouches that sucked inward when she talked. Once Carl had bet Joey that she kept acorns in her cheeks, like squirrels, and Joey had dared Carl to sneak into her bedroom and pinch her cheeks to find out.

"No," he said. "No, I never noticed. I never even noticed Dad wasn't eating with us. So how should I know where he eats?"

Mrs. Rosenthal shook her head. The loose gray hairs wavered before her eyes like a grasshopper's feelers. "Oy, what a kid you are! What a son. For three weeks now your own father skips not only his dinner, but his breakfast too, and you didn't even notice."

"So? It's a crime or something? Who am I supposed to be, Dick Tracy?"

"No, smartypants. You're supposed to be intelligent, that's all. Though God help me, I can't see any of it. But where do you think your father eats his meals, hey, smartypants? You think some other boardinghouse he's going to, because the prices are cheaper? You think he's eating out in a restaurant, everybody else is out pounding the pavements but your father got a raise, in the middle of the Depression he's making enough money, restaurants he can afford?"

Carl stared at the bobby pins struggling to hold down the gray knotty lumps of Mrs. Rosenthal's hair.

"He's not eating, smartypants, that's why you've got an empty head for not noticing. He's not eating because he doesn't have enough money to pay for both of you, so he stopped eating. And you're such a fine son you didn't even notice! A head like a sieve you've got. Like a sieve!"

Carl floats upstairs to cradle his head in the starch-smelling sheets again, in his pink room with the walls papered in chains of bonnets and flowerpots. Shouting drifts up from downstairs, and then the anger in his father's voice stirs him to listening.

"My business is my business," his father shouts. "You keep your big nose out of it."

"In my house I'll push my nose in whenever I feel like! What am I, a stranger, after seventeen years boarding with me, all of a sudden you can turn around and treat me like a landlady? Listen, I'm the closest thing that boy has to a mother, and don't you forget it! I'm the one who sat up with him all the nights he was sick and you were working overtime at Acme. I'm the one who wiped his bloody nose and told him next time not to go near the *goyim*. I'm the one who mends his clothes and makes sure he get to school on time and has to sit and eat with him two hours after my own dinner because you're too stubborn to come home and eat with him yourself. You think it's a decent way to bring up a kid, to leave him to eat by himself?"

"I have a choice, maybe, you're telling me all this? I'm the one who brought down the Stock Market? I'm the one who put half the men in New York out of work? I'm the one who shut down Acme Garments three months ago, who hangs NO WORK signs on all the dress factories on the East Side? What am I supposed to do?"

"You could eat, for a start. You could come home and eat. With your son. So you're out of work, so all right. So I know it, so I know also it's not your fault. You're not a stranger asking for credit, seventeen years I've known you. It's not long enough I can trust you for some food until you get work again? Come home and eat, don't worry about what it costs. I'm not starving; I can feed all of us until the stores shut."

"No. No debts. I'm not making debts. Carl's meals I can afford, once in a while I get some handbills, a job on a truck, it makes a little money. Him I can manage. But no debts. I don't want to owe nothing. How do I know how long this is going to last?"

"How do you know how long you'll last, not eating? You think you're a camel? Even camels eat; it's only water they go without."

"Camel, shmamel, I'm not eating, that's all. So let's stop talking about it, I'm not eating, and that's all. And don't say anything to the kid, either, you hear? Don't say a word to the kid. He should go on like he is, he shouldn't know anything about anything."

Carl creeps back to his bed, and wonders about the Crash

and the Depression. He wonders what they mean, those words, and why his father should be out of work, like Joey's father, and Marcus's, and Jerry's, and Sam's. Why can't somebody do something, he wonders, and listens to hear if they will start arguing again, his father and Mrs. Rosenthal. Then he is walking home from synagogue on a cold evening about a week later, and his father is asking him does he want to move, is he tired of Mrs. Rosenthal's.

"Tired?" Carl says. "Why should I be tired? I like it. I like my room. I like Mrs. Rosenthal."

His father shrugs his shoulders and they walk another block. "The food," his father says. "You haven't noticed the food, it doesn't taste so good any more?"

"You haven't been eating her food," Carl bursts out. "You haven't been home for a month, so how could you know what her food tastes like?"

"I eat, I eat. Don't worry, I eat. I just eat later now, that's all; I got to work longer hours at Acme, so I eat later. But I eat."

Carl walks on. He wants to tell his father that he knows about the Acme, that his father doesn't have to pretend, that he knows his father stopped eating to stay out of debt. But he keeps silent, afraid that his father will be very angry. They stop at an intersection. Carl stares across the street.

"If we moved," he says finally, "where would we move to?"

His father steps off the curb into the street. "I don't know. Somewhere in the neighborhood. Be nice to have a change. Changes are good for you, keep you from getting too used to things. And besides, Mrs. Rosenthal is an old busybody. Always poking her nose around. We'll go somewhere where the landlady minds her own business, where you have a nice room and some good food, for a change."

Carl shakes his head and kicks at a stone.

"Well?"

Carl kicks the stone again, and sends it scudding into the street. "Nothing."

But next morning Mrs. Rosenthal is waiting for him in the dining room, her face set like a storm cloud, wrinkles streaming in heavy black lines from all the corners.

"You're moving. Your father told me this morning. A week

from this Wednesday you're moving out, you're going to Gold-farber's over on Third Avenue. A real hole you're going to live in, cockroaches you'll have for company in the mornings!"

Carl races across the room, buries his face in Mrs. Rosenthal's lap. "I don't want to go. I don't want to go. Please, please, Mrs. Rosenthal, tell him not to move. Tell him, tell him, he'll listen to you. Tell him I don't want to go, tell him. I'll do anything. I'll get a job after school, I'll stop eating breakfast, only I don't want to move. Please, please, Mrs. Rosenthal, talk to him. He'll listen to you. Please, Mrs. Rosenthal."

And Carl breathes more deeply as he moves into the final part of his dream, drifts out of Mrs. Rosenthal's arms, away from the dough and apple smell of her apron, into the streets, where Ralph, Marcus, and Joey wait for him.

"There is, there is!" Marcus yells. "I went there yesterday with Dickie, they sell five chocolate balls for a penny."

They stand on the street corner at recess, their sandwiches wrapped in brown parcel paper and shoved into their pockets.

"You're lyin'," Ralph says. "Nobody sells five."

"Betcha! Betcha! Next door to the movie, the little shop with the clowns' faces in the window. They sell five for a penny."

They make their bet, Ralph and Marcus, a penny for the winner, and the four set off at a trot, down Houston Street to the movie. They cut across a weed-choked lot and slow to catch their breath near the end of a line of shabbily dressed men that stretches toward the back of a truck. Carl stares at the line of men, dreading what Marcus's voice must surely say.

"Carl!" Marcus shouts. "Ain't that your father?"

And again Carl stares at his father through the same tear-blurred eyes, tries to turn away, and as always, is rooted to the sidewalk. His father turns from the head of the column, from the dirty-jacketed man dishing out the soup with his huge ladle.

"Carl," his father says.

Carl turns and races down the street, races down all the streets that lead him away from his father. His father's voice shouts and pleads in his ears. Carl. Carl!

The sun is stronger through the window. Carl shields his eyes and realizes that the blinds are open. The toilet handle cranks from the bathroom and then the water rushes into the bowl. Carl glances at Millie's side of the bed and sees the covers rolled back, the bed empty. So, he thinks, it's time to get up. But his head is cobwebby and clouded with pieces of his dream; his forehead feels flushed and there is a pulse beating at his temples. He holds his hand against the cool metal of the bed frame, brings the palm to his forehead, and relaxes back against the pillow. I should see Dad, he thinks. I should go see Dad.

Three

The old man lay, staring up at the ceiling which Feinstein had never bothered to paper or paint, until it was almost time to get up and go to the synagogue. No voices broke into his silence, no forms leaned against the stove or swung their stockinged legs against the radiator. The old man lay on his back, perfectly still except for the slow rise and fall of his breathing, and listened to the pounding of his heart. It made a dull steady throb in his ears and a dim thunder that he felt in his stomach, and in the hour that he lay awake, after dawn, if he tried very hard, he could concentrate on that thunder and shut out most of the aches and twinges that his body rediscovered each morning. The old man had awakened earlier than he had to and listened to his body wake itself for so many mornings that he was no longer interested in discovering new pains. So he lay, half dozing, and stared at the patchy gray ceiling that Feinstein had not even promised to fix.

Usually, the old man thought, when I show him something that's wrong, like the paint peeling off the radiator, or the window that's so stuck even a *goy* couldn't push it open, at least he makes an effort, at least a promise he makes that he'll do something about it. He nods his head, like he's listening to what I'm telling him, like it's a very serious business that he'll take care of as soon as he's finished reading the paper. Absolutely, he says, when you tell me about it, it makes me so ashamed I never saw it before I could almost trade my eyes in. Right away I will have it taken care of. Tomorrow, even. First thing in the morning. So even when he doesn't do anything about it, at least he pretends I'm right, at least he pretends that it matters, what I say. But about the ceiling, no. When I told him that when I look at it lunchtime—when God knows, the light isn't good, but you can see your hand in front of your face—at lunchtime, I told him, the ceiling's at least three or four different shades of gray, with splotches where the plaster is peeling off, and holes and scratches where termites and ants or even rats have been eating away—all he did was laugh. Listen, he said, a ceiling's a ceiling. Why worry about it? You don't have to walk on it. All it does is cover you up. Who looks at a ceiling? If it bothers you, just don't look up!

Don't look up! So what should I look at when I'm lying in bed? I got a TV I can switch on? Movies I can run on the wall, I should have something to look at? Maybe I should look out the window. But what's out the window? Out the window is only the other side of the street, and the woman with the red *shmatta* around her hair, and her cat that crawls out on the window ledge and stares at me. A bargain I have, my beautiful view from the fifth floor. Besides, the window's so dirty I can't even see out of it. That's another thing Feinstein keeps promising, to clean that window.

The old man lay and listened to his heartbeats. The light streaming through his windows began to define the stained blue of his quilt, the scarred wood of his bureau, table, and chairs. When the old man could make out the bubbles in the ceiling and the lightest of the gray patches, he closed his eyes, squirmed to the edge of the bed, and eased his feet over the side. A spear of pain shot up his back.

Ach, the old man mumbled. His eyes were still tightly closed. He slid his legs along the floor, shuddering at the coldness of the bare boards against the soles of his feet. As he slid his legs he twisted his body, until finally he sat on the edge of the bed. He bent forward, pushing the breath out of him, twisting his lips at the pain in his stomach, and groped with his right hand until he found his shoes and socks. He opened his eyes, straightened, breathed deeply, then bent to slip on his socks and then his shoes. He fumbled too long at the ends of shoelace which had broken so many times the old man had little unknotted string left, and the pain flashed in his back again. Ach, he grunted. He tied a bow in his right shoe, a knot in his left. Probably, he thought, I won't be able to get the knot undone, so I'll have to slip the shoe off, and tomorrow morning I won't be able to get it on again. So, he thought, tomorrow morning I'll worry about it. If I remember, I'll take a pair of shoelaces from the supermarket.

He pushed himself to his feet. The boards creaked beneath his shoes, his knees trembled, and he reached out to steady himself against the wall, remembering mornings when he had crumpled onto the floor, whimpering and finally screaming with pain until Feinstein climbed the four flights of stairs and helped him up. And when Feinstein didn't come, the old man thought, all the times that I fell and he didn't come, I still got up, somehow, and got my clothes on in time to open up the synagogue. He braced himself against the wall, and gradually his knees steadied, so he could push himself across the room to the kitchen chair on which he had draped his underwear and shirt and suit. He tugged at the drawstring of his pajamas until the bow came undone and the pajama pants slipped to the floor, but as he stepped out of them his shoe caught in the folds of the left leg. So, he thought, so sometimes even the knot sticks, so don't get angry. Carefully he bent down to free his shoe, trying to move slowly, waiting for the pain to shoot up through his back again. He pushed the cloth off the tip of his shoe and straightened. Good, he said. Holding the rim of the chair with his right hand, he slipped on his undershorts and then drew them up to his waist. He worked his undershirt over his head and tucked the long tail under the waistband of his shorts.

Underwear is too much trouble, he thought. I should wear my pajamas all the time, put my clothes on over the pajamas in the morning, and take only my clothes off at night. But it would be uncomfortable, and after a while they would smell too much. So I could get them washed. I got two pairs pajamas. But pajamas are too long, they would stick out under my pants when I walked. I would trip. Worse, people would laugh at me in the streets. Look, the old man has pajamas on under his clothes. So what's so funny? What, it's a crime to wear pajamas under your clothes? Listen, some people don't wear nothing under their clothes; they wear the same suit and shirt for years, with nothing underneath! They're afraid to take a bath even, because they would have to peel the clothes off their backs. So don't laugh at me! It's a free country. If I want to wear pajamas under my clothes, I'll wear them. It's my business!

Maybe I could sleep in my underwear. I wouldn't have to bother with the pajamas. I got more underwear than pajamas. I got three pairs underwear. But at nights I would be too cold; it's too cold even with the pajamas. With only the underwear, I'd freeze in the nights. More heat I'd never get from Feinstein, even if I told him I was sleeping naked. He's so cheap even his own place he keeps like an icebox. He does me a favor, he sends me up a little heat so I shouldn't forget what heat is. More I'd never get from him.

The old man had struggled into his pants and shirt, then paused at the window before he stretched his maroon woolen sweater above his head. He put his arms into the sweater and then pulled it down over him, tugging it below his waist and then folding it up. He turned the sleeves up and patted the folds into place, picking at the loose threads and patches with his fingers. He stopped over a new hole and ran his fingers around it. Moths, he thought. God knows how they live in a room that's so cold; they must come from Iceland. They must be starving, too; I didn't think there was any wool decent enough to eat left on this sweater. So have a good meal, moths. Soon I'll be dead, you'll have the whole sweater to yourselves. And my suit, too. Not that I think it's worth eating. But then, I wouldn't know. I'm not a moth.

The old man wondered as he shuffled to his kitchen table whether there were Jewish moths and *goyishe* moths, and if Jewish moths kept kosher and only ate from Jewish clothes. His shoe clinked against something under the table. He backed away and looked down, saw the tea glass on its side. The tea was still dark against the floorboards, and the top of the table still held some of the liquid. The old man bent down to pick up the glass, reached carefully under the table, and rolled the glass to him. He set the glass on the table and went to the sink for a rag, wiped the floor and then the table, and dropped the rag back into the sink.

The spoon is somewhere, too, the old man thought. Later I will look for the spoon. He went to the bureau and fished his teeth from the glass of Polident and water. Suppose, he thought, that they don't go away next time? Suppose they don't go away when I tell them to? Then what will I do?

I won't think about it. I just won't think about it. He clicked first his upper and then his lower plate into his mouth, turned to the sink, and splashed some cold water on his hands and face. Maybe I should pour out the Polident and water, he thought. No, it's only two days old. I'm not in business for the Polident people. Let it stay.

He dried his hands on the towel hanging from the nail above the sink, and shuffled back across the room for his suit jacket. Five floors beneath his window, the street was its usual dirty morning gray. The old man dimly registered footsteps and the swoosh of tires. Had he listened, he might have heard the lapping of the tidal waves against the concrete and wooden breakwaters that ran the length of the river. He might even have heard the bells from the buoys rocking in midchannel, the short booming hoots from tugs swinging out to head some liner into port, the long mournful wail of dredgers and barges moving slowly into the bay. But the old man had taught himself not to listen. He heard what he had to hear: footsteps on the stair, a knock on the door, steam spouting in the teakettle.

So now he looked a last time out of his window, across the street at the window ledge where the cat of the woman with the red *shmatta* crawled and stared. Today the window was shut and the shade was drawn. No cat appeared to stretch its claws and yawn at the old man.

So, the old man thought. Already it's time I was at the synagogue, not standing and staring out of a filthy window. After morning service, I'll come back and stare. For hours, if I want. As if it makes a difference. He dug his left hand into his jacket pocket, turned from the window, and shuffled across the room; opened the door, stepped into the hall, shut the door behind him, and started down the stairs.

At the bottom landing he stopped, and knocked at Feinstein's door. He heard the sound of the knocking echo through the hall into the kitchen, and knocked again. It's a waste of time. He won't come. Since when does he come to morning services? It's too early in the morning for him to drag himself out of bed. And what do I care if he does come? I'm getting so lonely in my old age, I can't even walk to *shul* by myself? I like him so much I have to bang at his door and beg him to come to *shul* with me?

The old man knocked again. Inside a door opened. He heard the soft pad of footsteps.

"So all right, all right. Don't break the door down. I'm coming."

He was in his bedroom. Sleeping. Probably I woke him up. So what? Serves him right, he's not a young girl, to stay in bed till lunchtime on a Sunday morning. Besides, he should be going to *shul*. Suppose we didn't have a *minyon* and we needed him?

The door opened. The old man stared at Feinstein's puffy face, at the blue robe wrapped around his fat belly.

"It's time for *shul*," the old man said. "You coming?"

"*Shul?*" Feinstein blinked. "*Shul?*"

"What else? You been going to church lately, you forgot what synagogues are for? Yes, *shul*. Services. Prayers. What a Jew's supposed to do three times a day, what the Lord commanded Moses in the desert of Sinai, what the—"

"All right, all right. So I'm not exactly brilliant first thing in the morning. You woke me up."

"What do you want to stay in bed for, you got a maid to serve you breakfast?"

"Listen," Feinstein said, "what I do with my Sunday mornings is my business. I don't ask you no personal questions, don't you ask me none. And since when do I go to *shul* in the mornings, all of a sudden you got to bang on my door and wake me up?"

"That's the trouble. You don't go to *shul* mornings no more. This morning," the old man said, "when I came downstairs, I thought, for a change, you should come to *shul*. So you'll miss some of your beauty sleep. Big deal. You don't need it, beautiful you never were. So come. Take a look at the world in the morning. See what it looks like."

"What are you, a tourist guide?" Feinstein mumbled. "Somebody nominated you for the Junior Chamber of Commerce? It don't look no different in the morning, this city; dirt's dirt, dogshit is dogshit, cars is cars and cats is cats."

The old man turned away, started down the last three steps to the front door and the street.

"Listen. Don't feel bad I'm not going," Feinstein called. "I don't mean it personal. I don't like *shlepping* to morning services any more, that's all. I guess I'm getting too old. But—"

The front door slammed off the rest of Feinstein's words. The wind bit into the old man as he paused outside the door, and he huddled deeper into his jacket. *Goy,* he thought, you should be a *goy.* Too old to go to *shul* in the morning. I'm ten years older than you, am I too old to get up every morning? What do you need sleep for, you got dances or parties to go to at night? A *goy,* that's all you are, a lazy, good-for-nothing *goy.*

He set his face against the wind and shuffled down the street, his hands plunged deep into his pants pockets. At the corner he turned right. Perletz was at his stand; his newspapers were spread out across the wooden counter. The old man moved slowly toward the stand and undid the top buttons of his jacket. He shook himself to make sure the jacket fell loosely from his shoulders, patted the outsize pouch he had sewn into the lining, and approached the stand.

"Morning," he said.

"Morning," Perletz nodded.

The old man stared into Perletz's wrinkled little face and then turned to glance over his shoulder at the sky. The *Sunday Forwards* were stacked in their usual place. "Colder today. Looks like some snow we might get."

"No. I don't think so. Cold, yes. But no more snow."

"What do you mean, no more snow? You think it's too late in the winter for snow? Listen, I can remember when we had snow in April! April, as sure as I'm standing here, five-foot drifts we had. Nothing moved—cars, buses, taxis—nothing."

Perletz glanced down to check some figures on a tablet in his hand, and the old man's hand reached out toward the *Forwards.* He checked himself. Better wait, he thought. Soon someone'll come.

"So," he said. "How's business?"

Perletz shrugged. "How should business be? I live, thank

God. I don't starve. But a millionaire I won't be, either, not from selling papers. I got no worries and no surprises. Every morning the same papers come. They get delivered by the same drivers. I cut the same cords with the same wire cutters, put the same papers into the same piles, and sell them to the same customers. Sometimes I lose a customer, sometimes I get a new one. Every day I get a dozen, two dozen strays. Every day the same customers stop to talk. Every day they say the same things. So how should business be?"

The old man shook his head. "It's a hard life," he started to say, but before he got the words out, he sensed someone approaching the stand. He moved closer to the counter and loosened his jacket.

"A *Times,* please," he heard. As Perletz reached down to hand a *Times* across the counter, the old man slid the top *Forward* off the stack, slipped it under his jacket, and felt it slide into the pouch. Perletz was rooting in his cigar box for change for a dollar. The old man stood as Perletz counted out the change, nodded a thank you as the customer, *Times* folded thickly under his arm, moved away.

"So," the old man said as Perletz turned back to him, "I should be going. The synagogue doesn't like to be kept waiting." He forced a chuckle from somewhere in his throat, but Perletz didn't smile. He turned to shuffle away, then turned back. "You wait and see. It'll snow. Watch and see if it doesn't snow."

Perletz nodded.

Four

PERLETZ

Listen, don't start. A lousy fifteen-cent *Sunday Forward* I can afford to give away, so don't start. What should I do, reach over the counter and grab his arm? Yell "Thief! Thief!" until a policeman comes running up to arrest him? Get him thrown in jail for a lousy fifteen-cent newspaper?

It's not just a lousy fifteen-cent newspaper. Sometimes, during the week also, he comes and steals a *Forward*. Sometimes he steals one every day.

So what? So he steals one every day. So if every day he steals one, and every Sunday, too, I lose seventy-five cents a week. Three dollars a month.

That's nothing? You can afford to give away three dollars a month, just because an old man's a thief? You get up every morning at five-thirty to let an old man steal three dollars from you? What're you running, a business or a charity?

First of all, listen a minute. He doesn't take a paper every day. If he did, if he stole a paper every day and Sunday, I would lose three dollars a month. But he doesn't. So I lose less. That's first of all. Second of all, it doesn't hurt me. Sure, I'm running a business, but I give to charity, too. I give more than that to charity. So let's suppose he's one of my charities. Suppose instead of giving ten dollars to *Keren Ami* or the Old People's

Fund or the Society's drives, I give him his papers. Where's the difference? It's better my way. When I let him steal, at least I know I'm giving to a charity I can see. How can I see where my money goes when I give to those fancy-shmancy national charities? Cohen comes around collecting for the Allied Jewish Appeal, so I give him five dollars. I know what happens to that five dollars? Does the Allied Jewish Appeal send me a letter saying, Dear Herchel Perletz, We thank you very much for your five dollars, which we used to buy a pair of shoes for a barefoot little Yemenite Jew? When he takes that paper and I don't say anything, at least I know what my charity's doing for somebody else.

Big deal, your charity. So what's it doing for somebody else? How much is it doing for him, because you let him walk off with a paper? You're helping his life, maybe? You're making him happier?

I'm giving him a paper to read. Free. I'm letting him steal it. He must want to read it, or else why should he bother to steal it? Listen, he just doesn't walk up and take a paper. He goes to a lot of trouble. I don't know if he goes to all his trouble because he still doesn't realize I'm letting him steal the paper, that I'm not going to stop him. But he goes to a lot of trouble. He comes up to the stand first, and he talks to me. Every time, he talks to me. He talks to me about the weather, or my business, or his feet, or the synagogue. He watches my face to see if I'm listening. Maybe he even thinks I'm interested in what he's saying, maybe he thinks I'm a friend. I don't know. All I know is, he talks, and he waits. I look down sometimes, or I go to the other side of the stand, and pretend to arrange some papers. To give him a chance to take the *Forward* and hurry away. But he doesn't. Today even, just now, I looked down at my tablet, and he reached out to take a *Forward*, and then stopped. He always stops. He's very careful, he waits for another customer, no matter how long it takes. And when I go to wait on the other customer, then, only then, he moves. I think he must believe that I don't see him easing that paper off the pile, folding it, slipping it into his jacket. He smooths down his jacket, and then he smiles at me, like he's really put one over on me. Then he goes. Only then, he goes.

So what? So he's a careful old thief, and a little stupid, so what? So you make him happier by letting him steal a paper? It's a big thing in his life, that paper?

Listen. All the time I ask myself, what does he have? Every time I see him come around the corner, I wonder to myself, what kind of a life does he have? What kind of a man is he, to go to so much trouble to steal a paper? Can he be so poor, seventy-five cents a week he can't even afford? All right, I say, maybe he is so poor, maybe he can't really afford to buy a paper. So why does he care so much he has to steal one? When a man is a thief, he steals money, he steals food, he steals cigarettes, liquor, cars. But a paper? What kind of a thief steals a paper?

So I think about him. Everything I know. First, that he's a *shamos* at the synagogue. So, I think to myself, he must be religious. It's not a nice job, being a *shamos;* early every morning you have to get up, you have to open the synagogue, clean it out, pick up after all the members. And the pay is nothing at all. So he must be religious, I think, a very religious man. Maybe when he was a boy in the old country, he wanted to be a rabbi, but his parents couldn't send him to a *yeshiva.* They were poor, they didn't have the money. But his father taught him everything he knew, and when he got older, they sent him to the *Chasid,* and the *Chasid* taught him. He spent all his time with his nose buried in books, so instead of growing up straight he grew curved and crooked, so his back looks like a pretzel now.

Perletz, Perletz, you're a silly fool, you've got a heart like a valentine and a head like a Hollywood movie. A man steals papers from you and you turn him into the Vilna Gaon. He's not stealing books, idiot, he's stealing a newspaper. Anyone can read a newspaper, you don't have to be a scholar. You don't have to be in love with books to read a newspaper. People only read newspapers, Perletz; they don't study them. Some people even use them to cover wet floors. Or to wrap up smelly fish.

All right, so maybe I'm silly. But every time he comes I think to myself, what kind of a man is he? Why does he work so hard to steal a newspaper? What kind of a life does he have? I even asked Rosenthal, who owns the secondhand dress shop on Houston Street, and belongs to the *shul.* I asked him what he knew about the old man. Nothing. Nobody knows nothing. For fifteen years he's been the *shamos* at the *shul;* every morning, every evening, he opens up and closes up. More nobody knows. He lives in a little room around the corner, four floors on top of Feinstein. One room, that's all. What kind of life does he have? What does he do? Does he spend all day reading the newspapers he steals?

Why do you bother, Perletz, why do you bother your head with empty questions? Maybe he sees you the same way, a skinny little man who stands on the corner and sells newspapers. Suppose he asked you what kind of a life you lead? What could you say to him?

I'd say a lot to him. I'd tell him about my business. I don't mind selling papers. It's not the most exciting job in the world, but I don't mind it. It has its advantages. You learn the news before anybody else. If you care about the news. I admit, I don't care any more what happens in the world. It'll all blow up someday soon, and that'll be the end of it. But still, every day, there it is, everything important that happens in the world, spread out in front of me. It's a nice feeling. Almost like being on top of things. And everybody who comes to me wants to find out what's in those papers. Except that they don't, really. When I first started, I used to think that people bought papers because they wanted to read the news. They don't. They want to read the comic strips, or the gossip columnists. Or do the puzzle. But I think maybe the main reason people buy papers is because it's a habit. Makes them feel connected. Everybody's walking around this city wondering how he fits in. Stick a paper under his arm, and he's part of things.

So I'd tell him about selling papers. And about my apartment. That's one thing I care about, my apartment. Ten years it's taken me to fix it up the way I wanted, but it's worth it. I come home after a hard day's work, I make a light under the teakettle, I pour myself a glass of tea and I stretch out on the sofa. Maybe I get up to pull the curtains Doris made for me, and maybe I turn on the reading lamp. I look at the picture over the coffee table, that Sammy got for me. Very modern, he said. First I didn't like it much, but like Sammy says, you got to live with pictures for a while, then slowly they come to mean something to you. You come to see what they're all about. He says it better, what does he say? They relate to you. Relate. So I relate the picture to me. Now, when I stare at it, I see a face, a figure. Sometimes it's even the same face, the same figure I saw yesterday. It's relating.

The rug. I'd tell him about the rug. Three months I spent, bargaining with Horowitz for that rug. And finally I talked him into giving it to me for seven dollars fifty cents. A genuine Oriental rug for seven dollars fifty cents! So it's a little stained in places, and the part I got shoved beneath the sofa has the tape ripped off and is fraying at the edge. So what? Nobody sees that, nobody knows that except me. So it doesn't reach the other wall, so the chair with the blue slipcovers sits with its front legs on the rug and its back legs on the floor, that's a tragedy?

Ach, it's a waste of time, talking like this. So I got my business and my apartment, it means something? Millions of people got businesses and homes, are they happy? Sometimes I think nobody's happy; what does living have to do with happiness, anyway? Happiness is a dream, that's all; the old man probably thinks he's happy because every day he manages to steal a paper. I ought to fix him. I ought to tip off the cop on the corner and get him arrested the next time he tries it.

But I won't. I'll let him walk up to the stand and steal a paper every morning he tries to. And I'll never say anything. God knows what kind of a *mensch* he is or what kind of a life he leads, because I don't. But if he thinks he has to steal, I won't stop him. Let him go on thinking he's fooling me, I don't care. What kind of a world is it, that a Jew should be a thief for a lousy ten-cent newspaper?

Five

The old man huddled against the cold wood of the synagogue's doors and drew out his heavy ring of keys. The long, blackened brass door key refused to turn, then slipped slowly into place and snapped the locks open. The old man leaned his shoulder against the right-hand door. This morning, like most mornings, it took almost all the strength he could manage to lean himself against the door and push until his weight and the wind and his muttered prayers swung the door slowly inward. The door creaked open. The old man slipped into the moist stillness of the darkened synagogue, lit the lights, and let the door swing slowly shut.

Beneath the four dirt-coated globes of yellow light, the pews and aisles seemed hazy, indistinct. The old man moved along the side walls, easing the fraying velvet curtains back from the windows. Gray early morning light filtered through the smeared panes. The old man pulled the curtains back from the last window and started down the near aisle, glancing at every pew to make sure that all the prayer books were resting in their holders, that no prayer shawls lay discarded on the benches. But the benches were empty, the holders full of prayer books. The old man had checked the synagogue the night before, and had known, even when he began, that he would find nothing out of place. Still, he thought, a *shamos* is a *shamos*; he has a job to do, same as everybody else. Every night and every morning, he's supposed to inspect the synagogue. So I inspect the synagogue.

From the window ledge cut into the back wall, he took down the box of prayer shawls and set it on the last pew for the members who did not care to bring their own. Or no longer had them. Then there was nothing else to do. The old man eased himself down on one of the benches, rested his head in his hands, then pushed himself up and stumbled along the aisle. He climbed the five steps to the pulpit, and stood behind the reading table, with his hands grasping the sides, the way Rabbi Davis stood when he talked to the membership. The old man stared out into the empty synagogue and cleared his throat, then glanced up into the balcony. When was the last time I saw a woman up there? Women must die younger than men. Or else they don't bother to come to *shul*, once they get old.

In the fifteen years the old man had been *shamos*, very few women had ever ventured into the synagogue. The congregation was small and regular; a score of old men, from the nursing home and the few surrounding streets where a room was cheap enough to die in, struggled each day to the synagogue, to pray, gossip, stop for a glass of tea before returning home. The morning service was the shortest of the day; the men wandered in with sleep firmly marked on their faces, slid out of their heavy coats, wound themselves into their prayer shawls, and rocked themselves through their prayers. Even Rabbi Davis never bothered to mount the pulpit, but prayed from a bench near the front.

This morning, as on every other morning, the old man stood at his special bench in the far right-hand corner, in front of one of the wooden pillars that stretched from floor to ceiling, and raced mechanically through his prayers. He was not slow, for the repetitions of more than sixty years had turned whole sentences into a few sharp sounds and a jumbled slur, but by the time he had whispered his final "Amen," and closed his book, more than half the members had already left.

The old man sat down on his special bench, and rested his head in his hands. So I can go home now, and go back to sleep again. Or at least, I can go home and lay on my bed and try to go back to sleep. But suppose I can't sleep, suppose they come again? Maybe they'll let me alone, for at least the rest of the morning, maybe they'll let me alone? Maybe they won't come back any more today? But what will I do, if they come and they don't go away when I tell them to? What will I do?

I won't think about it. I'll go home, and I'll lay on my bed. And I'll close my eyes. And even if I don't sleep, the rest will do me good. That's all. The rest will do me good. But what kind of good will it do me? Does it matter, how much I rest? My body gets better, because I rest a couple hours? I'm getting closer and closer, and there's nothing I can do, resting doesn't help. "Oh God," the old man whispered suddenly, "please, God, I don't want to die."

Don't be silly! What's going to happen, you'll be excused? For thousands of years, everybody grows old and dies, God is going to make you an exception? Dying's dying. It happens to everybody.

"Not to me, please, God. Not to me. Oh, God, I don't want to die." Stop it, he tried to shout to himself, to the cold fear that was spreading from his stomach. A prickly crawling feeling moved downward into his buttocks, and his calves and thighs began to tremble. A liquid coldness, like ice water, flooded upward from his stomach into his chest. Stop it! How old are you, three? All of a sudden you just realized you're going to die? What can God do? What can anybody do? Being afraid doesn't help anything. Why all of a sudden should you be so scared? You didn't know yesterday? You won't know tomorrow?

The old man sat with his head in his hands, and gripped the hard wood of the bench with his knees to keep his legs from shaking. He swallowed again and again to keep the ice water in his chest from rising into his throat, and told himself that dying was simple, that dying was like going to sleep and not waking up, that dying was not-feeling, and why be frightened of not-feeling any more? Dying will be a blessing to you, you should pray only it should come quick, that's all. With all the aches and pains you got, dying will be a blessing. You won't have to suffer any more. You should thank God He's finally getting you out of all this trouble.

But suppose, he thought, suppose Zitomer is right, and the *goyim* are right; suppose dying isn't just going to sleep?

Suppose, afterward, you go someplace, because of what kind of life you lived. Then— The old man shook his head. No, not again. I can't think about it again. First with Zitomer, then with Rabbi Davis, and all those nights I couldn't sleep, when Naomi and Smetyanov and Shmuel Yaakov and all my other dead laughed and shouted across my room. No. It's enough. Far inside his head, the old man heard the beginnings of Naomi's laughter, felt the stubby bulk of Shmuel Yaakov begin to move. He opened his eyes and raised his head. The synagogue was empty. The members were gone.

Ach. Serves me right for thinking so much about nothing. Dying's dying, that's all, he thought, and pushed himself to his feet. Someone had left a prayer shawl on one of the side benches, and the old man gathered it up and shuffled along the pews. The prayer books were back in place, and the old man found no more discarded shawls. He started to shuffle toward the light panel, then stopped near the door that led downstairs to the assembly room and the rabbi's office. I should go to the toilet. Not because I have to go so very bad now. But last week I didn't have to go so bad, either, in the synagogue; but by the time I got home, it was all I could do to hold it in. A fine sight I would be, wetting my pants like I was a little boy. Or like Nathanson. He thought nobody knew, but I knew. I saw him. Sneaking out of the synagogue with his jacket wrapped around him. But I saw the wet. Filthy old man! What's wrong with you, you couldn't even think to go downstairs to the toilet, you had to wet yourself right in the synagogue! Look, it's all right for you to talk, you couldn't help it, but I had to clean up the wet under your seat, I had to wipe it up. Listen, the toilet downstairs isn't a palace, the Waldorf-Astoria we're not, but it'll do, even the rabbi uses it. At least it's better than the synagogue floor.

The old man chuckled all the way down the stairs to the toilet, remembering Nathanson's red face and the way he tried to hide himself inside the jacket, with the dark wet stain spreading across his pants leg. What a pig, what a dirty old man! You should be so ashamed you should stay in your room and never show your face inside the synagogue again. The old man had opened the toilet door and stepped inside before he realized that someone was sitting in one of the compartments. The two compartment doors had slipped off their hinges long ago, and each hopper sat, smug, round, and white, in its empty compartment. But now a man squatted on one of the seats, and grunted as the old man stepped into the room.

"Oh," the old man said, "I—I'm sorry. You should excuse me, I didn't know anybody was here. I'm going. I'll wait outside."

There was no light in the room except for a transom that led up to the street, and in the shreds of gray daylight that flickered into the room, the old man had not recognized the figure who squatted on the seat and grunted. The stale air was heavy with the smell of excrement, and as the old man turned to the door, he heard a hefty splash.

"Aaah," Rabbi Davis grunted. "Whew! I had to work for that one. Wait!" he called to the old man, who was halfway out the door. "What're you running from? You came down here to do something, so do what you came to do. Don't go away because of me."

The old man stood with his back to the compartment. Rabbi Davis! Of all people to walk in on, Rabbi Davis! "Well, I think I better go upstairs. Later—I think I should come back later. Upstairs, I forgot—I mean I left—the *talesim*—out. I better go put them back."

"Nonsense," the rabbi shouted. "Stop being silly. We're more than grown men, there's nothing to be embarrassed about. Come in and stop being silly. Come in and do what you have to do."

The old man closed the door and edged toward the urinal, trying not to look into the compartment where the rabbi sat. Oh God, he thought, why did I have to come down, why couldn't I go straight home? Even wetting my pants like that silly fool of a Nathanson would be better! Suppose the rabbi thinks I did it on purpose, suppose he thinks I followed him down here on purpose so I could catch him? I never go to the toilet in the mornings, suppose he starts to wonder why all of a sudden I should come down, when he's right in the middle of—

The old man stood at the urinal, unbuttoned his fly, and attempted to relieve himself. But nothing came. Come on, come on, five minutes ago you had to go so bad you couldn't even wait till you got home, now you can't go at all? Come on, come on. Suppose the rabbi's listening; if he doesn't hear anything, what's he going to think? He doesn't hear anything, not even a trickle, he'll be sure you came down to embarrass him. So come on, come on, the old man told himself, remembering, as he fidgeted at the urinal, the time he went to the nursing home for an examination, and they had asked him for a sample. The attendant had given the old man a bottle and led him to a small gray-walled cubicle, almost a closet.

"Just fill the bottle," the attendant said. "Fill the bottle and then come back."

"Fill the bottle?" the old man said.

"For a sample. We need a sample."

"Listen," the old man said. "You should excuse me, I know I'm an old man and not very smart, but of what do you need a sample? What should I fill the bottle with?"

The attendant in the white jacket stared at the old man, then threw his head back and laughed and laughed and laughed, until the sound bounced off the gray walls and pounded into the old man's ears. Finally, after the attendant had regained his breath and fought off the last few ripples of laughter, he patted the old man on the shoulder.

"Of your urine. We need a sample of your urine. For testing. Just fill the bottle." And he walked away.

The old man had set the bottle down, unbuttoned his fly, picked up the bottle, and held it in what he assumed must be the proper position. But nothing happened. The old man had fidgeted, shifted his feet, taken deep breaths, thought of huge glasses of water. Still nothing happened. The old man had sworn at himself to relax, had thought of all his favorite drinks. Nothing. Fifteen minutes went by, a half-hour. The old man thought of bathtubs, swimming pools, lakes, rivers, oceans. Still nothing. The rain of the Flood, pouring down on Noah and his family and all the animals of the Ark. The earth covered with water, only the small wooden boat bobbing on the waves. But still nothing happened. Finally the attendant came back.

"Well?"

The old man adjusted his fly. "I—couldn't. Nothing came."

The attendant grinned. Then he smiled. Then he began to laugh.

"You sure you're trying the right way?" he said. "Oh well, don't worry. Take the bottle home and come back when it's full."

The old man took the bottle and shuffled out of the cubicle.

"But don't take too long," the attendant shouted after him. "We're moving in a few months."

The old man had waited until he was about three blocks from the nursing home before smashing the bottle on the sidewalk. The glass shivered into splinters beneath the old man's feet. He ground them into the sidewalk. He kicked the larger pieces into the gutter and swore never to go anywhere for an examination again. But the sound of the attendant's laughter had stayed in his ears.

Come on, come on, come on, the old man urged, certain that at any moment, the rabbi would begin to question him. What kind of a synagogue is it, when a rabbi can't even go to the toilet without being followed by his *shamos*?

The old man finally decided it was useless, and was beginning to readjust his fly when a sharp tearing of paper sounded behind him. "Oy," the old man said, so startled that he began to relieve himself, and had to fumble his fly open, wetting his undershorts, his pants, and his hand. He stood at the urinal and listened to the steady scratch-scratch of the paper. I should say something, he thought, so that the rabbi shouldn't think I'm listening. But what could I say? I wish I could whistle. Since I got my false teeth, I can't whistle any more. But I should do something. He heard the chain being pulled but no quick flush of water.

"Damn," the rabbi said. The chain again. Still no water. "Stupid toilet. Come on, flush." The chain again. This time the water rushed into the bowl, and the old man breathed deeply and adjusted his fly for the second time. He stood at the urinal a little longer, so the rabbi should have enough time to raise his pants in private, then turned to the sink. He let the cold water run over his hands. Behind him the rabbi moved out of his compartment.

"There," the rabbi said. "That wasn't so bad, was it? Nothing to run from. If two grown men, old men, can't take care of their—natural functions—without a door between them—"

The old man nodded. He moved to the side of the sink and wiped his hands on the roller towel which was almost never changed. He was still too ashamed to look at the rabbi, so he finished wiping his hands and opened the door.

"Wait."

The old man stood at the door.

"Wait," the rabbi repeated. "I've got Zitomer upstairs. Come and talk to him with me."

The old man backed out of the door as the rabbi moved toward him. "Zitomer?"

The rabbi nodded. "Zitomer. I sent him a note the other day, and asked him to come and see me this morning. He should be in my office by now. So come. You're one of his friends, and you are the *shamos*. So you might as well come up to the office and listen. Just to keep things fair. So Zitomer won't go away and make a mountain out of what I tell him, or a miracle."

The rabbi brushed past the old man and started toward the back stairs that led up to the cubicle that served as his office. The old man stood by the door of the toilet. I'm not a friend of Zitomer's, he wanted to say. Don't think I'm a friend, just because one night I walked to his store with him. I don't think any better of Zitomer's crazy ideas than you do.

The rabbi stopped at the foot of the stairs. "What're you waiting for? Don't you have the time to stay? You have to go someplace?"

The old man shuffled forward, shaking his head. "No. I got noplace special to go."

"So come. What's there to think about?"

Together they climbed the stairs to the office. Zitomer was standing outside the office door, with his back to the stairs, but he turned as they reached the landing.

"So, Zitomer," Rabbi Davis said. "Good morning."

"Good morning," Zitomer said. The old man stared at Zitomer's face and thought it looked thinner than the last time; thinner, and more drawn. "And good morning to you," Zitomer nodded to the old man.

"I asked him to come along," Rabbi Davis said. "As *shamos*, he has a right to be here. And besides, I didn't think you'd mind."

Zitomer shook his head. "Why should I mind? I got nothing to hide. You could have the whole congregation here, they wouldn't bother me."

"I doubt they'd fit into my office," Rabbi Davis chuckled.

"You want to come in and sit down? I think maybe we can all three just manage."

The old man let both Rabbi Davis and Zitomer move into the office. Rabbi Davis squeezed past his desk and settled himself into the leather chair behind it. Zitomer took the chair next to the filing cabinet, directly facing Rabbi Davis. The old man edged into the office and sat gingerly in the chair near the door.

"Aaach," Rabbi Davis sighed, and settled himself more comfortably in his chair. "I'll tell you very simply why I asked you to come, Zitomer. A few days ago a committee from the membership came to see me. It doesn't matter who they were, you can probably guess. You've visited all their shops. Well, the point is, Zitomer, they're fed up. They're fed up with your visits and your preaching and what you do to their business. And they're not only fed up, they're determined. That's why I called you in. Unless you stop bothering them, they're going to make trouble for you. Bad trouble. Official trouble. They're not sure yet what they're going to do, but they're talking about issuing a complaint against you. So that the next time you walk in their stores, you'll be arrested. Now I don't want that," Rabbi Davis said. "It's true we had to ask you to leave the synagogue, but I certainly didn't do it for any personal reasons. So I wouldn't want you to wind up in jail. That's why I'm telling you this. They mean business. If you don't stay out of their stores, they'll make trouble for you."

The rabbi looked down at the rusted letter opener in his hand, then up at Zitomer.

"You could have saved yourself the trouble, Rabbi Davis. You think I didn't know? You think they don't tell me the same thing, every time I go into their stores? I'm not going to stop. You got me thrown out of the synagogue; the only way I can talk to them is to go into their stores. What I do to their business! I don't do nothing to their business. Five, ten minutes I stay in a store, no more. Ten minutes at the most. I talk in a soft voice, I say what I came to say, and then I leave. What kind of trouble does that make for their business? You know why they want to get me in trouble? I'll tell you why. Because I embarrass them in front of their customers. I tell the truth about how they run their business, and it embarrasses them in front of their customers. That's how I'm bad for business; I tell the truth. It's the truth they're afraid of, not me. Let them get the truth thrown in jail."

"Zitomer, Zitomer, they won't throw the truth in jail, but they'll throw you in. They're not children, Zitomer; they mean what they say. They'll fix it so next time you walk into one of their stores, you get arrested. I'm telling you, Zitomer, they're not kidding."

"So I'll be arrested. So what? I've never got arrested before, it'll be something new. Maybe it'll even make the papers. Old man, fifty-six, arrested trying to talk some sense to his friends."

"They're not your friends, Zitomer. They're not anybody's friends. They're just little Jewish businessmen, doing what they have to, trying to stay alive."

The old man leaned forward to rest his face in his hands. His chair creaked.

"Look, Rabbi Davis. There's something I've been wanting to ask you since even before you got me thrown out of the synagogue. I don't care what the members are trying to do, I'm not worried about getting arrested. But listen, Rabbi. All the time I was talking from the pulpit, and even when I talked in the Saturday discussion, I had an idea—more, I was sure—that you understood. That you understood what I was saying. Now you sit there and you say to me, 'They don't have any friends, they're just poor Jewish businessmen, trying to stay alive.' That's what I'm saying, Rabbi, that's what I'm saying. It seems to me that you know what I'm talking about, that you agree with me, even. And yet you got me thrown out of the synagogue. When all I tried to do was to get those little Jewish businessmen to follow the Ten Commandments. I don't understand, Rabbi Davis."

The old man sat, his back curved forward from the back rungs of his chair, his head in his hands. He heard the rabbi's drawn-out sigh, and the creaking of his chair.

"Zitomer, you ask so many questions, Zitomer. But you're lucky, this one has an answer I can give you. Because you're right, Zitomer. I understood what you were talking about from the first moment you climbed that pulpit and began to speak. And what's more, Zitomer, I agree. If we all follow the Ten Commandments, the world would be a better place. Without a doubt. And I agree that if all men realized that they were brothers, we could all lead better lives. Absolutely. But where we're different, you and me, Zitomer, is that you think it's possible, and I don't. You think you can change people's lives by preaching to them, Zitomer. And I don't. No, wait, don't interrupt. You asked me a question and now I'm answering it. For all your life, Zitomer, you lived like a Jew, like all the rest of those little businessmen still live. And none of it, the Commandments, the Torah, the *Niveyim*, the *Kisuvim*, meant anything to you. You came to *shul* twice a day and you prayed, because you always came to *shul* twice a day and prayed. When the holidays came, you observed them, doing what you had done the year before and the year before and the year before that, for as long as you can remember. And you weren't unhappy, Zitomer, you weren't unhappy. You were doing what we call living a life, Zitomer, living a Jewish life. But one day, Zitomer, one day you had a revelation. Suddenly you see that life can be more than scraping and cheating and sniveling for money, or bowing and mumbling in the synagogue. You understand that all men can be brothers, and you rush to the synagogue to tell us about it. And you're surprised when the membership doesn't take you up on its shoulders and hail you Messiah. Zitomer, Zitomer, Zitomer. What happened to you is a great and wonderful thing; at fifty-six you stopped being a thing and became a man. But how many things become men, Zitomer, and how many things stay little Jewish businessmen? You're the first man who ever insisted that the Ten Commandments were given to be obeyed? You're the first man who ever realized that all men are brothers? Zitomer, Zitomer, our history is full of prophets who soured unto death because they preached the same things to the people, and the people refused to listen. The history of the world is written with the blood of men who believed that all men are brothers. Every decade in the history of any country or any people can produce the bones of a man who believed that things could become men, and died mistaken. People are animals, Zitomer. Men are animals. Ninety-nine men out of every hundred want only enough to eat, a decent place to sleep, a woman, maybe, and a way of living that protects them against the outside world so well that they don't have to think. Ever. And that's what Judaism's about, Zitomer. We bind each man with so many laws, so many commandments, so many rituals and observances, that the whole of his waking hours is taken up with the doing, and he lives in a world with all the questions answered, and no pauses for thinking. Because ninety-nine men out of every hundred are afraid to think, Zitomer, and for those men Judaism is a way of life. A pattern for things. And into this pattern, into this sealed universe, you come with your revelation that all men are brothers, you come with your questions nobody can answer. You come with your demand that each man should take up his life and look at it, and decide whether he is living it as he should. You wonder why I threw you out of the synagogue? You would destroy every one of these things, these sheep, Zitomer. They're not strong enough to think. The Commandments weren't written for them, Zitomer; the Commandments were written for men. These poor little sheep, living their days inside a meaningless pattern they never questioned, dealing in their petty lies and cheats and thefts inside their tiny business, you think they matter? They're the world, Zitomer, and the world's rotten! Rotten through and through. And you can't change that rottenness by preaching, Zitomer. All you can do is make each little sheep uncomfortable, until I come along and patch up the fences of their pasture again. You can't help them, Zitomer; you can't change things so they don't have to lie and steal. You can't make them strong inside, so they don't need a law to tell them how to behave. So let them alone. Even their sins are so small, so sheeplike, why should you worry about them? None of them are even alive enough to harm anybody else. There is so much real evil in the world. Let them sleep."

The old man's face had remained hidden in his hands, but he had listened. A board creaked. The old man looked up.

"I don't agree," Zitomer said. "I don't agree at all."

Rabbi Davis nodded.

"Ask him then," Zitomer said. "Ask him what he thinks. Ask him whether he thinks all of us are sheep; whether the way we live, with thousands of rules and laws and commandments, is the only way to live."

The old man saw Rabbi Davis begin to frown at Zitomer, then turn to him. The old man shook his head even before Rabbi Davis spoke.

"Well? What do you think about all this? You think Zitomer's right, that men—the members here—have a chance to change themselves? You think Zitomer does any good, telling them that their lives are rotten, that they cheat and lie and steal instead of trying to follow the Commandments? You think any of them can make a new life for themselves, so late in their own lives?"

The old man went on shaking his head. "Why are you asking me? I'm not a scholar, I never studied. What do I know about these things?"

"It's not a question of being a scholar, of studying," Zitomer cut in. "It's a question of what you think life is all about. And what you think people can do with their lives."

"And I'm supposed to answer," the old man shouted. "I'm supposed to know what life is all about! Sometimes I think you are *mishuga*, the kind of questions you ask. Who's got the right to say what life is all about, who can answer a question like that? In the Torah, in the Commandments, that's where the answers are. God gave us all the answers we need; that's all we have to know. It's all written down, everything; what we're supposed to do, what we're not supposed to do. We made ourselves, we got the right to say what life is all about? God made us. God gave us the Torah. He tells us what life is all about. He tells us what we're supposed to do. That's not enough for you?"

"I think," Rabbi Davis said, "that all of us are getting just a little—"

"But do you believe it?" Zitomer shouted. "Any one of the members, the men he calls sheep, could have said the same things you just said. But do you really believe it? And if you believe it, even then do you live the way you believe? So God told us what life is all about, did he, and he gave us a whole *megillah* of laws and commandments to obey? Do you obey them? Do you keep them? You, you're just like everybody else, you live a good, pure, Jewish life, hey? You follow every one of God's Commandments because that's the way to life a life. Don't you see what I'm trying to tell you!" Zitomer shouted, and slapped his open hand against his knee. "You're just like everybody else, you break more commandments than you keep. You're like all of us, we're all liars and cheats and hypocrites. You don't really believe what the Torah says life is all about; you don't really believe that all we have to do is obey the Commandments, follow the laws, and do unto others as you would have them do unto you. You don't believe it, you don't do it. We say all men are brothers, but what we really mean is that if we don't take advantage of our brother first, we know damn well he'll take advantage of us. What we really believe in is doing everything we can to keep our heads above water, even if it means standing on our brother's shoulders. And you," Zitomer shouted at the old man, who was on his feet at the door, "how can you stand there and tell me what's written down and what we should obey, when in my own kitchen you sat and you told me how you stole and lied and cheated your way from—"

"Liar!" the old man screamed. "Liar! It's lies, lies, all lies. I never said a word; I never came to your kitchen. You're making it up. It's all lies. Rabbi, you shouldn't believe a word of it, nothing that he's saying is true," the old man sobbed. "It's lies, lies, all lies. Every word is a lie."

The rabbi's chair scraped back as he hurried around his desk to the old man. The old man stood, propped against the door frame, his hands covering his face, his body shaking with his weeping. Rabbi Davis reached him and put his hands on the old man's shoulders. "Now please," he said in a soothing voice. "Now please, please, don't get yourself upset. There's nothing to be upset about. You got yourself all worked up for nothing. Here Zitomer, you, and I were just having a friendly little chat and all of a sudden, an argument. Like a thunderstorm. It's nobody's fault, we just didn't understand each other. Zitomer didn't mean what he said; he got excited. After all, it's been a month since he's been inside the synagogue. It's no wonder he said some things he didn't mean. So it's no reason to get upset. So come, dry your face. Here, use my handkerchief and dry your face."

The old man let Rabbi Davis pull his hands from his wet face, accepted Rabbi Davis's handkerchief, and dabbed at his eyes.

"That's better. Now, listen to me. You go home, now; go right home and get some rest. Don't worry about closing up; I'll take care of the lights and the door. You get home, now, and rest for a few hours. And if you don't feel like opening up for the afternoon service, then don't bother. I'll manage."

Patting the old man's shoulder, the rabbi eased him out of

the office door and down the back stairs to the synagogue's rear entrance. He opened the door.

"You shouldn't listen," the old man mumbled, "to anything he said. They were lies."

"Of course I won't listen. I didn't call him here to have an argument; I called him here to give him a warning. All I'll do now is go up and tell him to go. I won't even let him say anything."

The old man nodded. He stood in the entrance and blinked at the rabbi. Thank you, he wanted to say, but all he did was stand and stare at the rabbi.

"Go ahead now," the rabbi said. "Get some rest. And remember what I said. Don't worry about the afternoon service. I'll manage."

The old man turned from the door and shuffled on to the sidewalk. The door closed behind him. What will they say now, he thought as he set his steps for home. Rabbi Davis will go back upstairs to his office and sit behind his desk. Zitomer will shake his head, and the rabbi will cluck his tongue. Then Zitomer will tell the rabbi everything that I said, that night when I went with him to his kitchen and talked my tongue away. Oh God, why did I have to talk to him? Did it do any good? Did it help me any? They still come when they want, and soon they will go when they want. They don't listen to me any more!

A car hooted. He stopped at a corner. Far inside his head, he heard Naomi begin to laugh. The light changed. No, he thought. I won't think about it. He started across the street. I'll go home. I'll go home and try to sleep. And if I fall asleep, I'll do what the rabbi says, I won't worry about afternoon service. But I won't think about it. He reached the other side of the street and the wind sliced into his open collar. He pulled his jacket tighter and buttoned the top two buttons. The *Sunday Forward* flapped against his chest from the pouch inside his jacket. Or maybe, he thought, if I can't sleep, I can read the paper.

Six

Millie is drying her face with the fluffy green towel she likes when Carl walks into the bathroom. "Morning," he says, and stoops to kiss the back of her neck, which smells of Palmolive soap and water and the slightly salty taste of Millie's skin.

Millie rolls her shoulder under his lips, pats his arm with her toweled hand, and smiles into the mirror at him. "Morning," she says. "Sleep well?"

Carl nods. He knows it is not meant as a question. Millie allows him only an instant to reply before she continues with what she wants to say.

"I started to wake you when I got up, but you were turned all the way away from me, hunched over on your side and breathing so deeply I didn't have the heart to wake you."

Carl nods again. The dream, he thinks, but he doesn't say anything. He has learned that some things he can explain to Millie, and some things, particularly the way his mind works when he is not overtired from work or worrying about next month's payments on the mortgage, he must keep to himself. For Millie, everyone is simple; people who have what Millie calls "thinking troubles" are guilty of paying too much attention to themselves. "I don't see," Millie always says, "why everybody makes such a huge fuss about living. You get born and you grow up and get married and raise children and grow old and die, that's all. No matter how much you worry, it happens to all of us." So when Carl begins to wonder, on the days when his back is not pricking him from the weight of his tool kit, or he has had an easy afternoon and doesn't begin to feel the bone tiredness seep into him soon after dinner, about what living is all about, and why he, Carl, son of a Russian immigrant, should be a TV repairman and have a son who is maybe going to college, he tells none of it to Millie.

Millie stares at him from the mirror. "You okay? You sure you feel okay?"

"Yeah," Carl says, and runs his hand across her waist, crumpling the limp cloth of her pajamas. "Why shouldn't I feel okay?"

"I don't know. You're quiet, that's all."

Millie moves away from the sink and Carl turns on the hot water tap and stares at the water flowing over his hands. The heat moves up his wrists into his arms and the water gurgles into the outflow pipe.

"Maybe. I was thinking."

Millie chortles. "Thinking! Excuse me! On a Sunday morning, yet. Well give the thinking a rest till after you eat your breakfast. I heard David get up over an hour ago, he must be starving already. So hurry up and get washed. You got all day to think."

She pads out of the bathroom. Carl soaps his hands, rinses them, stares at the dirt he can never scrape out from under his nails, and the crisscross pattern of cuts, scars, and scratches that laces across his fingers. He makes a fist with his left hand and watches the muscle below the joint of his thumb swell into a hard round ball. A workman's hand, he thinks. Not pretty. If I went on *What's My Line*, they would look once at my hands and know immediately that I was no white-collar worker. What would they think I was? Would they guess? Do you work outdoors or indoors, they'd say. Both, I could answer. It's true. Antennas you got to put up outside. I don't do many antennas any more; almost everybody already has one. Streets look like some kind of jungle's growing on the housetops—antennas. But still, I work outside and I work inside.

He soaps his face and rinses, decides not to shave because it's Sunday and the extra twenty-four hours' growth will mean a smoother shave Monday morning. The toothpaste is almost gone. He rolls the tube up to the metal plate at the top, sets it on the sink, and presses till a thin white stream of paste edges reluctantly onto the toothbrush. He stares at himself scrubbing away in the mirror, and thinks, as he always does, that the white foam on his lips makes him look like a mammy singer. Like Jolson in *The Jolson Story*. Then he remembers that they got some young *goy* to play Jolson, and he shakes his head. Hollywood! Couldn't even get a Jew to play Jolson. Had to find some good-looking young *shagetz!*

He scoops cold water into the cup of his hands and gargles, his head thrown back against the taut muscles of his neck, the water bubbling and gurgling in his mouth. "Ggguuuurggghh-hilllll," he trumpets, feeling the laughter begin to tumble in his stomach. "Ggggghhhhhuuuuuuurrrrggghhhlll—wwwwaaa-aappppssshhh!"

"Hey, crooner!" Millie shouts. "Perform later. C'mon!"

Carl chuckles as he wipes his face. A smear of toothpaste still lines a corner of his mouth. He reaches a thumb to flick it off, watches his face in the mirror, remembers the chocolate balls and Marcus and Joey and the soup pot. I better tell her, he thinks. She won't like it, but I better tell her.

So he goes into the bedroom, where he finds Millie already dressed. She's got her old blue slacks, too tight to button at the sides now, stuck together with a big safety pin, and an old red striped jersey that's faded and hangs down too long flops over her heavy ass. She steps away from the mirror and slaps Carl's stomach as he passes.

"Whoa! No wonder you're not in a hurry for breakfast. You've got a nice little storehouse down there. You planning to hibernate?"

Carl remembers Mrs. Rosenthal's pouchy cheeks and his bet with Dickie. "Listen," he says. "I've been thinking. It's been a long time since I've seen Dad."

Millie stops. She's almost out of the room, but she stops at the door and turns around to face Carl. Her expression doesn't change, she is still grinning, but Carl sees the way her eyes have narrowed, and watches her hand begin to pick-pick-pick at the safety pin holding her slacks.

"So?"

"So," Carl says, "I think maybe I'll go see him today."

Carl stares at Millie's face, at the top of her head where the short curls are fizzing out of their normal order. Nobody speaks. The floor creaks as Millie shifts her weight.

"All right," Millie says. She shrugs her shoulders.

Carl moves to the chair by the window and tugs at the drawstring of his pajamas. He checks to make sure the Venetian blinds aren't open too wide and then lets his pajama pants slide to the floor. He steps out of them, into his undershorts, and then unbuttons his pajama top.

"You don't mind?"

He hears the sharp click of her tongue against the roof of her mouth, and then the short exasperated sigh. "Carl. Please. Let's not start again. Not today. It's a nice day. The sun's shining. I didn't even worry whether David put a scarf on when he went for the paper. Will it do any good if I say something? Will you listen? Does it matter what I say? You want to go, go; that's all. Just leave me in peace. Go, come back, dinner'll be ready for you. Get yourself all upset, come home and be grumpy with me and David; I don't care. But don't talk to me about it. I got nothing to say."

Carl pulls his undershirt on, steps into his brown gabardine trousers that are pink across one knee because once Millie tried to wash them, and poured in too much bleach. He takes his green plaid flannel sport shirt from the back of the chair and sniffs at it. Doesn't smell bad, he thinks, and puts it on, leaving the flaps to dangle loose over his slacks.

"And David?" he says. He waits. It has to come. Me, that's all right. I can go. She doesn't like it, but she puts up with it. But not David. With David, it's different.

He buttons his shirt. Still she doesn't say anything. He leaves the top button open and turns. She is still standing by the door. Her eyes are narrowed, she has stopped grinning.

"Why? Why do you have to aggravate me? Why all of a sudden do we have to have a rotten filthy Sunday morning? I knew! I knew from the minute you walked into the bathroom, something was stirring in that head of yours. Thinking. I bet you were thinking. Never a minute's peace. One peaceful Sunday I can't even have for myself."

So, Carl thinks, here we go again. "And David?" he says.

"And David, what?"

"And David, too? You don't mind if I take David, too?"

"Oh, Carl, you make me sick. How many times we been through this before?"

She moves back into the room, and Carl watches her image caught in the double mirror. "Why? Just tell me that. Why? I don't even ask any more why you think you have to drive thirty miles on a Sunday to see an old man who swore for years that he didn't have a son, and then let you come to see him only when he got too sick to argue. I don't even ask any more why you have to go and sit with a crazy old man who mumbles curses at you for all the things you couldn't do for him when you were a kid! But why do you have to *shlep* David? Tell me that, just tell me that! Why do you have to take David, on a Sunday morning when he could be reading, or playing ball even, and *shlep* him thirty miles to the East Side, lead him through a crummy stinking neighborhood and up four rotten flights of stairs to a crummy hole of a room, to sit and stare at a crazy old man who happens to be your father!"

"Just for that. Just for that!" Carl senses his voice growing louder, and fights to keep down the surge of anger that begins to build in him. "Because he's my father. He's my father and he's David's grandfather and it makes him happy for a little while when we come to see him. That's all."

"It doesn't make him happy. He's so crazy and bitter, nothing could make him happy."

"It makes him happy. I know. It makes him happy. We come up and we sit and I tell him about the business and you and David, and then David sings for him, maybe the Blessings, maybe even the *Kiddush*, and it makes him happy. He doesn't say it, he doesn't show it, but it makes him happy. I know."

"You know! All of a sudden, you've got so much wisdom about your father. Where'd it all come from? Why didn't you use some of it years ago, when you walked out on him and went to Philly? Why didn't you realize, then, what it would do to him? Did your wisdom tell you he'd curse the day you were born, rip up your letters and throw them away without even opening them? Even the ones with checks in them?"

"All right!" Carl shouts. "All right! Now stop it! What I did when I left him I had to do! And you know it. You got no right to throw it in my face! Because you're angry I'm taking David, that's an excuse? You think I don't know why you don't want David to come with me? You think I don't know? It's not even because you don't want David to know his grandfather's an old country Jew who lives like an immigrant in a ghetto. That's bad enough, but it's not that. You're jealous. That's what it is. You don't want David to come with me because he likes to come; he enjoys himself when he comes with me. And you don't like that."

Carl almost snaps his mouth shut, cursing his tongue, cursing himself for an ignorant stupid fool. He stares at her and tries to decide what to do, but before he can find the words that say he is sorry, that he doesn't mean it, he sees tears begin to form in the corners of Millie's eyes. She turns and hurries out of the room; he hears her feet on the stairs.

"Millie!" he shouts. "Millie!"

Her feet sound through the living and sitting rooms, into the kitchen. He hears David's voice and then Millie's short answer. So, he thinks, I've done it again.

Breakfast drags. They carry out a charade of normality for David, who, of course, Carl thinks, has noticed that something is wrong. But unless we put it into words in front of him, we can ignore it. We can pretend it doesn't exist, that this is just another Sunday morning, that Millie and I haven't been shouting at each other fifteen minutes ago.

Almost in spite of himself, he picks up the thread of the quarrel. Who am I justifying myself to, he wonders, Millie or myself? But his stomach is stirring; the dreams and the quarrel are seething inside him. He stares across the table at Millie. What am I supposed to do, he thinks. Tell me, what am I supposed to do? He sits in that little room and he's dying and maybe two men, three men a week come up to say something to him. He's sick and bitter and lonely and above all, he's my father. I'm supposed to say to him, I'm sorry. You're a crazy old man, you treated me wrong in the past, I know you're lonely and you'd like to see your son and grandson, but I won't come. I'm thirty miles away and I've got a car and a free Sunday but I won't come to see you. I'm carrying a grudge for the way you treated me.

David clanks his spoon against the side of his cereal bowl.

"David!" Millie snaps. "Can't you eat without making noise?"

David looks up, prepared to snap back, then sees the look in Millie's eyes and bends back to his cereal.

"Sorry, Mom," he murmurs.

He's dying, Carl thinks, he's dying. I'm supposed to carry a grudge? I'm supposed to say, listen, old man, die by yourself, you may be my father, but you should have treated me better? Millie, Millie, Millie, how can you blame him for the way he's treated me? Did he know any better? Did he have a decent life, even; never mind a good life, did he have a decent life? He came to America like all the rest, because the streets were paved with gold. And what'd he find? Nothing but bad luck and trouble and sickness; a wife who dies giving birth to his only child, and a child who grows up to be a *goy*, who wants to do all the things the *goyishe* boys do, instead of being content to grow up a Jew. A boy who leaves the East Side as soon as he gets a chance, and goes to Philly. Philly! What'd he know about Philly, what'd he know about any place in America except the East Side and Williamsburg? The rest of America was full of Indians, for all he knew. Or *goyim!* So after I ran away, he shouldn't be bitter? He shouldn't think I deserve to be cursed? And now, he sits alone in that little room and he waits to die, with only his misery and his sore bones to keep him company, I shouldn't go to him?

Carl sets his coffee cup down into its saucer. "David," he says.

The boy looks up. "Yes, Dad."

Carl feels Millie's eyes on him, senses how she waits, coiled.

"I've been thinking of calling Gran'pop. Find out if he wants us to come see him. Want to come?"

"Today?" David says.

Carl nods.

"Sure," David says.

"You don't have to," Millie cuts in. "Don't go just because Dad asked you to. If you've got something better to do, you don't have to go."

Carl nods. "That's right. Don't come if you don't want to. I don't mind going by myself."

"No, I want to come. We weren't even going to play ball today; Vincent went with his mother up to Metuchen to see some friend of Buddy's. And besides, they took the backboards down at Richie Kline's. They're being repaired."

"Okay," Carl says, and glances at Millie. She moves her spoon round and round in her half-filled coffee cup.

"Are you sure?" Millie says. "Are you really sure you want to go? What about your homework? You haven't done any homework all weekend."

"Oh, Mom," David fidgets. "All I got is some algebra, and I can do that in homeroom Monday morning. I told you before, near Christmas vacation they never give us much homework. Everybody's too busy putting on plays and all."

You satisfied? Carl thinks. You satisfied, or you going to push him further?

He shoves his chair back, and the scraping nose startles Millie. She drops her spoon into her coffee, and a few drops splash onto her jersey.

"Damn," she says.

"I'm going to call Dad," Carl wipes his mouth with his napkin, pushes his chair against the table, and walks into the sitting room.

The ring jangles in his ear as Carl settles himself into the armchair by the phone table. Feinstein will have to climb the stairs to get the old man, so Carl squirms in the chair, prepared to wait. The phone rings for a long time. Maybe Feinstein's out, Carl thinks. What does Feinstein do with his time?

"Hello? Hello, Mr. Feinstein?"

"This is Carl, Mr. Feinstein. Is my father in?"

"Good. Thank you. No, I don't mind waiting."

I wouldn't call if I minded waiting. Maybe he was angry. But he didn't sound too angry. Four flights of stairs is a lot for an old man to climb. Carl hears the water running in the sink, and the clink and clatter of silverware and dishes. Millie's washing up. Thank God, David remembered to stay and help her. But I'd hate to be him, in that kitchen now.

"Hello, Dad? Dad, this is Carl. Yes, Carl. How are you?"

"Yes, it's me. Carl. How are you, Dad?"

"Oh."

"That's too bad."

"That's not good, Dad."

"Look, Dad, it sounds serious."

"Please, excuse me for mentioning it, but—well, maybe you should see a doctor."

"Yeah, I know. I understand. But still—maybe a doctor would help."

"Please, Dad, don't be angry with me. Listen. Why don't you let me pay for a doctor? If it's serious, you got to go, that's all. And I can—"

"All right, Dad."

"All right, I'm sorry I said anything. Look, is it all right if David and I come to see you today?"

"Yes, David too."

"Will you be home?"

"We'll be there in about an hour. Maybe an hour and a half. All right, Dad?"

"Okay. Goodbye, Dad."

Carl hears the click of the receiver and stands with the phone in his hand, imagining the old man climbing the steps, back to his tiny room. God, Carl thinks, how much pride, how much stubbornness! It's too much to hold inside one man. It sounds like heart attacks. Probably. But he could collapse on the street, on an icy sidewalk in the middle of New York's coldest winter, and he wouldn't ask a passerby to help him up. He'd get an attack in front of a doctor's office, but he wouldn't go in. He'd walk barefoot for a year, across every frozen pavement in New York, before he'd take five dollars of my money to buy himself a decent pair of shoes. My father. I had to have the world's most honest Jew for my father.

Finally Carl puts the phone down and walks into the kitchen. David is standing next to Millie at the sink, drying a dish.

"Go on," Carl says, and takes the dish and towel from the boy's hands. "I'll finish up. You go upstairs and get ready."

The boy squeezes past his father and mother and scoots through into the sitting room. Carl wipes at the dish, scraping the towel clockwise against the damp surface.

"He's sick, isn't he?"

"Says so. His heart."

"Attacks?"

Carl nods. "He's so proud. I practically had to beg him to let us come. Such a blind, foolish, stubborn old man."

Millie puts a wet hand on Carl's sleeve. "Look. I'm sorry. About before. I'm sorry I made such a fuss."

Carl covers her hand with his own. "I'm sorry, too. I didn't mean what I said. I just got angry, that's all; I got angry and lost my temper. I had a dream, see; about the old man. I had a dream before I woke up."

"A dream?" Millie says. "What kind of a dream?"

Carl hears the doubting tone in her voice. He pats her hand and grins. "Never mind," he says. "C'mon, let's finish the dishes."

$\mathcal{Seven}$

FEINSTEIN

When you're old, you shouldn't live alone, it's not good. That's what I said when I moved in here fifteen years ago, and that's what I still believe. But it's also not good you should live with your children, either. That's what I said to my son before I moved in here, and that's what I still believe. "Stay with us, Dad," he said to me, my Irving. "Stay with us, we'll be getting a bigger house soon, we'll have even more room." "Irving," I said, "listen, Irving, you're a fine son, and Molly's a fine daughter-in-law, every night I thank God for the both of you, but an old man like me, with a young couple, with two young children, it's just not good, it's not the right way to live. I got my ways and you got yours, sometimes I don't understand you and sometimes you don't understand me. We live together, what happens? Tempers. Arguments. It's not good, Irving. Old people and young people, they don't mix, they live in different kinds of worlds. So I think it's better I find a place, maybe with two or three old men, and then I come to visit you, you come to visit me, no more arguments."

He understood, my Irving did. "All right, Dad," he said. "If that's the way you want it, okay, I won't argue. But remember, any time you want to come back, you got a home with us." "Irving," I said, and I was almost crying, I was so proud to have such a son, "Irving, don't you never forget it, you're a fine son, Irving, a fine son. I only hope you have such luck with your own children as I have with you."

But I never found any old men to live with, like I said I would. Only this apartment and the small room upstairs, the old man's room. A lot of company I get out of him. I could have rented it to a deaf mute, it would've been just as good. No, it's not good to live alone. What I should do, I should get married again. Be nice having a woman around, breakfast waiting for me, dishes washed, beds made. Mistake it was, not looking for a woman before I moved in here. Maybe I could find one without marrying her, lots of women around would be happy to share an apartment without paying rent. Feinstein, Feinstein, what're you thinking? A good Jewish woman is going to move in with you, sleep in the same bed with you, do your dishes and wash your clothes, without marrying you? So who says she has to be Jewish? What are you, *mishuga*? What's Irving going to say about you living with a *shikse*? What's the rabbi going to say? They'll throw you out of the synagogue like they threw Zitomer!

So I'd have to marry a good Jewish woman, it would still be better than living alone. It's lucky for me I'm the way I am, and not like some old people, that's all I got to say. I don't like living alone so much, but it doesn't drive me crazy. That's more than I can say for some people.

But it's time that's the problem, time that I've always got on my hands, that I don't know what to do with. I sit in the chair and I rock back and forth and I stare at the wall, thinking, but what do I got to think about? Problems I got, in such a simple life? Who worries about problems? My money's in the bank, I'll probably die before I use half of it up, and there's always my Irving, God forbid I should have to ask him, but he's there.

That's the phone. It couldn't be for me. Irving called yesterday, who else would call? I got nobody else to call me. Maybe it's Irving again, something's wrong? I better go answer it.

"Hello?"

"Yes, this is Feinstein. Who are you?"

"Carl? Oh, Carl. Yes, he's in, I heard him come back from *shul* about an hour ago. You hold on for a while, I'll go and get him down."

Four flights of stairs I got to climb to get the old man to

answer a telephone call he probably doesn't want, anyway. What a crazy way to rent an apartment, out of my head I was, to take it. Three rooms on the first floor and one on the top. I need his money, I had to rent out the top room to him? Better I should have let it sit empty, it would have been less trouble. Company I think I'm getting. Come down to my place any time you want, we'll sit in the kitchen and drink a glass of tea, I told him, but does he ever come? Once in a blue moon he comes, that's all. And when he comes, you think we talk? He sits there staring at the wall, and finally I run out of questions so I sit too, a pair of old men like a couple Chinese, sitting and staring.

I'll only knock lightly. He's probably sitting and staring out the window.

He didn't hear. I better knock again.

"Hey, wake up. Your son's on the phone. Carl."

What's wrong with him, he's deaf all of a sudden? Maybe something's wrong, he doesn't feel well. I better go in.

He leaves the door open. If I was on the top floor, would I bother to latch the door? But look at him, he's sitting there like a statue, the bed isn't made, and he's sitting on it like a statue, staring out of the window.

"Listen, your son's on the phone. You better come downstairs."

"What? What do you want?"

Mazel tov. At least he's alive. I'm a ghost, what, you never saw me before?

"What do I want? I haven't been standing here for fifteen minutes, telling you? Carl's on the phone, he wants to talk to you. You'll be lucky if he didn't hang up, he's been waiting so long."

"Carl?"

Carl? Is my son named Carl or is yours?

"Yes, Carl. If you don't hurry up, he's going to decide he can't keep the phone company in business. He should hang up, it would serve you right."

"Feinstein, you don't even know anything about your own phone. Carl's calling from Highland Park, you still think it costs money to call from Highland Park? Well, it doesn't cost a penny, Rabinowitz explained it to me. When you got a phone you get to make so many calls for nothing."

"Sure, sure. The phone company is in business so you can make calls for nothing. I get my phone bill every month because the phone company's got a grudge against me, everybody else gets to make calls for nothing. Rabinowitz is a prophet or something, all of a sudden he knows what he's talking about? He's an oracle already, just because he's half crazy? He's even got a phone, he's telling you all about it? To call from Highland Park to here costs money. By the minute, it costs. And if you don't hurry up and go downstairs, Carl will have to work overtime next week, to pay for the call."

Oy, look at the way he gets up. Like every bone in his body was stiff and creaking. If he moved any slower he's be standing still. The bones stick out underneath his shirt. So what's he doing now? A jacket he has to put on?

"Listen, downstairs in my apartment is nobody but me and the phone. And the operator can't see through the wires, she doesn't care if you come down in your shirtsleeves, you could answer the phone in your underwear, in your pajamas, nobody would mind."

"Feinstein, what are you in such a hurry for? It's not your son on the phone. Even if it does cost, Carl's got money, he can afford it. And besides, if you weren't so stingy and got some heat in your apartment, I wouldn't have to put on a jacket every time I come down. Last time I had tea with you I almost froze, I was so cold. What I should do is put my coat on, an icebox your apartment's like. But I haven't got it. I gave it to Rabinowitz. But if I had it—"

Finally he's going downstairs. Lucky he goes first, I don't have to listen to him. Grumble, grumble, grumble, that's all he knows, if it isn't the heat then the light isn't bright enough, or the tea's cold. Something wrong all the time. Sometimes, sometimes, when I look at him, I'm glad I live alone.

Lucky the phone's in the kitchen. I can stay here on the couch and hear everything. Maybe I should read something, he shouldn't think I was listening when he comes out. So yesterday's *Forward* is good enough, I haven't read all of it twice yet.

"It's my back again. It's getting so bad sometimes, I can't walk."

That's the truth at least. How he gets to *shul* every morning, God only knows.

"I have to stop and sit down wherever I am. Until the pain goes away."

"And my heart the same way. Only last week I had two attacks."

Thank God I'm in good health. The only thing I pray for is I should stay healthy until I die, and then go quickly, without pain. When you're sick like he is, it's better to be dead.

"Two attacks I had, the second one was so bad I thought it was the end, I started praying."

"Serious? It should only be the end, that's all I ask. All I want is it should be over, I should die in a little peace. But no, I got to suffer, I got to suffer all the time. It's not right dying should be so much pain and trouble. You think it's easy, when your back's breaking and your heart stops every half-minute? You think I get any sympathy, any consideration? With only Feinstein to talk to in the whole house? What do you think we do, go to a show maybe? On my pension, shows I can afford? Feinstein's so cheap, heat he can't afford in his own apartment! God knows why he keeps a telephone."

So Carl can call up and talk to you, that's why I keep a telephone. You have to tell all your fairy tales to Carl, you have to grumble to him like you grumble to me? God knows why he wants to talk to you, all he gets is grumbling.

"A doctor? What good can a doctor do me? He's going to keep me from dying, give me a pill to make me live longer? Punch me in the arm with a needle? No, doctors I don't need. I can die by myself, I got enough trouble without a doctor."

"Help? What kind of help? They're thieves, all of them, all they want is money. You know what doctors cost? Thieves, all of them, robbers! All of a sudden I got money to throw away on doctors?"

"Oh, so now all of a sudden you're a good son? You worried maybe I'll drop dead and not leave you anything? Well I got nothing to leave, so you shouldn't worry, you can save your money, you won't get a thing out of me."

"I never asked you for money when I was well and I never took any, now that I'm dying you think maybe I'm crazy too, all of a sudden I should start taking your money? I never took it before and I don't need it now, I don't want nothing from you, nothing."

What a way to treat a son. Serve him right Carl should hang up on him. Thank God my Irving and I get along the way we do.

"So come—what's stopping you? If you want to come, come, since when do you ask me about anything, since when does what I say matter? When you left for Philly did you ask me, did you stop to think about what I wanted, how I felt? Did you ever ask me about anything, you have to ask me now? If you want to come, come. To me it makes no difference. . . . Is the boy coming, too?"

Listen to him. To me it makes no difference.

"Where else would I be but home? I got dances and parties to go to, maybe? I got another house in Florida I can run to in the wintertime, to get away from the cold?"

"An hour, five hours, you think I care? Come when you want, if you don't want, don't come."

"So goodbye."

He's coming in. I should keep my mouth shut and not say anything, it's none of my business. But somebody should tell him he's got no right to treat a son like that.

"Next time you don't have to come up and get me. Just tell him I'm not in, that's all."

"Why do you treat him so bad? You got twenty more sons, you can afford to treat Carl so bad?"

"And you, you got no other business, you have to listen to other people's phone calls? You worried somehow I'm going to spend your money on the phone? What does it matter to you how I treat my son? He's my son!"

"I got a son, too. I could have lived with him, but I didn't. I could take money from him, but I don't. But the other things he wants to give, those I take. But you, you got a son who wants to give to you and you treat him like dirt. I think you don't deserve a son like Carl, and in my own living room I got a right to say it. If you don't like it you can go back upstairs."

Why do I bother? A waste of time, just gets me all upset. Him, maybe he likes to argue, but me it doesn't do any good. He wants to treat Carl like a dog, let him. Does he listen when I tell him fathers and sons don't have to live the way he does? Carl, I feel sorry for, but it doesn't help Carl for me to argue with him.

"What do you know about it, you can afford to butt in and feel big? All you see is the way he acts now, when I'm dying and he smells my money."

"Money he knows you haven't got, you tell him that every time you talk to him."

"You don't know, you don't know nothing about it, nothing at all. The years I spent, slaving for him, father and mother both I was to him, you don't know nothing about that. And did I work so he'd grow up to be a *goy*, did I slave so he'd run away to Philly, did I sacrifice for him to marry somebody no better than a *shikse*? A kosher home they don't even keep!"

"So?"

"So now I'm supposed to forgive him, I'm supposed to take his money, I'm supposed to be happy because he comes to see me?"

"Listen, I don't care what you do. But if you don't want to see Carl, tell him not to come. That's all. Just call him back and tell him not to come. I'll pay for the call, even to Highland Park. It's worth it, for a little peace and quiet."

So go ahead now, call him back. You don't want to see him, call him back.

"Calling him! What good's calling him? He says he's coming, I can stop him? He never listened to me before, he's going to listen now? If I say don't come, he'll listen?"

I'm getting too excited. In a minute I'll be screaming at him. It isn't worth it. I should have my head examined, trying to talk sense to him. I should shut up and let him go upstairs.

"Look, maybe you're right and it's none of my business. I apologize for what I said in the beginning, it's my fault the whole argument started. I just want to say one more thing, that's all, then we can forget about it, you can go back upstairs, and I'll go back to my paper. But it's no good making believe you don't want to see Carl. You want to see him, you want to see him and David, too! You don't fool me, I know how you feel. You don't even fool Carl. You're happy to see them, you want them to come. But you're such a stubborn old mule you won't admit it to yourself."

And now you expect him to go upstairs like a good boy. Feinstein, you're an idiot! Look at him staring at me, like he's going to explode in another minute, he's so angry. And look at me, my hands are actually shaking. I'll be lucky if my stomach cramps don't bother me the rest of the day. That's just what I need, for the old man and Carl to make me sick again. I don't have enough of my own troubles. Carl's battles I have to take on my shoulder, so I can make myself sicker. I won't eat, either; I get upset and I go without eating the whole day. Tomorrow I'll go down and buy a little piece of meat, fry it with some onions, it'll make me feel better. Even a bottle celery tonic I'll buy.

He's still talking. He's so excited he doesn't even know I'm not listening.

"Just a *goy*, they're bringing him up like a *goy*. He'll be lucky to have a *bar mitzvah* when he's thirteen. They think I don't see. Every time the boy comes, I see what they're doing to him, a good Jewish boy and they're making a *goy* out of him. Not a thing he knows, nothing, nothing."

Maybe if I just keep nodding and don't say nothing, he'll run down. How long can you talk to somebody that doesn't talk back? A record machine he's not, besides, even record machines run down. He should have a handle to wind himself up again.

"My own grandson, I shouldn't care? I shouldn't care what they're doing to him?"

You should care, by all means you should care, who said anything about not caring? Care all you want, pound your head against the wall, tear your hair out, but do it upstairs, so I can have some peace in my apartment. But why is he staring at the linoleum? It's cracking over there in the corner? It could be, it's cracking everywhere else. Please, have pity on my cracked linoleum, it only makes more cracks when you get excited and walk on it. Me, I know where all the cracks are, I don't walk on them. So go upstairs. There if the floorboards start cracking the roof will fall in and then you'll be on the fourth floor instead of the top. Finally. He's going. My head is so stuffed with all this talk, sooner or later I would have screamed at him.

"The trouble with you, you're half *mishuga*. You stay down here all day with no heat, reading yesterday's paper over and over, waiting for the phone to ring so you can come up and make fun of me. Sometimes I think you're trying to freeze me, the apartment is so cold when I come down to talk on the phone I can see my breath in front of my face. Stingy and half *mishuga*, that's what you are."

Next time you come down I'll turn the heat off altogether. I'll lock you in the icebox, in the freezing compartment. Go ahead, crawl up the stairs. It'll be a long time before I come up to your room again. Me, *mishuga!* If anybody's *mishuga*, it's you, not me. I treat my son the way a father should treat him, not like a dog. And besides, I don't have fits, and I hear people when they're talking to me. Except when they're like you, grumbling and quarreling all the time.

I'll latch the door, just to make sure he doesn't come down again. Freezing! It's not even cold in here. What does the thermostat say? Sixty-two. No, sixty-three, the red line's past the two marker. Warm enough for any sensible person. So. I should sit down and relax, try not to stay upset. It doesn't do any good to my stomach. Tomorrow, I'll buy a piece of meat. I'll fry it with onions. Celery tonic, too. I got to be careful, to remember the celery tonic.

Eight

The old man crawled slowly up the stairs to the top floor, pushed open his door, and shuffled into his room. The torn shade of his one streaked window was snapped into a sagging roll at the top of the sash, its pull-cord fraying downward into a listless dangling pendulum. The old man sat down on his bed and turned to stare dully out his window. Sometimes, after he had stared silently, motionlessly, for as long as an hour or more, a gull would come sweeping down the street and dip into the column of air space between the rows of buildings, propelling itself with a lazy graceful flap of its wings past the old man's window and back toward the harbor. Sometimes a flock of pigeons would wheel by, or the cat kept by the woman who wore a red bandanna and lived across the street would ease onto the window ledge, stretch itself, yawn, arch its back, wedge its claws against the rim of molding that defined the edge of the narrow parapet, and stare across at the old man. The old man would stare back for as long as it took the cat to back down and crawl inside again. He would stare very calmly, realizing that this was a battle between himself and the cat. He would stare straight into the cat's narrow eyes and think to himself, fall down, cat. Fall down, you hellcat. Fall down. But the cat never fell. It stared at the old man until it turned its back and slipped inside.

The old man hated the pigeons and the gulls with the same dull undifferentiating anger that formed his prayers for the cat's death. Once a pigeon had fouled the coat he had given to Rabinowitz, but that was longer than the old man's memory could reach. He hated the pigeons for the same reasons he hated the gulls, who had never done him any harm and could have brought him a breath of clean unconcerned beauty and the taste of an open sea on the tongue, had he cared to receive it. He hated the pigeons and the gulls that flew across his bounded universe, he hated the cat that stared into his window, he hated every dog that crossed his path, every mouse that scurried underneath his bed, even the few bedbugs that rooted in his mattress.

But now he sat on the bed and let the grayness of the day sink into him, and not a bird, not a cat, appeared. Fool, the old man thought. Nosy old fool. I forgot that he could hear, he probably has the phone in the kitchen so he can sit on his couch and listen to everything. I should have hung up, I should have closed the kitchen door, I should have gone down to Schreiber's store and called Carl from there, but I didn't think, I chattered like a monkey on the phone, and Feinstein sat there behind his paper, that paper he reads so many times he could tell you the news backward, and listened.

A small finger of pain crooked softly deep in the old man's back. He breathed as deeply as he dared, tried to relax the trembling muscles of his stomach, and waited for the pain to arc across his back and explode in the rasping hollows of his chest.

The finger beckoned, beckoned, began to steal swiftly away. The old man waited until its receding echoed only a ghost of a tremor where a pain might have been, then nodded to himself, as if some act of will, some conscious choice, some assertion of himself, had reprieved him from that particular session of agony.

But I am getting careless, the old man thought. I'm too old to care any more, that two men know so much about me and my business, I don't even belong to me, any more. Ten, fifteen years ago, I would have moved away, today, this minute, but instead I let Feinstein listen to what I say to Carl and I don't even care he hears. And Zitomer? The old man rested his head in his hands, rubbing the heels deep into the sockets of his eyes. I am still ashamed for that night with Zitomer. Sick I wasn't, crazy I wasn't, in cold blood I sat in his kitchen at the back of his store, stirring my tea with the long-handled spoons that you can steal from Woolworth's in summertime when they serve iced tea, and I told him not only everything that troubled my mind but so much about the past that even if he never tells anyone, I can never look him in the face again, or hold up my head like a *mensch* when he's in the same room.

It was a cold, quiet night; the steam from their tea and their breath fogged the glass of Zitomer's kitchen window. Zitomer had talked all the way back from the synagogue, and the old man had tried to understand and to constrain his own confession. The urge to talk, to spill all that he held inside him, had listened to and relived on sleepless nights when the wind howled outside his one window, stirred him to restless movements that shifted the tea glasses, clanked the teaspoons, jarred the table.

Finally, Zitomer finished; the slow downward procession of the words to almost a whisper told the old man that Zitomer was done. So I can begin, the old man thought. But he did not know how. He stared at the scuffed, stained hardboard floor, and made small neat circles with the splitting tips of his black shoes. Zitomer stirred his tea with the long spoon, sipped, blew, stirred again. He sipped some more and stared at the old man over the rim of the frosted glass. Finally he sat the glass down on the wooden kitchen table, smacked his lips several times.

"Something's troubling you?"

"Yes," the old man said. "Something's troubling me, that has been troubling me for a long time," and without preamble, without even wonder that he could tell to Zitomer what had been bottled up inside him for so long, he began to talk. "You see, Zitomer, I am not a very good man. Maybe nobody's a good man, but soon I am going to die, no use lying to myself, everybody dies, and my time's coming, I can feel it in my bones. So what I keep thinking is, what will happen to me after I die? If I just die, just lie there in the ground, that's not so bad, how can it be bad not to know anything, not to be anything? But suppose God doesn't forgive me, suppose he's angry at all the things I've done, suppose there's a place for people like me, suppose the *goyim* are right and there is a hell? Then I'll go there, Zitomer, I'll go there. Because you don't know, you don't know the things I've done. In the old country, in Russia, I ran away from my parents with all the money I could find in my father's tobacco jar, I got a job on a small farm near Charnitsev, and I played with one of the kitchen maids until I finally got her to sleep with me, in the sweet hay in the top loft of the barn. The other fellow I worked with, a big clumsy lout named Shmuel Yaakov, was sweet on Marfa, so when Marfa got pregnant I blamed it on him, I swore blue in the face that I'd never touched Marfa, that it was Shmuel Yaakov that had her, and he, poor fool, admitted it and agreed to marry her, because he loved her. Marfa kept her mouth shut, I'd found another girl by then, and besides, it wouldn't have done her any good to refuse to marry Shmuel Yaakov, because I was out of Russia the next month. Smetyanov, the farmer I worked for, decided to take his family to America, and caught as I was with Marfa and her father, I begged, I pleaded with Smetyanov to pay my passage. I told him I'd do anything, I'd work for him in America, I'd remember him in my prayers. Finally he took me along. But when we got to New York, I gave him the slip and disappeared. And," the old man whispered, staring down at the hardboard floor, "I took the family's silver set with me, to sell. So I could start my life in America with some money."

The creaks and groans of the decaying beams of the old house sounded loud in the silence after the old man's whisper. Zitomer sucked at an unlit pipe and stared at the old man with quiet, waiting eyes.

"Well, that's only the beginning. In New York I found a job for myself and settled down to live. But it was hard work. I worked at a dress factory, pushing heavy carts of material up and down the rows of machine operators; every day, pushing that cart miles, over a cold cement floor. So I decided there must be an easier way to make money than by working so hard for it. You could marry somebody whose father had it. A butcher around the corner from the boardinghouse I lived in had a daughter, Naomi. I used to talk to her sometimes when I went past the shop. Why not, I thought, the old man's got plenty of money out of that store, the daughter's not bad-looking, I could use a wife, why not? So one day I went around to the butcher's in my one good suit. I waited until almost closing time, when there was nobody left in the store and he was already beginning to scrub down the big wooden cutting blocks that get caked with fat and blood after a day's business, and I told him that since I had no mother and father to come and speak for me, I had to come myself and tell him that I would like to marry his daughter. Well, he was surprised; he looked me over a few times, he asked me a lot of questions, and finally he shook his head.

"'Well,' he said, 'I don't mind telling you that you're not exactly what I expected as a husband for Naomi. In the first place, I think she's still a little young to be married, and secondly, I don't mind telling you I was thinking of somebody with a position, somebody that could take care of her the way I do. But you're a decent, hard-working young man, I can see that. And frankly, Naomi's a little headstrong, she's got all these modern notions about how women should pick their own husbands, and she's always telling me that in America you don't marry off your daughters, you let them find their husbands. So I say to her, you want to find a husband yourself, so find him. I only want you to be happy, that's all. So it's up to Naomi, not me,' the butcher finished. 'If you want to call on Naomi, I give you my blessing, but it's her you'll have to ask, not me.'

"The rest was easy. Naomi was headstrong, but she was vain, too; once I learned what she liked to hear, I knew just how to get around her. Soon she was telling her father she wanted to marry me. Her father argued, said I had such a poor job I couldn't even support myself, let alone both of us. But Naomi only shouted louder: why couldn't he help us, he had plenty of money? The butcher fought for a long time, but Naomi wore him down, and finally he agreed to give us a hundred dollars as a wedding present, and take me on as an assistant in the shop.

"It didn't work, me and that shop. Naomi's father was honest. Honest! Can you imagine it, an honest butcher? Long lectures he used to give me, about the trust of your customers being more important than the money you made from them. And every day he scrubbed those scales till they gleamed. No thumbs, no extra paper on the scales. And always give the customer what he wants. God, how I hated it. All those fat, stupid women, staring over the counter watching me cut their meat. A little more, Mrs. Bloomstein? Trim the fat, Mrs. Yoselmann? Yes, no, please, certainly, to fat stupid women nine hours a day, every day except Saturday. And you couldn't even cheat them. Every time I saw I could have added an extra quarter-pound here, nicked a quarter, thirty cents there, I swore at Naomi's father until my mind was so angry with him I could scream. Finally I started using my thumbs on the scale, not much, just a little with the customers I really hated. Then I started making little mistakes in the prices, in the addition, when I was certain they were too stupid to notice. Once in a while, with the sharp ones, I made a mistake in their favor, and when they pointed it out to me, Naomi's father only trusted me more. So I got a little careless, I started pocketing the extra money, and finally a couple customers complained. But I covered myself so well all Naomi's father could do was suspect me. He couldn't prove anything, but he watched me like a hawk, waiting. So I had to be honest again, let all these women beat me, get the best of me. I did as much chiseling as I could, but it wasn't much, every time I was at the scale I could feel him behind me, watching. Finally, I couldn't take it any more. I quit the store and went back to work at the dress factory. But this time I was smart. I worked out a deal with one of the other cart-pushers, and we lifted a good ten dollars' worth of material every week. We even got a watchman fired because he couldn't stop the thefts."

The old man smiled at the memory of the little Polack watchman, too scared to search under the loose heavy coat, where rolls of material were tucked into the pouches in the lining. Then he looked up toward the bare bulb hanging from its black cord swaying very gently in the draft from Zitomer's door that never quite closed, and saw Zitomer's face still staring sadly and patiently at him. The old man remembered why he had started the story, and the weight of his care came back to him.

"So that's why I'm troubled. There's more, even, but that's enough, enough for you to understand that if God doesn't forgive me, what can I do? Forgiveness from these people I can't even ask, most of them are dead! And," the old man whispered, again looking down at the floor, "sometimes, in my dreams, in the daytime even, they come back to haunt me, to torment me for what I did to them."

The room was quiet again. The old man stared at the floor until the tears that had begun to cloud his eyes washed back into the corners, and then looked up at Zitomer.

"So," Zitomer nodded. "It is a lot to carry on your head, what you tell me. It is a lot to think about, that much wrong. What can I tell you? Everybody buries inside themselves things that they done, that they can't forget. Me, too, I got my own list of what I done to other people, that I can't forget about. And what can I do? Like you, the people are all dead, I can't even tell them I'm sorry. Not that saying I'm sorry would help, even if they weren't dead. But it would be something."

Zitomer shook his head.

"I don't know. Life is hard. Maybe God doesn't expect us to be perfect. Maybe he only wants us to try. But who knows where the trying stops? What do you say when you've tried and failed? What do you say about all the years when you didn't even try? What can I say about the thousands of lies I've told, the hundreds of customers I've cheated?"

"Everybody's weak. God knows we're weak."

"Maybe. But weakness can be an excuse," Zitomer said. "I know that. It's not that we're weak, therefore God must forgive us. It's that we try our best, and then, when we fail, we try to understand why, and we promise ourselves and God not to let it happen again. And then we tell God that we're sorry and ask forgiveness."

Maybe, the old man thought, it's never too late to say that you're wrong, that you're sorry. To ask forgiveness. And if I can't ask it of Shmuel Yaakov, of Smetyanov and Marfa and all the rest, I can ask it of God.

"I can't worry about the past," Zitomer said. "Sometimes I feel I only been living since that afternoon in my store, when I gave the *schwartze* that car for sixty cents. I only got maybe five, six more years to live, and I got to live those right, so how can I worry about all the years I lived wrong?"

The old man sat, his head in his hands, feeling the warmth from Zitomer's stove seep into him, thinking that if only he could stay with Zitomer and listen to Zitomer talk, the voices would go away, and the dreams would not trouble him, he would be able to live out the rest of his days in some kind of peace.

"You make me happy inside."

"I make myself happy as well," Zitomer answered. "For the first time in so many years, I hate to go to bed each night, and I wake in the morning like a spring chicken, bouncing out of bed so quick you'd think I had a nice plump little girl to run to."

The old man chuckled. Then he imagined Zitomer's lean wrinkled body and almost bald head bundled into bed next to the rosily beaming face of a bouncy young girl, and he started to laugh. Zitomer joined in, and the two of them rocked back on their wooden kitchen chairs until Zitomer's chair passed the invisible line of balance and knocked against the wall.

"My sides," gasped Zitomer. "Oh, my poor stomach."

The old man wiped his eyes and let his laughter subside into a giggling cough. And all the way home, he felt the release of that laughter, and the warmth of Zitomer's kitchen and Zitomer.

But that night was six weeks past, and what the old man remembered now, as he slumped on his bed and stared at the lifeless winter sky outside his window, was neither warmth nor laughter, but how much of his life and the secrets he carried inside him he had given away to another man. Lucky for me, he thought, that so many of the members think Zitomer is crazy. Even if he tries to tell them about me, they won't listen. Maybe even the rabbi didn't listen, this morning in the synagogue. And in the end, it doesn't matter, what he knows and what Feinstein knows. I'm going to die soon enough anyway, I should bother my head about what they know.

He forced himself off his bed with a slow, quavering push of both his arms, finally swayed himself to his feet. I should put some water on, he thought, for tea, in case Carl and the boy want some. It's a cold day outside, maybe they would like some hot tea. But lemon I'm out of, I don't have any lemon. So all of a sudden they can't drink tea without lemon? I guess I should run out and buy some lemon, just for Carl and the boy? They can drink tea without lemon.

He filled the teapot with water and set it on the stove. Behind him the cracked porcelain clock that Feinstein had donated ticked away. I wonder what was the last time I wound it, the old man thought. What does it matter? What do I need time for, to tell me anything I don't already know? I'm in no hurry that a kitchen clock can do anything about.

But he turned anyway, to look at the clock. Forty minutes, more or less, before Carl and the boy come. The bed waited, undone, sheet and blanket curled into a dingy pattern of lines and hollows, twists and ridges. He swept back the blankets, smoothed the sheet, tucked it under the mattress. Then he folded the blankets, cornered the loose edges, fluffed the pillow, and whirled the bedsheet so that it settled slowly and gracefully into place. He fussed with the pillows for a minute more. There was nothing more to do. The sink was empty, the table was clear, the two chairs were in place, only the glass of Polident and water stood on his bureau. I will leave it for another night, he thought. It is only two days old, it still has some strength left.

The old man stood by the window again, but still nothing stirred. So he went to the kitchen table, sat in one of the flat-white wooden chairs that Feinstein had provided, and pulled at the warped drawer of the kitchen table until it creaked open. He took his carefully sharpened pencil and the almost finished letter to the secretary of his burial society, and set them on the table.

It is about time for me to finish the letter. It is getting closer to the time I'll need it. So.

He licked the pencil point, stared at the rigidly lined progression of his cramped handwriting crawling across the page.

Arnold Seligman, Esq.
Secretary,
Solomon Ibn Gabirol Society
568 East 14th Street
New York, New York.

Dear Secretary Seligman,

I got your last letter with the receipt, the letter that said I was done paying to the Society, that I didn't owe nothing more. Well, I told you in my last letter, I thought I was paid up two months ago, but I guess maybe you got better bookkeepers than me, so instead of complaining I paid the extra two months. But now that I'm all paid up, I'm writing to say how I want everything to be. It's not that I'm trying to be fussy, it's just that I don't think I got too much longer, and I have to tell you how I want everything done.

The old man licked his pencil again. Maybe it is not exactly formal, he thought, but it is all right, it is good enough for him to understand.

> When it comes my time, I want you should bury me quickly. I don't want any service in your chapel. I want you to bury me as fast as you can, with only Rabbi Davis, from the Beth Israel Synagogue on Fourth Street, where I belong, and the friends that Jacob Feinstein, my downstairs neighbor, will notify, at the funeral. That's all the people I want at the cemetery, there shouldn't be any fuss, maybe Rabbi Davis will want to say a few words, that's all right, but no more. I don't need *Kaddish* to be said for me by the Society, because Feinstein will say it for me at Beth Israel and Nathan Rabinowitz, another friend, will say it in his home.

I don't have to tell him who's going to say *Kaddish* for me. He doesn't care who says *Kaddish*, as long as the Society doesn't have to worry. He's an officer, my personal business he only wants to know as much as he has to. The old man started to cross out the lines, then realized it would make too much of a mess of the letter. I don't have an eraser, he whispered to Seligman, or else I would take away the lines. But I'm sorry. I'll leave them in, but you should understand I realized it wasn't necessary to tell you about the *Kaddish*.

> PLEASE, ON NO ACCOUNT don't tell my son or nobody else in my family until after I'm buried. I don't want my son at the funeral. I don't want any of my family at the funeral. I only want those people I mentioned. After I'm buried, you can tell my son, but don't tell him before the funeral.

I wonder what he'll think, reading that, the old man thought. Maybe that I don't like my son, that's all. Or maybe my son don't like me. Anyway, what does it matter what he thinks? It makes a difference? I'm a paid-up member and I got a right to run my funeral the way I want it.

> I ask you, please, to do everything I ask the way I want it. Maybe it seems like I'm causing you a lot of trouble, but I don't

mean to, it's very important to me, what I asked. And after all, I'm a paid-up member, I got certain rights. And what else have I ever asked from you?

Thank you very much.
Yours sincerely,

and the old man signed his name, forming the letters slowly, squinting over the nudgings of the pencil to make sure his signature looked the same as always, so that Seligman would have no doubt who had written the letter.

He started to fold the letter to put back in the drawer, to read it once more before he sent it off. Then he remembered about the stone, unfolded the letter and spread it out.

P.S. In a few more weeks I will be done paying for my stone, which Levin the stone-cutter, 125½ Avenue A, is making. Please get in touch with him when the stone is needed, and he will carve the final date and send it to the cemetery. Everything else that should be on the stone he knows.

Now the letter was finished, but the old man felt it was too much like business to end it that way, so he added:

Levin is a good man and will have the stone ready in time, so you shouldn't worry. Thank you.

Yours very sincerely,

signed his name again, folded the letter, and put it back in the drawer.

He started to push the drawer shut, then fumbled around the corners until his fingers found the small folded paper that announced Zitomer's expulsion from the synagogue. He took the paper out. It was creased, so that some of the corners were bent; it was dirty from finger stains and the caking of the dust inside the drawer. He opened the letter and read it through, although he had read it so many times in the last three weeks that he knew everything, from the Dear Member followed by his typewritten name to the Yours Sincerely at the end, above Rabbi Davis's sprawling signature.

Such a simple letter. For such a big thing. Again the old man wished that they would call him Dear Sexton, or even Dear *Shamos*, instead of just Dear Member. All right, so being a *shamos* isn't so important, but who else gets up at six every morning, opens the *shul*, turns on the lights, folds the *talesim*, counts the prayer books to make sure nobody walks out with one, and then closes up after *Maariv* in the evening? Maybe it's not such an important job, but somebody has to do it, and I do it good enough so they could pay attention to me once in a while. Not that they should invite me to the officers' meeting, like the one they had when they decided to throw Zitomer out of the *shul*. I'm thankful I didn't have any part of that. When Cornfeld started screaming I could hear it clear all the way upstairs where I was cleaning. From downstairs, with all the doors closed, I could hear him.

"I'm not going to stand for it," Cornfeld screamed. "Nobody in his right mind would stand for it! An idiot, I tell you, an idiot! Thursday afternoons he comes marching into my store, full of customers.

" 'Cornfeld, I want to see you,' he says, loud enough so all my customers can hear.

" 'Later, Zitomer,' I say, 'I'm busy now.'

"But does he listen? Does he go away? Like hell he does. He stands there, in the middle of my shop, and he shouts:

" 'Cornfeld, you're a thief, you're a *ganif*! You think I don't know how much markup you get on the stuff you sell? You think I don't know where it comes from, or how you get it? Some day, Cornfeld, they'll catch you; it's ten years in jail for selling stolen goods. And what do you need it for, Cornfeld, you got to cheat everybody to live? You don't make enough, you need so much money? You don't even spend it, Cornfeld, you don't even give it to charity, you lock it up in a bank. Cornfeld, Cornfeld, with all the people in the world who're sick, who're starving, does that money give you pleasure, all locked up in the bank?'

"I could have killed him.

" 'Get out of my store,' I screamed. 'Get out of my store or, so help me God, I'll have you arrested, I'll get you thrown in jail and let you rot. Get out!'

"He walked out the way he came in, like he owned the place.

"'Remember, Cornfeld,' he said at the door. 'The Ten Commandments don't tell you to steal from your neighbor. They tell you not to. And somebody you'll have to answer to for all those broken commandments, Cornfeld.'

"So finally I got rid of him, I got him out of the store. But what did my customers think? What did my salesgirl think? Suppose the word gets around, what he said, you think I got a chance to stay in business? You think Variety Clothing Shop and Liebman's flea-bitten little hole will keep quiet about what he said? It'll be all over the East Side in a week! I'm ruined, ruined! And all because of that crazy nut of a Zitomer!"

"My store he came into, too," another voice said, and the old man, finished now with the folding and counting of the pile of prayer shawls, moved as close as he dared to the door leading downstairs into the assembly room, where all the meetings and discussions were held.

"He came in on a Tuesday afternoon, when thank God, business was slow, there was nobody else in the shop.

"'Riskin, I want to talk to you,' he said.

"'Well, I don't want to talk to you, Zitomer. I heard enough from you in the synagogue; in my own shop I'm a free man, I don't have to listen to your nonsense.'

"He just stood there and looked at me, with a smile on his face like he was talking to a little boy who couldn't understand.

"'Riskin, Riskin, I know where your heart is, you can't fool me. You think you can fool me? You know I'm right, don't you? You know what I said was right. Nobody needs to make the kind of profit you make, Riskin. People got to have fruits and vegetables to live, but you don't have to suck them dry, Riskin. How many times you told me about shortweighing and shortchanging?'

"I tried to argue, to interrupt, but he wouldn't let me.

"'Listen,' he said. 'For thirty-five years I was the same as you, and now all of a sudden I've changed. Why? Some of the others say I'm mad, but you know me, Riskin, you know I'm not mad. Then why did I change? Why do I go around talking like this, barging into people's shops and preaching to them? I'll tell you, I'll tell you why, Riskin. For five thousand years we been persecuted, we been chased from country to country, kicked around like dogs, cheated and slaughtered. And all that time, what we had, what we could have given to the world, was the truth of the Ten Commandments. Because when God gave them to us, Riskin, he gave them to us to live by. Not to study, or to write learned commentaries about, but to live by. And now I know, Riskin, that the rest of the world is in as bad a shape as we've always been, and all we have to do, all any of us have to do, is just get back to the truth of the Ten Commandments, to live the way God wants us to. It's such a simple thing. Ten Commandments, and the first one doesn't even tell us to do anything. But we can change the world with them; we can show the rest of the world what they mean; we can be the people that God meant us to be—the children of the Covenant!'"

"Enough," said Rabbi Davis. "We could spend all day talking about what Zitomer says, but we know too much about that already; we all heard him that night in the synagogue. Now what we have to—"

"Listen, Rabbi, he came into my shop too, not once, but twice."

"And mine also, lunchtime, if you please, when I'm behind the counter trying to make some extra sandwiches so we don't run short; he comes in—"

"Look, I can't stop Zitomer from coming into your shops," Rabbi Davis shouted. "Only the police can do that. What we're talking about today, what we're supposed to be doing here, is not talking about what Zitomer said in your shop or your shop or your shop, but about whether he's got a right to stay in the synagogue."

The old man had stepped quickly back from the door, bumping his heel against the edge of a pew. Even the thought that the sound might carry downstairs to the meeting did not frighten him as much as the idea of throwing Zitomer out of the synagogue. How can you throw someone out? Take away their membership, I suppose, but what does that mean? That a man can't come to synagogue to pray? That Zitomer can't walk into Beth Israel any more? Ever? What could a man do, without the synagogue that was so much a part of his life? The old man moved closer to the door again.

"It's no good, that's all; we just can't go on this way. If he would agree to keep his mouth shut, to come to the synagogue only to pray and keep his mouth shut until the service is over, not a word would I say about what he argues afterwards." Rabbi Davis cleared his throat. "But to interrupt a service. And not once, he's not satisfied with once, he has to interrupt not only the service but the discussion, too. Twice, he has to open his crazy mouth. Twice! What am I supposed to do, I can't shut him up. One of these days I'll get so mad I'll throw a prayer book at him! How would you like that, your rabbi throwing a prayer book from the pulpit? No, it's got to stop, that's all there is to it. I've talked to him many times, pleaded and begged with him just to keep quiet, not to interrupt the service. But he won't listen. 'What good are services,' he says, 'everybody can pray, but no one follows the Commandments.' I'll give him Commandments!"

The old man had not stayed to hear any more, but had tiptoed back softly to the synagogue door, switched off the lights, and struggled out into the cold evening air. The rabbi would win because he always got what he wanted, nobody could argue with the rabbi. The rabbi always knew what was best for the membership. So Zitomer would find a letter waiting for him next morning, announcing that the officers of Beth Israel had decided he was no longer a member, no longer allowed to come and worship in the synagogue.

The old man sat with the soiled letter hanging loosely in his fingers. Zitomer, Zitomer, what do you do now? How can a Jew be a Jew without a synagogue? Another *shul* you could go to, but you won't—you'll sit and wait until they realize that you're right and send someone to apologize, someone to invite you back.

The wind rattled the loose panes of his window. The old man looked up from the table and the letter. It's a crazy world, when a man knows only one thing for most of his life, and then changes his mind near the end of it, so they throw him out of the *shul*. Because Zitomer isn't crazy. I should be as crazy as he is. I'd be a lot better off. That night in the synagogue, the first night he spoke to us, there was a silence for his words; the membership sat without stirring, and listened.

That was a strange night, the night Zitomer spoke. If I had known what Zitomer wanted when I heard him and Rabbi Davis talking, what would I have said? No, Zitomer, don't speak.

It'll change your life, Zitomer; better stay quiet. But it was too late, then, to stop him.

"But why, Zitomer? Why all of a sudden you have to talk in a Friday night service?" Rabbi Davis shook his head. "Can't it wait till tomorrow afternoon, you can bring it up downstairs in the discussion?"

Zitomer shook his head.

"No, no," he said excitedly. "It can't wait. It's a revelation, I tell you, a revelation. If I have to sleep on it, I'll split myself apart thinking and worrying. Please, Rabbi, please, just ten minutes, five even—"

"All right, Zitomer, all right," Rabbi Davis smiled and nodded. "After the *Kiddush* you can have a few minutes, before I talk about tomorrow's portion of the Torah."

When the rabbi called Zitomer to the pulpit and explained to the congregation that Zitomer had asked to speak because he had something important to say—"A revelation," Rabbi Davis said with a smile, "he has a revelation for us."—the members were silent for a few seconds, then broke into whisperings and murmurings. The old man sat in his special seat in the far right corner of the first row, looked at Zitomer's flushed face, and licked his lips. Zitomer had always been a quiet man, both in his store and in the synagogue. Though he came regularly to the Saturday discussions, he hardly ever spoke, preferring to listen carefully to the varied commentary and occasionally nod his head. Many of the men, the old man thought, probably don't know what his voice sounds like; I bet some of the members don't even know who he is.

Zitomer swayed at the pulpit, his hands bunching the velvet cloth, waiting for the whispers to stop.

"Brothers," he began. The old man was surprised that his voice was so strong and clear. It seemed to lift out of him and come singing down to them. "Brothers, forgive me for coming up here and taking your time like this, but I got something on my mind, it's important. It's so important I wanted to say it to all of you, here, in the synagogue. I'm not a speaker, I never got much education, so you should excuse me if I mix things up a little, or don't speak proper." He paused for breath and again the old man noticed how red his face was, and how his hands shook on the cloth.

"Some of you that know me, know how I keep a little shop—papers, candy, cigarettes and toys I handle—not much, but it makes me a living."

"A business lecture we're getting," somebody in the front row complained. Four or five members laughed.

Zitomer nodded.

"It's about business I'm trying to talk. But not just about business. About living, and how life shouldn't be a business."

Then only the faint ring of laughter echoed among the old dusty balcony beams. The members were silent.

"Anyway, I sell penknives, and cap pistols and balls and marbles to the *schwartzes* that come in—my store's down in the colored section. So today, this afternoon, when I'm getting ready to close, a little *schwartze* comes in and wants to know how much is this model car I keep in the window. Now I got the cars, a gross of them, for forty-five cents apiece from an old supplier who went out of business. But I usually sell them for a dollar, ninety-eight cents—I can get that much for them. So I say to the kid, 'Ninety-eight cents it'll cost you, sonny,' and he looks very sad at me, so I know he wants the car but he ain't got the ninety-eight cents. But I take the car out and show it to him, figuring maybe he'll go home and bother his mother and father until they give him the rest of the money. But while he's looking at it, I start to get this funny feeling inside, almost like my heart is turning over. So I put my hand over my heart, thinking maybe I'm getting an attack and I should sit down, but instead I'm asking myself why I'm making fifty-three cents off the poor kid? I try to shake the feeling off so I look at the kid, but he's still staring at the car, holding it in his hand and staring at it. And the feeling gets stronger, some voice inside me starts saying, 'You're stealing, Zitomer, you're stealing.' And then I remember 'Thou Shalt Not Steal.' I can't even remember which Commandment it is, but I can see it cut into the tablet. Thou Shalt Not Steal. So I start to think about it. Okay, I say, the reason I'm making a hundred per cent profit off the kid is because I can, I bought those cars dirt cheap, they're worth more than I paid for them. Why shouldn't I make as much as I can off the kid? What am I in business for, to be nice to little *schwartzes* or to make money?

"But I didn't believe it. I said those words that I always lived by, but I didn't mean them any more. I stood there with the little *schwartze* still looking at the car in the palm of his black hand, and I thought, all my life I been stealing from people and calling it business. And then I saw it wasn't only the way I live, it's the way all of us live. We run our lives like a cheap store, stealing, cheating and lying every chance we get to make more money. Thou Shalt Not Steal, the Lord commanded us; Thou Shalt Not Bear False Witness, but we don't pay no attention, we're too busy making money. There I was, making fifty-three cents off a poor kid, when I only needed fifteen, twenty cents to pay for my overhead and what I needed to live on. But still, I tried to argue against it. I'm not a saint, I told myself, I'm a businessman. I'm running a store, not a charity. The world's a hard place, it's a shame. But I can't change the world. I got to live with things the way they are.

"No good. The more I tried to explain to myself, the worse I felt. I couldn't say anything to change the feeling. Then I realized that the boy is still standing there with the car. So I looked at him. 'Listen, sonny, how much you got?' He opened his hand and I counted—two quarters, three dimes. 'Here,' I said. I patted the car in his hand and I took both quarters and one dime. 'Sixty cents it'll cost you, sonny. Now go home and be a good boy.' I patted his head and he ran out the door."

Zitomer stopped and took a deep breath. The sudden dead silence shocked the old man's ears; he had been so absorbed in Zitomer's words that he had forgotten the voice that spoke them. But someone stirred in the middle rows.

"That's very nice. So you made a little *schwartze* happy, you have to come and waste our time telling us about it? Shapiro keeps a grocery store, but he don't get up every Friday night and tell us how many stomachs he fills."

Zitomer waited until the laughter had stopped. There was very little laughter, he waited only a few seconds.

"Look, I didn't come up here and tell you a story about how I made a boy happy. That's not important. Why I told you was because I realized, all my life, I've been stealing. All my life, and all your lives, too. All of us have been breaking one of God's Commandments, not by accident, but on purpose. And what for, I said to myself. What for? I've lived sixty-two years poor, always scraping, always just getting along—what do I need a hundred per cent profit from a lousy model car for? Those gross of cars are going to make me rich? My papers, my candy, I sell for just a penny over cost—who could sell them any higher? Nobody would buy! So why not sell everything that way? What else do I have to do but live? I have to skin a poor little *schwartze*? Make a million dollars? On a hundred forty-four model cars?"

The old man had sat and stared at Zitomer as whispered discussions broke out all over the synagogue. How, he had wondered, does a poor Jew who runs a toy store get thoughts like that into his head? But Zitomer was frowning at the noise, impatient to continue.

"I said before, all of us, all of us, are guilty. Of stealing. Of breaking one of the Ten Commandments. You, Horowitz, and you, Shapiro, and Michaels, Kaplan, Schriebstein, all of us break one of the Ten Commandments every day, and we never think about it. It's part of our lives, it's the way things are. It's business. What are we Jews for, if we let ourselves break one of the Ten Commandments and it never even bothers us? What else is more important for a Jew than keeping the Ten Commandments? Did God give them to us so we should be successes in business?

"I thought about all this after the boy left. I sat down and I said the Ten Commandments to myself, and for the first time, I listened to them, not the way we *daven*, the way we pray so that the words are a babble and getting done is all that matters. I listened to the words and I asked myself, what do they mean? And it's so simple, because the Commandments are so simple; God's way of telling us how we should lead a good life. So I asked myself, Zitomer, in all honesty, how many do you break? And you know what? Every week I break four of those Commandments, and when my parents were alive I broke five. Sure, I don't worship graven images, commit adultery or murder, but I take the name of the Lord in vain, I steal, I bear false witness, and I covet. Almost all the time, I covet what don't belong to me. And yet, I said, I'm a good Jew, I come to *shul* twice a day, always I have kept the holidays and given money when I could afford it and when it was asked. But I knew then, once and for all, that it wasn't enough. It isn't enough! Those Ten Commandments the Lord gave twice to Moses, not once, but twice. And me, Zitomer, an unknown little New York Jew, breaks four or five every week! Is that why the Lord gave them twice to Moses? So I could break five Commandments and not even be bothered? So I closed up my shop, I went in back, ate, washed and dressed for *shul*. And I knew, I knew even when I looked at myself in the mirror while I was knotting my tie, that it couldn't be the same. No more for me. No more lying and cheating and stealing. And I promised myself that I would come up here and tell you what happened to me. Because I thought, when I was coming here, if every Jew felt what I felt, if it happened to every Jew in the world what happened to me, then we'd be the people of the Book, we'd be God's chosen people, we could live the Ten Commandments, and bring God's word to peoples all over the world. Yes, I thought to myself, that's why God gave us the Commandments, and look what we've done to them. We've got to change, all of us, we've got to live the only way for a Jew to live, by God's Commandments."

Zitomer had finished. He had stared down at the silent, motionless membership, pushed his skullcap further back on his head. Then he turned from the pulpit and walked down the stairs to his seat.

The old man sat, stunned. Above the sudden babble of voices, he thought, again and again, how many Commandments have I kept? How many have I broken? He could not answer. But I have been a good Jew, he thought, all my life I have been a good Jew. It must count, to be a good Jew. What more can I do now?

Then he listened to the words of the voices around him, whispering that Zitomer was a fool, a dreamer, an idiot, an idealist! The Commandments never said anything against business. Or about starving yourself. To sell without taking a profit was communism—what did communism have to do with the Ten Commandments? What was Zitomer, anyway, a Red? All of a sudden he was a sage or something, he had a right to preach about the Ten Commandments?

"Whose business is it, anyway, what Commandments I keep and what I break?" Horowitz had demanded. "That's between me and God; it's our worry, not Zitomer's. I keep a kosher home and I keep the Sabbath and the holidays—that's all anybody has to worry about. That's the way the Lord commanded us to live—if you want to talk about Commandments."

The old man listened to the accusations and the arguments, muddled in his own mind, wanting to agree with Zitomer and not wanting to agree, unsure about who was right, about what the Lord expected of a Jew. The members were still arguing when Rabbi Davis returned to the pulpit and stood waiting to begin his talk. He coughed, then cleared his throat, and the membership reluctantly quieted.

"Before I begin talking about tomorrow's portion of the Torah, and tell you what we will discuss in the afternoon, so you can go home and prepare for it, I want to thank Zitomer for coming to us, because I think there is meaning and importance in what he said. Sometimes we forget about the Ten Commandments too easily, that's very true. The other things we do as Jews, the rituals we observe, the holidays we keep, the prayers, are every bit as important. If we only lived by the Ten Commandments, there would be nothing Jewish about us. But the Ten Commandments are also important, and I want to thank Zitomer for reminding us." He nodded to Zitomer and began to talk about the portion of the Torah.

After the service the old man had moved through the fringes of groups excitedly discussing Zitomer's speech. He heard Zitomer's voice and stopped to listen.

"I'm not saying we have to be perfect. But we have to try, the least we have to do is try. So we fail, so what? We fail because we're only simple people and life is hard; great people, prophets and kings, have been failing for years, all of a sudden little people like us are going to succeed in leading a good life? But just because the world's a hard place to be good in, that means we shouldn't try? It was a hard world when God gave Moses the Ten Commandments, too, but Moses took them down to the people. Twice he took them down. And now we shouldn't try to obey them? You think God cares how many times we come to the synagogue or how many ceremonies we perform, if we lie and cheat and steal when we get home? We make a mock out of ourselves!"

Five voices tried to shout him down.

"Didn't you hear what Rabbi Davis just said?"

"The laws are as important as the Commandments!"

"What are you, a *goy?*"

"You want to break up the religion? You want to make us all atheists, or *goyim?*"

"Listen," Zitomer shouted. "I tell you God won't care how many laws and rules you keep if you break His Commandments. He gave them to us to keep—not to write on fancy stone tablets and look at in *shul.*" He pushed his way out of the group, moved slowly toward the corner where the old man waited.

"How do you know what God cares about? You're God's special messenger, you got a private pipeline to Heaven?"

Zitomer kept walking.

"Yeh," another voice taunted. "What you got, an inside track, He's let you in on what He's thinking?"

Zitomer was so close the old man heard his angry muttered "Fools!" before he turned.

"That's right. I told you I had a revelation this afternoon— maybe it came from God! How do you like that—eh? It wouldn't be the first time, either; Moses, Isaiah, Ezekiel—and now poor little Zitomer. I've got lots of company. Nobody listened to them at first, either. But I'll tell you the real reason why you don't listen to me, why you're fighting with me. Because you're all a bunch of liars and cheats and thieves, that's why, and you're afraid maybe I'm right. Because, if I'm right, you've got to change your lives, you've got to stop all the stealing and the cheating that's so much a part of you that you have to think all men are the same, there's no point trying to change. You're scared that maybe I'm right, that all your prayers and rituals won't do a bit of good when you're before God, and that's why you're fighting me. Because if I'm right, you've got to do something. And none of you want that. So go ahead, all of you. Call me names, call me Red or *goy* or *mishiginer.* Go on stealing and lying and cheating, then come to the synagogue twice a day and pray. You won't get away with it. The day of reckoning will come. You'll be judged, and not on how much money you gave to the synagogue, either."

There was only shocked silence as Zitomer turned away. The old man waited until the members started to argue again and then plucked at Zitomer's sleeve.

"Zitomer?"

Zitomer looked up, a red flush splotching his face.

"What do you want?"

"Quietly, quietly. I would like to come to your place, to talk with you—about some of the things you said tonight."

"You would, heh?" Zitomer said. "What for? You got a little fear, maybe—"

The old man motioned with his hand for Zitomer to stop, glanced over at the crowd of members.

"I'm sorry," Zitomer said, "I'm sorry, I didn't mean to say that. It's just that I'm too angry to talk anything but spite. Yes, come home with me, by all means come home. We'll sit in the kitchen and have a glass tea, and we can talk."

The old man had gone back to the prayer books and the prayer shawls, folding, rearranging and counting, as he did every morning and every night, fingering the familiar worn surfaces while his mind wrestled with what Zitomer had said, what the members had argued. Zitomer waited outside the synagogue while the old man locked the heavy wooden front door, and then they set off through the quiet streets toward Zitomer's store.

The old man puffed as he walked, forcing his shorter legs to keep up with Zitomer, not wanting to ask Zitomer to slow down because Zitomer had not spoken and his face was so obviously troubled.

"Are you angry?" the old man finally asked. "Because they would not listen to you?"

Zitomer continued walking, staring with a set angry face into the darkness of the street ahead, spotted by little pools of street lamplight. After a long time he sighed.

"No," he said, as if the old man had just that moment asked his question. "At least, I'm trying not to be angry. Because I told myself before I spoke, you have to be ready for what they will say and do. But I hoped anyway—it was only afterwards when I realized how much they wouldn't understand, how much they didn't want to hear, how little and frightened all of them are, that I felt how much I wanted them to listen to me, how much more I hoped that they would see what I believed was possible. I knew they wouldn't, but I didn't want to believe it; in my heart I hoped that I would move them, that I would open up their hearts and they would understand. Because there is so much good we could do together, if only they would understand. We could build new years onto the ends of our lives—we could begin to use our time and money to help others beside ourselves. We could make a difference to so many people's lives, right here on the East Side we could be an example, to show that people don't only care about themselves. Even once, tonight, up there on the pulpit, when they were all quiet, I felt in my hands that I had such strength, such control, that I could make them do whatever I wanted, that I could move mountains with them, that with them I could change Jews all over the country, all over the world. But I was wrong," Zitomer laughed. "I dream of changing the world and I can't even change a handful of tired, scared old men."

The old man pushed back the kitchen chair and shuffled to his window, the letter that announced Zitomer's expulsion from the synagogue still in his hand. The bitterness and the pain didn't stay in his voice. By the time we got to his store, pictures he was painting for me about how men could live in peace with themselves and their brothers, all over the world. And I listened. While he talked, I listened, and I believed it was possible. All the way to his store, as we walked and he talked and I forced my feet to keep up with him, the feeling that I wanted to talk, to tell Zitomer everything that was troubling me, grew stronger and stronger, until I thought that if he did not stop talking, I would have to break in, to shout at him that he should listen to me. Then he stopped, and though I knew I had to begin, I didn't even know how. Something's troubling you, he said, and before I even had a chance to think I was telling him. Everything.

The cat crawled out of the window across the street, but for once the old man did not stare back. I didn't understand how I could talk to him so easily. And I still don't, now; except now it doesn't matter. It's too late, I can't talk to him any more. He'll never forgive me, after what I said today, in Rabbi Davis's office.

I didn't understand so much. For a week after that night, I sat and wondered how he could live, without the synagogue. What does he do with himself; who does he talk to? And finally

I walked down to his store, to see for myself what kind of a life he led, without the synagogue.

"Come in, come in," Zitomer shouted. "Welcome, welcome, come in and rest yourself, sit down and have a cup of tea. I never thought you'd be coming here, to see me. The *shamos* isn't supposed to set a bad example for his *shul;* if somebody finds out you came, you'll get fired!"

Two of the men bent over the chessboard behind Zitomer's chair snickered without raising their heads. The old man didn't smile. He had been afraid to come, afraid precisely because the membership would not understand and would be angry with him, and so he had put off coming each time something inside him had whispered it was time to see Zitomer. But finally he picked a dark, dreary day, scuttled as quickly as he could down back streets and alleys to Zitomer's shop.

"I didn't come to be made fun of," the old man said.

"No, of course not. I'm sorry. Forgive me. It's just sometimes, my bitterness, it gets away from me. I carry it around in here," Zitomer touched his chest with the heel of his right hand, "and I try to forget it, but sometimes I feel so sour with it, as if my whole chest was on fire, and if I don't say something out loud the taste rises until it creeps in the back of my tongue, so that I want to spit and spit and spit until the taste is gone. But sit down, sit down, sit down and talk to me."

The old man sat next to Zitomer, on one of the low three-legged stools that had sprung up all over Zitomer's shop. The shelves were almost bare, the counters were disassembled and stacked against the walls.

"What's happened?"

"What do you mean?" Zitomer said. "Oh, you mean the shop? I sold it. Couldn't see any reason to stay in business any more. So I sold all the stock and as much of the display and fixtures as I could get rid of. I got enough money, all together with what I saved, to keep me as long as I'll be around; I can't go to operas or ballets any more, or eat lunch at Longchamps'. But the food there I never liked much anyway."

This time almost all the men laughed.

"Comes the revolution, comrade," one of the men at the chessboard said, "and we'll all eat at Longchamps.' Every restaurant will be at least Longchamps. Ain't that right, Dawidowsky?"

The old man looked closely at the bald head that slowly rose from its contemplation of the chessboard.

"Very funny," Dawidowsky said, "very clever. Now if you could manage to be half so clever at chess as you are at making wisecracks, maybe you'd give me a decent game once in a while. Check!"

"Check? What'd ya mean, check, how could it be check? You're moving the pieces already? A fine thing, lift my head for a minute and you switch the pieces on me."

The old man had put the name and what was left of the face together, and remembered Dawidowsky. Once, long long ago, almost at the beginning of the old man's second turn in the garment factory, the union had tried to organize a major walk-out, and Dawidowsky had come to the old man's factory, to talk to the members. Dawidowsky had made a stirring speech, had called them all brothers, had appealed to their decency, their self-respect, the bonds that forged them to their struggling fellow workers. "Come out with us," he pleaded. "Even if your wages aren't as bad as ours, let us get beaten and you'll get yours cut next. There's only one way to beat them, comrades, through the unity of every working man."

All the shop workers had cheered until after Dawidowsky had left the platform. Women wept, men rolled up their sleeves and swore that this time nobody would stop them from showing the bloodsucking capitalists who was boss. Two days before the strike, the men found a notice pasted to the time clock when they reported for work in the morning:

> ANY EMPLOYEE NOT REPORTING FOR WORK
> WEDNESDAY MORNING WILL BE DISMISSED.
> NO REHIRING WILL BE CONSIDERED.
>
> *The Management.*

The strike came and went, the old man's factory remained solidly at work.

But Dawidowsky was a Red, the old man remembered. The boss came around and told us afterward, that Dawidowsky and all the officers of the union were Reds. And I remember when Dawidowsky came around and talked to the Red in our shop. He's been a Red all his life.

"But what do you do now? What kind of a place is this? It looks like a tavern, without beer," the old man said.

"That's not such a bad idea," a man with a badly bent back and a grayish-white beard chuckled. "You hear, Zitomer? What we need is a keg or two, a counter with a footrail and some sawdust on the floor. Then we'd really have some good discussions."

"It's a sort of club, I guess," Zitomer said. "A club for people like us to come and sit, and talk. I made up my mind to sell the whole store, after the night I talked in the synagogue. But while I was still selling off the stock, people started to drift in. All kinds of people, people who heard about what I said in the synagogue, people who saw me going around the shops, trying to pound some sense into the members' heads. So they came around to the shop to talk, to talk to me because I had an idea, I had something I believed in. Soon every day came four or five people in here, talking, arguing. So one night I called a meeting. I told them to bring everyone who might come to the store to talk, everyone they knew who cared about something more than making money. So I called the meeting for eight o'clock, and at seven-thirty it's already so crowded when I open my kitchen door that I can't get into the store. I ask everybody, if I keep the store instead of selling it, and clear out the counters and put chairs and stools around so that you can be comfortable, would you come here? To talk, to argue, to discuss, to be together? They all said yes. So I got rid of the rest of the stock, took apart the counters and stacked them up against the wall, bought a few cheap stools and chairs, and here we are. The Bowery Discussion Club," Zitomer laughed.

The old man looked around the store again. Besides the two bent again over the chessboard, and the man with the beard and twisted back, there was a small fat man reading a paper, and two men on rickety chairs in the front corner, leaning toward each other, deep in argument.

"You see," Zitomer said, "this isn't exactly what you might call a revolution. Or even what I meant when I said in the synagogue that all we needed was a little change. What I'm finding out is it's not so easy to change people as I thought. Most of them," and he opened his hand to indicate the rest of the men, "knew that a long time ago. People don't care about things, they don't want to change. Sometimes they don't even want to think. Takes a long time, to make a difference. These men here, they've been working for what they believed in all their lives. Mostly in little ways, but at least they got something, they got an idea, they believe in something more than money. Sure, they don't believe in the Ten Commandments, hardly anybody agrees with anybody else. But here, here in this shop, we can sit and we can talk about what we believe with each other, argue about religion and Communism and everything else. We can try to show somebody where he's wrong, and he can try to show us. Sometimes we even have discussions on one subject and everybody joins in; sometimes we invite friends. In the evening I make tea, and we sit around the radiator, because it gets cold, and tell stories about the old days."

"But what good does it do?" the old man said. "What good do you do, all of you, sitting in here talking, drinking tea, playing chess? You can't change anything, you can't do no good, all you can do is to talk to each other to keep from going crazy."

The old man called Dawidowsky looked up from his chessboard until his eyes met the old man's. The old man looked down at the floor.

"It's hard to explain. There are some things you can't measure by what good they do. Me, I've been a Communist all my life. Since I've been sixteen, anyway. Well, what good has it done, me or anybody else? No revolution ever took place, and sometimes I think none ever will, America'll blow herself up first, and the rest of the world with her. But so what? Sure, it makes a difference but it doesn't mean I was wrong. Or that I wasted my life. You think I'd change for anybody else's, or do it differently if I had it to do over again? The hell I would. What I learned, what I know now is that ideas are worth something even if they don't accomplish nothing. Look, I'm going to die soon, I know that, all of us know that. We don't kid ourselves, there's no use in that. So sometimes I tell myself, what's the use of worrying, you'll be gone soon, it won't matter any more. But I don't feel that way, not most of the time. I care about the idea. Only about the idea. I've been a Communist and worked for Communism and I believe in it as an idea, not as something I did. Or didn't do."

"What he means," the man at the back of the room said,

only his eyes visible above the top of the paper, "is that we've believed in ideas so long we've finally come to see that ideas have a life of their own, outside of us."

"Exactly," Dawidowsky shouted, slapping his knee with his hand. "Ideas have a life outside of us. They matter, not so much us. We're going to die, but the idea don't die, it moves on. So we come here, we talk, we argue. We look at our ideas, at other ideas, and we try to understand them better. Because we care about them. Because, in some ways, they're more important than we are. Because they never die."

"So," Zitomer said. "He didn't come here to listen to speeches, he came here to talk to me. So shut up already."

The eyes of the man behind the paper disappeared again, and Dawidowsky chuckled and winked at Zitomer before turning back once again to his board.

"It's not that I mean to be rude, but I thought that since you came, it must be because something's on your mind."

The old man shook his head.

"No," he said. "I came because I couldn't understand how a man could live without the synagogue."

But the old man stayed the hours through the afternoon. He listened to arguments about things he had only dimly heard of, and could not begin to understand. He listened to a discussion between Zitomer and Dawidowsky about Zionism and Israel, and was amazed when both agreed that the creation of an independent state was the worst thing that could have happened to the Jewish people. Finally he found himself outside the door, Zitomer grinning down at him.

"It makes my head spin," the old man said. "So much talk. Even in the *yeshivas* you don't hear so much talk."

"Sometimes talk is good," Zitomer said. "In the synagogue, it was bad. Here, I think it's good. But it's not dark yet. I'll walk a little way with you. So tell me, how are things in the synagogue? Do they still talk about me?"

"What do you think, they can forget about it? After all, you're still going around to their stores, aren't you?"

Zitomer stopped to knock one of the wet limp leaves that littered the pavement off the top of his shoes.

"So what do they say?

"That you're crazy. That you're mad. That you should be

locked up, so you don't bother innocent people and lose them customers. That it's a good thing you've been thrown out of the synagogue, or else they'd be hearing speeches all the time."

"I only made one speech. But that was a good one, that first night in the synagogue. The feeling from the afternoon was still inside me. Sometimes when I stopped speaking, even when I just had to catch a breath and didn't want to stop, I could feel how quiet they were, how much they were listening. It was only when I was done, and reality, dollars and cents reality, came back to them, that they started to shout me down."

They stopped on a corner, underneath a red light, next to a shop that sold chickens and smelled of feathers and dried stale blood.

"This is as far as I can go," Zitomer said. "I must get back to the store. We have an important meeting tonight. To decide whether to have officers. We need a chairman, especially, but the anarchists are objecting."

The old man smiled back at Zitomer.

"Are you angry with me, because I didn't do anything, when they threw you out of the synagogue?"

"What could you do? You're not even an officer, you couldn't stop them. Besides, you would have made trouble for yourself, and what for? They would have got me anyway; nothing would have stopped them. No, there was nothing for you to do."

"So," the old man said. "Good. I thought maybe you were angry. After all, I am the *shamos*. But you're not. So goodbye."

"Goodbye," Zitomer said. "Come to us again, whenever you want to. You are welcome."

But I can't come any more. Not after what I called him this morning. The wind rattled the pane of his window, the cat still guarded the ledge. I can't ever walk down to the store and sit with Zitomer, listening to the talking I don't understand, from men whose whole lives are a mystery to me. Crackpots, all of them. Crazy old men. But somehow, sitting and talking and drinking tea and playing chess, they're happy. And Zitomer was happy with them, I could see it. I wondered how he could live without the synagogue, but he doesn't need the synagogue. He doesn't need Rabbi Davis or any of them.

But I couldn't live like that. How could I live like that? Even if I could apologize to Zitomer, and he would forgive me, I couldn't stay in the store with them, talk to them. What would I say? What would I talk about? I didn't even understand half the words they were using, let alone what they were saying. Besides, there's the *shul*. I'm the *shamos*. They can't find another *shamos* overnight.

But the membership, they should listen to him, they should listen to what he says. I don't know enough to say whether he's right, but when he talks—he has something, something I can feel in my bones. And they feel it too, because when he talks they keep so quiet, and there's always those few minutes when he's done, before anybody speaks. They wait for him to start and they sit and listen, and then, when he's done, they collect themselves, they become themselves again, and they jump at him.

Like the discussion. Zitomer had come to the Saturday afternoon discussion the day after his speech from the pulpit, and had sat silently through the long boring hours. The rabbi had announced as the topic the ram that Abraham had substituted for Isaac, and so they debated the fine points of the ram, what it meant, why it was chosen, what Talmudic scholars had written about it. Zitomer had listened as the talk pecked and pointed its way through opinion, quotation, scattered bits of information, and the old man saw that sooner or later Zitomer would speak, that he had not come to sit so silently. Finally there was a pause, and Zitomer cleared his throat.

"Brothers," he began, and the silence was the same as the night before, as if everyone had known he would find voice and say that word, and had been waiting.

"Brothers, this is all very wise and learned, and perhaps it is a good way to spend Saturday afternoon—but after all, what difference does it make, whether the ram was short-horned or long-horned, black or white? What does it matter to us today, what breed it was, how tall it stood, what it symbolized? What's important isn't the ram, but that the Lord stopped Abraham from killing; the same Commandment he gave to Moses: Thou Shalt Not Kill. And that's what we should spend our Saturdays talking about—how we can help each other to obey the Commandments, what we can do to make a better world for everybody."

He caught his breath so quickly nobody had time to interrupt.

"There's so much we could do. We could begin right here, in the synagogue. We could agree to stop cheating the customers, work out ways to make our profits stretch further, figure out how to sell as cheap as we could to live. Then we could work on ways to keep salesmen and customers and distributors from cheating us. We could discuss lying, about why we lie to each other, why we covet our neighbor's property. We could try to understand what makes us angry, jealous, afraid. We can plan better things to do with the money we give the synagogue than to spend it on velvet coverlets and silver candlesticks. Fancy foolishness—what do we need decoration to pray? God will listen to us better in a fancier synagogue? We could give most of our money to charity, they could use it more than silver candlesticks."

He stopped, the same shocked silence surrounding the gap of his voice. The old man looked at the many faces red with anger. Harsh words would come quickly. Then the rabbi banged on the table as a signal that he would speak, and the old man watched the faces rearrange themselves for listening.

"Zitomer, yesterday I didn't say anything about the misleading things you said, because I thought the good things, the things we should be reminded of, were more important. But now I'm going to correct what you just said. First of all, this is a discussion on today's portion of the Torah, you have no right to bring your personal opinions in here and shout them out at us. But secondly, the Ten Commandments are not the end of Judaism, Zitomer, they're only the beginning. The Commandments alone are not enough for a Jew to live by. We have a whole Torah, Zitomer, Five Books of Moses full of laws and proclamations, all telling us exactly how we should live. And everything in these books is God's word, Zitomer, as much as the Ten Commandments. You can't pick and choose, Zitomer, it's not for you to decide. Are you a judge, can you say which is more important? No, you are not!" the rabbi thundered as Zitomer started to answer. "Who are you to judge God? You're only a Jew, and a Jew obeys, that's what he does. There are thousands of laws to obey. Not ten, but thousands. Even what we're doing here, this discussion, is written down as a proclamation, I can show you where," the rabbi said. "You can't make a religion over to suit yourself, because you have a feeling about the Commandments. Follow them the best you can, suit your own conscience. But follow God's word in all the other laws, too. And don't try to judge which of His words are most important. Who are men to try and judge God?"

The rabbi ended with a final gesture of his hand that said, no questions, plainly telling Zitomer and the rest of the table that he would hear no more. He pulled the open Bible to him, ready to continue the discussion, but Zitomer's chair scraped as Zitomer pushed himself up and stood facing the rabbi.

The rabbi began to read, stopped, stared at Zitomer, frowned.

"Well?"

"Well," Zitomer said. "For a start I don't believe God wrote the Five Books of Moses. I don't believe they're His words or His laws. I believe only the Ten Commandments are God's word and I know they're more important than all laws and rituals. What else can I do but live the way I believe—or at least try."

He stared down at the rabbi, then at the members ringing the table.

"You are all afraid, all of you. Even you," he said to the rabbi. "But I'm not. Not any more. The pity is that there is so much good we could do if you were not so afraid." He stood for a moment more, then quickly walked upstairs and out of the synagogue.

And since that day, except for the one afternoon in Rabbi Davis's office, he hasn't been inside the synagogue. The old man stared at the mimeographed letter in his hand, then turned from the window and shuffled back to the table. He folded the letter into its soiled square, then let it fall into the drawer. He pushed the drawer until it sagged back into place. They're late, he thought. Carl can't even come from Highland Park without being late. A lot he cares about me, he can't even come on time. The steam bubbled from the kettle. They can both have tea without lemon, he thought, and moved to the stove, to turn off the gas beneath the kettle.

Nine

Four flights of creaking wooden stairs, and though David has raced up each flight and whipped around the banisters at the landings, Carl, too, is puffing by the time he reaches the top. David scuffs the tip of one shoe against the calf of his leg as he waits outside the door.

"Knock," Carl says.

But David stands, with both hands in his pockets. So Carl puts a hand on his son's shoulder, and taps gently on the door. They wait. Behind the door they hear shuffling footsteps. The door opens.

"Hello, Dad."

"Hello, Gran'pop."

The old man stares at them, the door only half open, his body blocking the room. Then he eases the door back and motions them in. Carl half pats, half pushes David into the room, and the old man shuts the door behind them.

"*Boychik*," the old man nods. "Carl. So sit down."

Carl motions David to the kitchen chair, but David shakes his head and goes to the window. At home I never notice whether there's dirt on the windows, David thinks, but Gran'pop's window's so dirty you can't even see out of it. Like fog. David digs his fingers into the rust of the window handles, but doesn't tighten his muscles to tug upward. The window won't open. Probably it hasn't opened for years. Gran'pop's room would smell a lot better if we could get this stupid window up, David thinks. But he and Carl have tried more than once. It won't budge. Okay, David thinks, big deal. You want to stay shut, stay shut, see if I care. He begins to pick at the strips of hard white paint flaking off the woodwork. The wood beneath is grayish and spongy on his fingers.

"So," Carl is saying. "Not much is new. I got a new truck. God knows how many years it'll take me to pay it off. I got the *schwartze* that used to work with me and a neighborhood kid working the old truck, and I'm by myself in the new one."

"I don't trust *schwartzes*," the old man grumbled. "I never trusted them. Lazy. Good-for-nothing. Never work if they can help it."

"Oh, Willie's a good enough worker. Better when the sun's in; the hotter it gets, the slower he gets. But I trust him okay. He does his job. It's the other one I'm worried about; a big fat kid, a real loudmouth. I only gave him the job because his father asked me to. Couldn't I do something for Larry, Larry wanted a job close to home, something interesting. So what the hell, I figured, I'll teach him something about television sets. So I taught him simple installations; how to set up antennas, tube testing, adjusting. You think he thanked me? Not a word. A whole week I spent training him, you'd think he was doing me a favor working for me."

David peels off the paint in thin flaky strips, watches the window opposite to see if the cat that belongs to the woman with the red bandanna will ease onto the window ledge and stretch its claws over the parapet. The last time he and Carl visited Gran'pop, he made faces at the cat for almost a half-hour. But today the shade is drawn and no light cuts through the rips and holes.

"But it's not bad, business is better. I got all the work I need to keep me busy. We're not rich, understand, but we're comfortable. Millie wants to move. She says she's tired of Highland Park. She wants to move farther out, towards Metuchen. She keeps worrying that more *schwartzes*'ll move across the bridge from New Brunswick, and the value of the house'll go down. And she wants David to live in a better neighborhood."

"What's wrong with where we live now?" David says from the window. "I don't want any better old neighborhood; I like it where we are."

"You don't take after your father, *boychik*. Your father liked his old neighborhood so much, he ran away the first chance he got."

The old man coughs, bobs his head to force the tickle from his throat. The bedsprings creak beneath him. Carl stretches his arms around the back of the kitchen chair and curls his fingers along the rungs.

"Millie asked to be remembered to you."

The old man nods.

"She says she's sorry she couldn't come, but she has too much work to do." Both Carl and David realize that it was the wrong thing to say almost as soon as Carl finishes. But the old man is too quick.

"So who asked her to come?" he growls. "She shouldn't bother feeling sorry, I'm not sorry she didn't come. You can tell her that, *boychik*, I'm not sorry. And if you didn't come, I wouldn't be sorry, either. It's no favor you're doing me, believe me; I got better things to do than sit in my room and talk to you."

Oh, stop, David thinks. How much else do you really have to do? He shrugs his shoulders, but the prickly feeling creeps higher up his back. He kicks at the baseboard. Why do old people have to be so fussy all the time? Always picking, always fighting.

"David!" Carl says.

David looks up.

"What're you doing?"

"Nothing."

"You're peeling the paint off again, aren't you?"

David stares at the splinter in his hand.

"Yeah."

"What'd I tell you about that?"

"Listen, if he wants to peel the paint off, let him peel the paint off. Who's he hurting? Feinstein's so cheap a landlord, heat he can't even afford in his own apartment, let alone mine. Three years ago he promised to paint the whole place. Three years ago! Every time I remind him, he promises me a painter's coming up the next morning. A painter! The only painters I ever see are the ones who paint the white lines down the middle of the streets. So you peel the paint off that window if you want to, *boychik*. I don't care."

"He shouldn't do it. It's not right. He's always picking at something, all the time. Every time I tell him not to, and every time, pick pick pick. Now you stop it, David. Understand?"

"So what's he supposed to do, stand with his hands stuffed up his backside, listening to us? What fun is it for him, to come here? What did you bring him for, what good does it do to *shlep* him down here? I didn't ask, I didn't tell you to."

"I don't have to *shlep* him down here. He wants to come. He likes coming."

David stares at Gran'pop and wonders what to say. I should say, it's true Gran'pop, I like coming. Except probably you wouldn't believe me. He hears a noise from across the street that sounds like a shade snapping upward, and he wants to turn to the window, to see if the woman with the red bandanna has opened her shade and window and let out her cat. But Gran'pop still stares at him, so David stares back, feeling that he is being examined, that Gran'pop is asking some question, and the wrong answer is to look away.

Finally Gran'pop looks away. David edges to the window, but the shade across the street is still drawn.

"He's doing very well in Hebrew school," Carl offers behind him. "He's at the top of his class. And he's way ahead of his *bar mitzvah* class, too."

David squirms. The familiar tickly feeling that comes on him when somebody older talks about how smart he is touches his stomach. Let it alone, he almost says, wondering if the only reason they send him to school is so they can brag about how smart he is. Let it alone. But he is pleased, too, because he is smart, and he is at the head of his class, though it means less— different, almost—when they talk about it. What do you know about it, he almost said to Mom once, after she told Mrs. Finkle how well he was doing in the sixth grade. I mean, I go to school every day, I do the work, I answer the questions. You never see the inside of our classroom, how do you know how good I do?

But now he stays quiet, part of him listening and part of him wishing they would shut up.

"So," the old man nods. "All week he goes to school with the *goyim*, and two afternoons a week he goes to Hebrew school. A *machaiyah*. It's a miracle he remembers he's a Jew!"

"He knows all the Blessings already," Carl puts in quickly. "Not only the Torah, but before and after the *Haftorah*, too. Maybe you'd like to hear him sing them for you?"

"What for?" the old man said. "I know them, too. And I knew them before I was thirteen. Before I was ten, even."

David, at the window, feels the silence, turns to see Carl, and then Gran'pop, look over at him. Gran'pop looks at the window and then at Carl, and then leans forward to rub his hands across his knees.

"Nu. So, *boychik*, come and sing the Blessings for us."

David turns from the window and his father nods yes, so he crosses to the kitchen table, pulls from his pocket the *yarmilka* that his father reminded him to take before they left home, and sets it on his head. He clears his throat and stares down at the floor, frowning. He doesn't want to sing the Blessings and so he hesitates, and scuffs at the floor with the tip of his shoe, until Carl's "David?" pushes him over the last reluctant edge into performance.

The *Haftorah* Blessings are the nicest, he decides as he finishes the second Blessing for the Torah. The Torah's too short, and the melody changes too fast, so you have to think too much while you're singing. But the *Haftorah* takes a long time, the melody's regular, and you can even jazz it up if you want to. Cantor Singer almost hit me once, he got so mad at what I did to the tune. It's fun, that's all. It's boring to sing it straight all the time. But I bet Gran'pop would get mad if I didn't sing it straight. *"Baruch, atah adonai, m'kaddaysh ha'shabbos."*

"Ah-ah-main."

So, David thinks, now that's done, and moves back to the window. Carl nods to him and glances over at the old man, who still sits hunched with his hands on his knees.

"So. Good, *boychik*. Very good. You didn't forget anything. It was very good."

"Thank you, Gran'pop."

"Boychik, you know how to lay *tephillin?"*

"Yes, Gran'pop."

"How many times a week you lay *tephellin?"*

"Once a week, Gran'pop. On Sunday mornings."

David looks across at his father, who is picking at the chair rungs.

"And how often you go to *shul*, *boychik*?"

"Twice a week, Gran'pop. Friday night and Saturday."

The old man still leans forward, searching the floor as if his questions were inscribed there. "You play ball on *shabbos*, don't you *boychik*?"

Carl's chair scrapes as he gets to his feet, moves across to David and puts his arm around his son's shoulders. "Look, Dad," Carl says, "it's not fair to—"

"And your mother keeps a kosher home, too, doesn't she, *boychik*?" The old man raises his head to stare at both of them, there at the window, and they see the tears at the corners of his eyes begin to slip down his cheeks. "And you don't play with *goyim*, do you? And you never stop to talk to any little *shikses*, or go to their houses, or hold hands with them on the way home from school? God help you, you'll grow up to marry a *shikse*. Listen, *boychik*, it's not your fault, I know it's not your fault. But I told you, Carl, I told you what would happen when you left me. When you walked out on me and went to Philly, Carl, with not two cents to rub together in your pocket, didn't I tell you, didn't I promise you what would happen? But did you listen? Oh, no. Not you. You knew better. You couldn't stand living with me one more year. One more month, even. You had bigger ideas." The old man's rush of words clogs something in his throat, and he begins to cough, showering a coarse spray onto the rug and forcing his words out between each cough. "So now you should be satisfied. Now you got what you wanted. A wife who's no better than a *shikse* and a son who plays with the *goyim*. That's not enough for you, even, you have to come here and rub it in my face? What are you trying to do to me?" the old man screams. "I'm dying, doesn't that please you enough? You have to rush me into my grave?"

The old man buries his face in his hands and rocks himself, in his grief, on the edge of the squeaking bed. Carl and David stand by the window, and David feels his father's hand bearing into the flesh of his shoulder. Finally the choking sobs stop. The old man wipes his eyes with the cuff of his shirt-sleeve. "So," he says. "You got no more *b'ruchas* to sing?"

David shakes his head.

"No more *b'ruchas*, no more *b'ruchas*. So, Carl, what else is new?"

Finally, David thinks. Dad has just said they must go for the third time, and the old man pushes himself off the edge of the bed.

"I'll come with you."

"No, Dad. It's too far. It's almost four blocks to the subway. We left the car on the other side of the tunnel."

"So it's four blocks. I walk five blocks to *shul* every morning, before you're even out of bed, and then I walk back. And in the afternoon I walk those same five blocks, and then I walk back again. You think I can't walk four blocks when I feel like?"

The old man is already on his feet, fumbling his jacket off the back of the kitchen chair that David refused to sit in. David turns from the window. Carl is standing by the kitchen table, frowning.

"Look, Dad. At least put your coat on. It's cold outside. The wind's raw."

The old man buttons his jacket, shuffles to the door, opens it. "Well," he says. "I thought you were in such a hurry to go. So let's go."

Carl motions to David, who moves across the room to the old man at the door. "Okay," Carl says. "We're coming. But listen, Dad. It's cold outside. Don't you think you need a coat?"

The door slams shut as Carl and David move out onto the landing and then down the steps.

"Every day I go out like this," the old man says. "I go out with my sweater and my jacket on top of that, and most times I don't even button all the buttons. Besides, even if I did need my coat, I couldn't wear it any more. Because I gave it to Rabinowitz. So I don't have it to wear."

Carl stops halfway down the second flight, and David races ahead.

"You gave it to Rabinowitz?"

"Now all of a sudden, even my clothes aren't mine, I can't do what I want with them? Did you buy the coat for me, you got a right to complain about what I did with it? I'll tell you again, just in case you're deaf, I gave it to Rabinowitz. He was cold, his blanket wasn't warm enough he should stay outside in his wheel chair, so I gave him my coat."

David circles the landing and starts down the last flight. The bottom door is ajar and he feels the cold air streaming up the staircase.

"Is that all right with you, that I gave away my coat? Next time I should write a letter asking you if it's all right, before I do something with my own clothes?"

"Oh, Dad," Carl says. "Why do you have to be like that?"

"Be like what? I'm not being like anything. I'm the same as I always was, Carl. I didn't change. I didn't run off and leave my family and go live with the *goyim*. I can see why you think I changed, Carl; you've been away a long time."

"Dad, it's only two months since I saw you."

"Two months! You should pardon me, two months! I thought it was a year, but maybe that's because time goes so much quicker for me, I have so much to do. Two months! I should say thank you, Carl. I never realized how often you came to see me. Two months! How many miles away do you live, Carl? A hundred? Five hundred? A thousand? Two months! I should thank God I have such a son, such a busy son, and so far away, that once every two months he actually comes to see me."

David pushes open the bottom door and steps into the quick draft and coldness of the street. He waits, holding the door open for Carl and the old man, but as their quarrel drifts down to him, he shakes his head, decides to move down the block so that he doesn't have to listen. The subway is only four blocks away, and he knows how to get there. It's stupid, he thinks, every time we come, the same fights, the same arguments, Gran'pop never changes. He just gets meaner. But it's not his fault. Dad always says that, but I know it anyway. It's not his fault. All you can do is feel sorry for Gran'pop. Dad says he never had a chance. Dad says he's sick. He looks sick. If he dies, we'll all come to the funeral, like with the other Gran'pop. And Uncle Mike. Mom'll cry.

David turns the corner, then comes back to stare down the street. Carl and the old man are about halfway up the block. Carl is bent toward the old man, and his hands are close to the old man's elbow as the old man shuffles along. But Carl knows better than to touch the elbow, to offer to support the old man.

He moves slowly along at the old man's side, nodding as the old man struggles to breathe.

"Look, Dad," he says finally. "Please, don't get angry with me, but, maybe you should buy yourself another coat?"

The old man shuffles along. His face does not change, and Carl, staring down, wonders if he has heard. They reach the corner and turn it, slowly. Carl glances up. David is far ahead of them, down the street.

"What am I supposed to buy a coat with? You think I got stocks, maybe; I made a killing on the market with my pension? I got money to buy a coat? Horse races I—"

"Listen," Carl cuts in. "You could let me buy you a coat. It would be my pleasure. I would enjoy it."

The old man stares down at the cracked concrete of the pavement. Carl watches his face contort, his hand tremble into tightening. Carl stands and watches until the old man sighs, and his face relaxes into its usual lines.

"Pain?" Carl says. "Very bad?"

"So," the old man says. "The *boychik* will be at the subway already. What are you standing here for?"

David reaches the subway entrance, and stands in front for a few minutes, counting the people plunging down the stone steps into the tunnel that leads to the change booth. He counts up to twelve men and three women, one of them very fat. Then he wonders about Carl and the old man, crosses the street, and turns the corner. Carl and the old man are about fifty yards away, talking to a man in a black suit and a tall, old-fashioned black hat. David watches them for a minute or two, then trots slowly toward them.

"So," the old man is saying, "Rabbi Davis, this is my grandson."

"David, this is Rabbi Davis," Carl says.

David holds out his hand. "Pleased to meet you, Rabbi."

"Happy to meet you," Rabbi Davis says. He stares down at David. "Well," he says finally, "you're a very big boy, David. How old are you?"

"Twelve years, seven months, and sixteen days," David says. "I forget how many hours."

The rabbi chuckles. "Well," he says, "you're very big for your age."

"I don't think so. All my friends are bigger than I am."

"Oh. Well, maybe you have very big friends."

David shakes his head. "I think I'm just little."

The rabbi glances up at the sky. As if the weather was written up there, David thinks.

"It's getting dark early these days," Carl says.

"Yes." The rabbi nods. "It is. Be dark soon."

"We'd better be getting on. We've got to get to the bus terminal and then through the tunnel to the parking lot. I never bring the car into the city."

"Well," the rabbi says. "It was nice meeting you."

Carl and David nod.

"I'll see you at afternoon services," the rabbi says to the old man. "Unless you're still feeling bad. If you are, don't come. I can manage."

"No. No," the old man says. "I'm not feeling bad. I'm all right. I'll be there."

"What's this about feeling bad? What's wrong? What's the matter?"

The rabbi looks at Carl, then at the old man. "It's nothing. Nothing, really," the rabbi says. "This morning, I didn't think your father was looking too good. I asked him what was wrong, and he said he had some stomach trouble. So I told him to go home, and to stay home the rest of the day, if he still felt bad."

"You didn't tell me about any stomach trouble," Carl says.

"I get a lot of trouble I don't tell you about. You think I keep a diary of all my aches and pains, so I can tell you about them every two months? I'd need a whole Torah to write them all down."

"Well," the rabbi says, "I must be going. Goodbye," he says to Carl and David.

David waits as Carl and the old man walk toward the corner and the subway, to watch the rabbi walk off down the street. A funny rabbi, he thinks. Wouldn't want to be in his confirmation class. I bet he never touched a baseball. Not like Rabbi Kellman. Zevi says Rabbi Kellman used to play first base for Millville High. Maybe he did. David looks up and realizes that Carl and the old man are almost at the subway entrance. He hurries to catch up. The old man edges very gingerly down the first few steps.

"You don't have to come down," Carl says. "It's a waste of time, coming down; you'll only have to climb up again. Why not say goodbye to us here?"

"Why not leave me alone, why not?" the old man snaps. "You're going into the subway, so I'll say goodbye to you there. Listen, Carl, how many times I got to tell you, I'm not dead yet?"

"All right. I never said you were. It's just that on the phone, when you told me about the attacks—I started to worry. Look, Dad, why don't you go to a doctor? For my sake. And for David's. And buy yourself a coat. Let it be a present from me. From both of us."

"Now I should go to a doctor for your sake? And for the *boychik*'s? What, the two of you have a business with doctors, some good I'll be doing you by going? Listen, *boychik,* you'll forgive me if I don't go to a doctor for your sake. What kind of nonsense you talking, Carl? I keep telling you, what good's a doctor going to do me? He's going to give me pills to make me live longer? He's got medicines to make my bones younger, so they don't ache so much any more? Listen, Carl, doctors are thieves and liars, but even they got no medicines to cure what's bothering me. And if I ever went to a doctor, Carl, I'd use my own money."

The old man chokes on the rush of his words and coughs. His body shakes, he holds onto the rail and coughs wrench out of him. A bit of a flush begins to rise in his face.

"Please, Dad," Carl says. He puts his hand on the old man's shoulder. "Take it easy. You're getting yourself all upset."

The old man pushes Carl's hand off his shoulder, coughs again, then clears his throat. He takes a few steps away from the wall and the supporting rail. "So. I'm all right now, you don't have to worry."

He moves back to the rail and continues down the steps. "But I got a right to get upset. Doctors. Coats, yet. You run away from me and for years you leave me alone and I don't even know whether you're alive, and all of a sudden, because I'm going to die, you can't do enough for me. Well it's no good, Carl, it's not my fault you all of a sudden remembered you got a father. You can't expect me to fall down on my knees and thank God you remembered you're my son. It's too late."

They reach the change booth, and Carl turns to the old man.

"All right, Dad. I'm sorry. It's enough. I'm sorry I mentioned it at all. But it's time to go."

Carl turns and motions David forward. "Say goodbye to Gran'pop."

"Goodbye, Gran'pop," David moves close to the old man to feel the wet beard scratchy against his cheek.

"Goodbye, *boychik*," the old man says.

"Now go down the steps," Carl says to David. "Here's a token. Put it in the slot and go through and down the steps. I'll meet you on the platform."

David feels the token drop into his open hand, but he stands and stares at his father.

"Go on," Carl says. "Don't stare at me, do what I'm telling you. I'll meet you on the platform."

David shrugs his shoulders, turns, inserts the token into the slot, and pushes his way through the wooden arms. But he glances back, from the other side of the turnstile, and watches as Carl says goodbye to the old man. He sees Carl slip something into the old man's pocket and then insert his token and move swiftly through the wooden arms.

"Come on," Carl says, and grabs his shoulder. "Don't you listen? I told you to meet me on the platform."

David glances back over his shoulder as they race for the stairs. There is a sweeper pushing a line of dirt and rubbish toward the old man, who stands at the turnstile and stares down at them. Then the top of the stairs cuts off David's view.

A train waits at the platform. Carl checks its destination and then edges David in. David chooses a window seat and Carl follows him into it. The doors close, and the train grinds away from the station. David watches the station's lights flicker away, tries to count the occasional daylight patches from sidewalk transoms. Three stations go by before he speaks.

"That was money you gave Gran'pop."

Carl nods.

"That's why you wanted me to wait on the platform. You didn't want me to see."

The train squeals into a long straining curve, and the lights flick off. David counts up to three before the lights come on again, and the sway of the car settles into a smoother run.

"You think it'll do any good, the money? Suppose he doesn't use it?"

The train grinds to a halt, and they sit and wait. Probably, David thinks, there is a red light ahead; we're near some kind of line crossing, and the express is coming through. The train jerks into motion, and David stares out the window until he sees the green light pass by.

"He can throw it away," David says. "He can always throw it away."

"No. He wouldn't do that."

"Why not?"

"Well—he wouldn't, that's all. Look, I gave him thirty dollars. That's a lot of money. He wouldn't just throw it away. It'd be such a waste, to just throw thirty dollars away like that."

"Then maybe he'll give it away," David says. "He could always give it away. Couldn't he?"

The train stops at a station, and David watches as the doors slide open. The engines hum as the train waits, and then the doors slide closed again. The station lights begin to fall back, and David watches as the tile walls become dark and the overhead lights dot to single bulbs. Carl's face is drawn, he is far away in his seat, so David does not interrupt. He checks the map on the window and counts backward from their stop. Only two more stations.

$\mathcal{T}en$

Roland Shockley, aged fifty-two, sweeper employed by the New York Transit Authority, leaned on his pushbroom and watched the old man stand by the turnstile, staring after Carl and David. The old man stood with one hand outstretched as if to pull them back, and Shockley shook his head.

"Hunh," Shockley said. "Now why they do that? Couldn't even say goodbye decent, had to go rushin' off. People always in such a hurry."

He pushed down his broom again, sending the ice-cream papers, candy-bar wrappers, receipts and line of dirt another foot across the tunnel's floor. When he looked up, the old man was still at the turnstiles, looking at the steps leading down to the subway platform.

Maybe he lost. Maybe they lost him on purpose, bringed him down here for a joke, and then left him.

He shook his head, twirling the broom handle to knock off some of the dust.

Possible. Anything's possible these days. All you got to do is read the papers. Every day another headline, somebody's done something mean and rotten to somebody else. Ain't nothing much good happening any more.

Shockley slanted the line of dirt toward the turnstiles, figuring on talking to the old man if he kept standing there. Then he became absorbed in the movements of a small roach. It kept trying to fight its way out of the heap of papers, dirt and debris, but each time it struggled out it ran headlong into Shockley's broom, and got swept back in. It worked its way out again and again Shockley's broom swept it back.

"Now ain't you a silly one! Don't it never occur to you to go the other way?"

The roach backed out of a smaller pile of sweepings and again ran into Shockley's broom.

"You really stupid," Shockley said. The old man backed slowly from the turnstile, still staring at the steps. He backed into Shockley, still absorbed in the roach's movements.

"Hhump!"

The broom handle jammed into Shockley's ribs and shoulder, then clattered to the floor.

"Hey!" Shockley said.

The old man swayed, lost his balance. His knees folded and slowly he sagged to the floor. Shockley caught his arm, held him so that he knelt on the stone floor, his knees marring the line of Shockley's sweepings.

"Hey," Shockley said again, "Don't you never look where you's goin'?"

The old man's eyes were closed. Shockley heard his heavy, hoarse breathing.

"You okay? How you feel, you hurt anywhere?"

The old man opened his eyes.

"*Schwartze,*" he said. "You *schwartze* bastard. Tripping me with that broom. I'll get you, *schwartze* bastard, I'll sue the company, you see if I don't. I'll fix you, *schwartze.*"

"Listen here now," Shockley said. "You got things just a little mixed up. You bumped into me, I didn't do no tripping with no broom. I'm just standing here sweeping up this here floor, and the next thing I know you's on the ground. So don't go blaming me, now, you hear, cause it won't work."

The old man shook his head.

"Listen, *schwartze.* The least you could do, after you tripped me, is help me up again. It won't do you no good to let me lay here; more witnesses I'll get."

Shockley shook his head.

"I told you once," he began, "I didn't—" and then stopped, engrossed in the tremor that twisted the old man and ended in a hacking cough. He's sick sure, Shockley thought. He bent down, grasped the old man carefully at his armpits, and slowly lifted him to his feet. The old man swayed for a moment, steadied himself, and pushed Shockley's arms away. He shuffled a few steps, then turned back to stare at the line of rubbish he had marred in falling. His hands went down to the bottom of his jacket and brushed feebly at the dirt.

"I'm dirty," he said to Shockley. "I'm dirty all over. You tripped me so I'd fall into your dirt, and now I'm dirty all over."

Shockley tossed the broomhandle from one hand to the other. Then he let the handle slip from his hand; it hit the floor and bounced twice, making a hollow, whooping sound. Shockley crossed the few steps to the old man and brushed the dirt carefully from his jacket. He hesitated a moment, then stooped to gently strike the dirt from the old man's trousers, using his open palm in a short chopping motion to flick off the dust. He straightened.

"You're not dirty any more."

Shockley watched the old man's face contort again as another coughing fit seized him; the old man bent with the force of his coughing and then spat out a heavy globule of mucus into the line of Shockley's sweeping. He straightened slowly, turned, and shuffled away.

Shockley stared until the old man's stooped figure disappeared into the shadows of the tunnel. Then he bent to retrieve his broom and started the line of dirt moving across the floor again. The roach poked up from the dirt and Shockley shoved it back.

"Don't you ever give up? All you got to do is learn to go the other way."

Eleven

RABBI DAVIS

"So, Rabbi Davis. Another cup of tea?"

She pushes the chair back and stands with the table pressing into her stomach, her housecoat open over the sloppy bulge of her fat because she's too lazy to sew the buttons on when they groan against her paunch and finally pop off. And her housecoat is streaked with splotches of cooking fat and egg that have dripped off her spoon and dozens of little trickles of food that never reached her mouth.

"Look, Mrs. Kauffman. How many years have I been boarding in your house?"

First she crinkles her eyelids under her filthy glasses, to stare at me. Then she runs that fuzzy tip of a tongue along her lip line, and I watch the moisture coat the flabby line of her lips.

"Fourteen years, Rabbi Davis. Fourteen years next Passover."

"And in all that time, Mrs. Kauffman, in all those fourteen years, after I've somehow managed to swallow all the scrambled eggs, all the fried fish, all the *keplatin* that you've fed me, have I ever asked, even hinted, for a second cup of tea?"

She raises her eyebrows till they arch above her glasses, puckers her mouth until the corners curl and sag and seem to melt into the lines creasing her chin, and shakes her head.

"Why are you always picking on me, Rabbi Davis? Why, that's all I want to know? Do I give you bad food, do I forget to lay out clean towels every Tuesday; do I come into your room and try to clean while you're working? An educated woman I'm not, Rabbi Davis, God knows I never pretend to be. But when I ask a simple question, why can't you give me a simple answer?"

"All right, Mrs. Kauffman."

"Is it so difficult? Does it hurt you to answer? Does it hurt you to say, no, I don't want another cup of tea? So I ask you, so what? Does it hurt you? It's me who does the asking, not you. If I want to ask, is it such a big deal to give me a simple answer?"

"All right, Mrs. Kauffman."

"And is it so impossible, one time maybe you might want a cup of tea? Is it so impossible that one—"

"All right, Mrs. Kauffman. All right, I'm sorry. I shouldn't have picked on you. No, Mrs. Kauffman, I won't have another cup of tea. But thank you very much just the same."

Why do I bother? Why do I ever bother? She could ask me the same thing, I haven't lived with her for fourteen years? I don't know, by now, that in Mrs. Kauffman's boardinghouse, her star boarder gets offered a second cup of tea after lunch, no matter how many thousands of times he's already said no? All of a sudden she's going to change, she's going to shake off the habits of fourteen years and take a good look at me and realize that I'm Rabbi Davis and I don't take a second cup of tea? She's any different than the hundreds of other maiden ladies renting out their one room to "business and professional gentlemen," and then calling themselves "landladies"? Landladies. Why not roomladies? Or boardinghouse keepers? You would love being called a boardinghouse keeper, wouldn't you, Mrs. Kauffman? Oh, Rabbi Davis, you'd squeal, you have such a filthy mind, for a rabbi. You don't have no respect for no one. Calling my house nothing better than a brothel.

"Oh, Rabbi, I forgot. There was a call for you, while you were in synagogue. Some man. A member. Ron, Roth—Rozner. Yes, that's right, Mr. Rozner. He said to tell you—I was going to write it down but he hung up too fast—he said to tell you that Zitomer came to his store three times last week, and if you couldn't do something about it, he'd go to the police."

"So let him go to the police! What the hell am I supposed to do about it? He thinks it's the Middle Ages, all I've got to do is accuse Zitomer of heresy and turn him over to the civil authorities? What business do I have with what happens in his store? The synagogue's my responsibility, and I keep Zitomer out of the synagogue. He wants to keep Zitomer out of his store, let him go to the police. I got enough troubles."

She pitpats away into the kitchen on her soft slippers, with the heels so run-down the slippers look like the skins of dogs that have been run over and then squashed on Southern highways. Zitomer. What a mess one man can make. They'll get him. He won't listen to me, he won't believe me, but I know my members. They'll get him and they'll fix him so that every time he opens his mouth to say all men are brothers, he'll laugh out of his backside instead.

Oh, I'm full. God knows how I manage on Mrs. Kauffman's cooking, but I'm full. Might as well read the *Worker* for a few minutes before I go out. Though God knows why I bother. I know what it'll say so well I could recite it by heart. Forty years ago reading the *Worker* was like reading the Torah, I used to tear into every paragraph. Now it takes me five, ten minutes, maybe, and I'm done. Only the names are different.

"Rabbi. Excuse me for mentioning it, but—well, Mrs. Horowitz, you see. She told me about Zitomer, that he can't come to the synagogue any more. That the membership threw him out."

Mrs. Kauffman! That was three weeks ago! You mean you don't know the whole story by now? And even a dozen extra little details, just to make it sound more exciting? I'm ashamed of you, Mrs. Kauffman. The whole network needs new faces. Fire all the old spies and gossips, change the party lines, make new contacts. What kind of a landlady are you, you have to come and ask me what happened?

"That's right, Mrs. Kauffman. The membership threw him out. Three weeks ago."

"Listen, Rabbi, you should excuse me for mentioning it, but isn't a synagogue open to everybody? Since when do you need a membership to come in and pray?"

"You're right, Mrs. Kauffman. A synagogue's open to everybody. You don't need a membership to come in and pray. But everybody in that synagogue has a right to pray in peace, and if one man keeps disturbing their prayers, then I think they have the right to ask him to leave."

Pitpat back into the kitchen. She's after something. Some little detail, in all the stories she's heard and told, doesn't fit. She wants to check up. Just my luck, I had to board with the biggest gossip in the East Side. So, she's back again.

"Listen, Rabbi Davis. Maybe I shouldn't ask this."

"You go ahead and ask, Mrs. Kauffman. Sooner or later you'll ask anyway, so ask now and save all the excuses."

"That's a fine thing. Always, Rabbi Davis, always you're picking on me. Sometimes I think you don't like me at all, Rabbi Davis."

"Mrs. Kauffman, whether or not I like you doesn't make any difference. I know you, Mrs. Kauffman, I know you. Fourteen years I know you. So I know when you're going to ask something that you have to lead up to first. All I'm saying is, don't bother leading. Just ask."

She smiles at me, as if we're sharing a secret about her, but I know how deep that smile goes. Sometimes, Mrs. Kauffman, I think you don't like me at all. And other times, I'm sure of it. And you know, Mrs. Kauffman, I don't blame you one little bit!

"So all right. What I wanted to know was about Zitomer. About what he did. What kind of disturbance did he cause, that the membership had to throw him out?"

"It was a sexual disturbance he caused, Mrs. Kauffman. He started out with a little exhibitionism, between *Adon Olem* and the benediction. Unsettling, maybe, but minor; nothing the membership couldn't handle. But then he graduated to more conspicuous stuff, cleverly spaced into the lulls in the service, a deliberate process of mimed enticement aimed at some of the younger members. When he started flirting with the *bar mitzvah* boys, the membership decided it was time to do something."

"Oh, my God, Rabbi Davis! That's horrible. It's horrible! Oh my God. And in the synagogue, yet!"

I don't know, really. Myself, I think the synagogue's a fine place for that sort of thing. First of all, it's warm; try it outside and you're liable to freeze yourself. And besides, in a synagogue, it's purer, somehow. There you are, lifting your eyes and your voice to heaven, and waving yourself around with your hands. I can't help grinning at the thought of it, though she'll know I'm playing with her. Look at her, sitting there with her shocked look, her mouth so open she'd swallow a thousand flies if her breath didn't smell so bad it'd drive them away. What does she think it means, to exhibit yourself? Does she even know it's about sex? Do professional landladies, maiden ladies, admit that word into their vocabulary?

"You're fooling me again, Rabbi Davis."

"Me, Mrs. Kauffman? Fooling you? A man in my position has the time, the inclination, to fool with his landlady?"

"Well, you are, Rabbi Davis. I can tell. You're always telling me stories and making fun of me, Rabbi Davis, and I'm always falling for them. I don't understand you, Rabbi Davis, I don't understand what pleasure it gives you, to make fun of a poor simple landlady. I never thought any rabbi would be like you. Always telling me stories, and some of them filthy, too. You think it's right, to tell me stories all the time and make me believe them?"

"Listen, Mrs. Kauffman. I'll tell you something that's not a story. A long time ago I gave up worrying about what was right and what was wrong, and decided to do my job the best way I could and live the rest of my life the way I felt like. I don't know anything about right and wrong, Mrs. Kauffman, and I'll tell you something else—I don't believe anyone else does, either. Once, when I was very young, in college even, I thought I knew a little about right and wrong, but my first pulpit taught me different. Now Zitomer comes running into the synagogue, after God knows how many years of running his candy store and minding his own business, all of a sudden he knows the difference between right and wrong. More, he has to tell the members. All the years he stood behind the counter and raised prices and short-changed all the *goyim* and *schwartzes* who came into his store might have taught him that maybe there isn't any right and wrong? Not Zitomer! Zitomer's got answers. Zitomer hasn't lived long enough to know that there are only people, some bad, some worse. No, Zitomer knows what people really are, Zitomer knows how people should live their lives. The Ten Commandments, he shouts, we must all obey the Ten Commandments. Yes, yes, Zitomer, I think to myself, and I let him come up to the pulpit and add his voice to the millions of voices that have told people to do this, do that, obey this, live different. I let him lecture about not lying and not cheating and not stealing to my beloved congregation, a greedy little pack of vultures who'd spit on the Torah before they'd let a blind man off with an extra penny's change. I let him tell all those shabby little money-making machines that they should act like people instead of money-making machines, and then I went back to the pulpit and talked about the Torah, which we treat as a piece of historical research rather than as a body of law to be understood and obeyed. But does Zitomer give up? Not Zitomer! Zitomer knows what men really are. After they laughed at him does he give up? Not Zitomer! After they throw him out of the synagogue, does he give up? Not Zitomer! They'll throw him in jail before they're finished with him, you think he'll give up then? Not Zitomer! He knows what men really are. He'd had a revelation. He thinks he can—"

The phone. For me, I guess. Somebody wants to talk to me. Somebody wants spiritual comfort. But I don't want to give any. Not today. Today's my day for comforting myself.

"I better get it, Rabbi."

"If they want me, Mrs. Kauffman, tell them I'm not in. I'm out. Take the message."

Sunday's the one day in the week I reserve for myself. I don't have to sit around answering phone calls on Sundays. All week is enough, answering calls from old men who don't have anything better to do and think that because I'm the rabbi I'm supposed to listen to them. Rabbi! Comforter of the aged. Wet nurse for a bunch of senile old men. All over the East Side they're huddled in their dirty little rooms, wondering how to fill all the empty hours that stare from their peeling walls. My walls aren't peeling and my life isn't empty, that's what the difference is. I've got my books and my papers and the shape of the world to think about, even though it doesn't make very pleasant thinking. But I've still got a mind left, and I've used it enough, through the years, so that it hasn't degenerated into a memory cabinet crammed with whole chunks of meaningless conversations. I didn't work for five, six days a week hovering over a machine and pulling the bobbin lever exactly thirty-four and one-quarter times per hour. I didn't work eight, nine, ten hours a day and then shuffle home, eat and go to sleep so I could get up the next morning and go to work again; I didn't take my paycheck to the bank or put the dollar bills in the little glass jar in the bottom drawer. So I have a brain left, and all they have is a set of habits they can't use. Their feet could still take them down the steps and around the corner to the bus stop, if only they still worked in the factory. Their hands could still thread a machine and guide the hem under the needle, but they have no machines in their dirty little rooms. The figures in the bankbook keep getting smaller, the dollar bills in the little glass jar finally run out. So they sit down to write a letter to the son or the daughter; they lick the pencil point and wonder what to say. If only they were back on their machine. What can they do with eight, nine, ten hours stretched out before them, now that their jobs are done, their machines are run by younger people? Retired. Retired from work, when work was all they had. So now they got the synagogue, eating, maybe a little shopping, a walk into the park. And a phone call to their rabbi.

"It's some lady who says she's Mrs. Marshall, Rabbi. She says she's Rabbi Samuels' daughter. She wants to talk to you. She says it's important."

Samuels' daughter? Maybe Samuels kicked the bucket? Choked to death on an overload of avocados or melons or whatever else they grow out there in California?

"What did you tell her, Mrs. Kauffman?"

"I said I wasn't sure whether you were in or not, that I'd go find out."

"Thanks, Mrs. Kauffman. All right, I'll talk to her."

"Hello?"

"Rabbi Davis?"

"Yes, this is Rabbi Davis speaking."

"Well, I'm Mrs. Marshall, Rabbi Davis. Rabbi Samuels' daughter. I don't know if he ever mentioned me to you."

"No, I don't think he did, Mrs.—wait a minute. Yes, he did. He once said something to me about a daughter coming to live in New York. Well, how are you, Mrs. Marshall?"

"I'm very well, thank you, Rabbi Davis."

"Good. Good. Well, what can I do for you?"

"I'm awfully sorry to disturb you, Rabbi Davis. But I got a letter from my father yesterday, and he asked me please to find your number and call you up to find out why you hadn't written to him. He said he's been writing you for the last six months, and you haven't answered any of his letters. He thought something was wrong, so he asked me to call up and find out if you were all right."

"Well, that's very kind of you, Mrs. Marshall. And it's very thoughtful of your father, too. But there's nothing at all wrong with me, Mrs. Marshall. I've just been very busy, that's all, you know how a rabbi's life is. No rest for the wicked. Heh, heh, heh."

"Yes, I understand, Rabbi. It's just that my father asked me, if I spoke to you, if you were all right, to ask you to please write to him. He says he misses very much not hearing from you. He says you're the closest friend he's got, that he's known you since college and seminary days."

"I'm sure Samuels must have closer friends than me, Mrs. Marshall. After all, I haven't seen him since he went off to California."

"No, honestly, Rabbi Davis. He says you're his closest friend. And I'll tell you something, I'm really worried about him. Ever since he took that job in Santa Monica, his letters have been so gloomy and depressed. I don't understand what's the matter. His work sounds interesting enough. California sounds wonderful. But he broods and broods. His letters get more and more depressed. He actually begged me, in this letter I got yesterday, to get you to write to him."

"Well—well, I'll try, Mrs. Marshall. That's all I can say."

"Try, Rabbi Davis? But surely—"

"Listen, Mrs. Marshall, I've been trying to tell you nicely that I won't write to your father any more, but you won't let me. So I'll tell you un-nicely. I haven't written to your father for six months, not because I was too busy or because I lost his address or because I was momentarily offended by something he said in one of his letters. I stopped writing to your father when he took that post in Santa Monica, and I don't intend to write him or speak to him or see him. And what's more, Mrs. Marshall, he knows perfectly well why I'm not answering his letters. He's known me too long to think that he could sell out completely and expect that I'd go on writing to him and calling him Comrade as if nothing had happened."

"But—Rabbi Davis! To stop writing to a man, to cut him dead—just over a disagreement in politics—"

"Politics, Mrs. Marshall? Politics? You think the way a man lives his life has only to do with politics, Mrs. Marshall? You think that when your father wriggles himself into a congregation where he doesn't have a scrap of work to do, and gets himself appointed official rabbi to three of the city's old-age homes that don't even have any Jews in them, you think that's a political act? You think what made your father and me close to each other, those years in Columbia and the seminary, when we were ready to lead riots through the streets, was a nice simple political agreement? Listen, Mrs. Marshall, when your father's letters came to me, sunburned and sleek from California, and I open them and read Samuels' gloating about his car that he tricked the congregation into buying for him, because he told them his leg isn't too good—"

"His leg *isn't* too good!"

"Because he told them his leg isn't too good, and after I read them I shove them into my pocket and walk down my filthy street to my little wooden synagogue that will probably fall apart some day, and inside are twenty, twenty-five stuttering wrecks of old men, waiting for me to lead them in prayers they don't even understand, I'm supposed to feel good about Samuels, riding the hog's belly in Santa Anna or Santa Maria or wherever else he is? I'm supposed to treasure the memory of my brother in socialism and feel equally happy about my brother in luxury? Now I'm willing to admit there's more than a trace of envy in what I'm saying, Mrs. Marshall. God knows I'd love to be sitting plump and handsome in some luxury flat, with a car in the garage and a congregation two blocks away who paid me handsomely and asked only that I make the requisite sounds in the proper places. But what keeps me from worming my way into a post like that, Mrs. Marshall, aside from my own limitations and the fact that at my age, with my reputation, nobody would take me—what keeps me out of a post like that is something I call belief, Mrs. Marshall; there're nicer ways of saying it, but what your father's done is to decide that the ease and security of his last few years is worth more than any set of beliefs. However treasured, however fervently

129

shared with his old faithful comrade Davis. So I hope he enjoys his beach cottage and his car and his congregation and his three old-age homes full of *goyim*, Mrs. Marshall. Because I don't intend to write him a postcard, even. And if that's politics, Mrs. Marshall, then I'm afraid everything's politics!"

Silence is nice, for a change. I can still hear my own voice ringing into the earpiece. So, Mrs. Marshall? Come, come, must say something. Can't let the side down. I'm a nasty old man, aren't I? Uncivilized, almost. I'm sure nobody you know would ever act this way.

"I—I don't know what to say."

"No need to say anything, Mrs. Marshall."

"I never—never—heard anyone speak like you. I think you're crazy, Rabbi Davis. I think you're a mean, crazy old man. I thank God my father got out when he did. He might have wound up like you."

"Mrs. Marshall, I couldn't agree with you more. I think Samuels' move to Santa Monica was the most intelligent thing he's ever done. And I'm sure this gloomy period he's passing through is only a temporary one. Any day now, you'll get a letter telling you how gay and cheerful he's becoming, pottering away in his little beachfront garden. So I'm sure, Mrs. Marshall, you wouldn't want any letters from a crazy, twisted old man to disturb your father's serenity. Better if we just forget the whole thing. But thank you very much for calling, Mrs. Marshall."

"But he needs you, Rabbi. He needs you!"

"Me, Mrs. Marshall? A mean, crazy old man? A twisted hangover from a dirty past? With his cottage and his car, sunshine all day, the Pacific on his doorstep, nothing to do and all the fresh air in the world to do it in, he needs me? I really can't believe that, Mrs. Marshall."

Silence again. Unfortunately, Mrs. Marshall, you are way over your head. You sound like Suburban League, Mrs. Marshall; Community Center, perhaps, and trips to synagogue on the High Holy Days, in the car. Husband commutes to work, you meet him at the station. What do you talk about, these days, at your sherry parties? Or is it cocktail parties? Broadway plays, probably, and the new comedians that they call "sick." Well it hasn't helped you much, Mrs. Marshall, your brain's as soft and cuddled as all the other executives' wives I've ever intersected. Your husband probably chisels on his income tax, would like to sleep with his secretary but hasn't got enough nerve and isn't quite certain how to approach her. You've got two children dressed in contrasting pastel shades, who sleep in two contrasting pastel bedrooms, on either side of the powder room. So you try to explain to your father just what I'm talking about, Mrs. Marshall.

"I think you're very wrong, Rabbi Davis. I think you're making a big mistake."

"Making mistakes, Mrs. Marshall, is one of those proofs of my fallibility and humanity which I most dearly treasure. I relish my mistakes almost as much as I enjoy the overwhelming number of times when I'm absolutely right. And if I weren't wrong occasionally, dear Mrs. Marshall, I'm afraid I'd be terribly dull. Is there anything else I can do for you?"

"No, Rabbi."

"Well, thank you again for calling, Mrs. Marshall. I'm sorry we haven't exactly seen eye to eye, as they say, but then those little things do happen. Heh, heh, heh. If you ever need any spiritual advice, Mrs. Marshall, don't hesitate to call on me. I'm always willing to aid one of my ex-comrade's relatives. And if you do try to explain to your father about me, Mrs. Marshall, just tell him I've still got the same synagogue. He'll understand."

Put the phone down quickly, and let the soft click tell her that I've actually hung up on her. I bet no one's ever hung up on you before, Mrs. Marshall. I bet you put the phone down and go into the breakfast room to your husband, with a puzzled frown on your carefully made-up face. Darling, I just don't understand. Well it's nothing you or anybody else would understand, Mrs. Marshall, unless you grew up the way I did, watching my father work himself to death, trying to keep his leather shop going so he could feed my mother and me and keep some clothes on our backs. Maybe you think nobody suffers in America any more, Mrs. Marshall, but my father wasn't smart. He was just honest and stubborn, and when you've got a little leather shop and the first manufactured shoe shops open in the town, honesty and stubbornness don't help. A smarter man would have gotten out, changed his line, done some dealing, but my father wasn't smart. Leather was all he knew, working in leather was all his hands were good for. So he hung on, and he fought the first small stores that sold ready-made shoes, the larger stores, and the chains—until finally we had one mail-order house and two department stores, and my father was still trying to sell handmade shoes and bags and briefcases. Well, I never forgot, Mrs. Marshall, I never forgot any of it. I never forgot the twenty-hour days he worked, because he was convinced he had to send me to college, so I wouldn't grow up to be an honest exhausted bootmaker in a town where everybody bought ready-made. I never forgot the way he shrank at his bench; from a man who used to tower over the table, he shrank to a twisted dwarf of a man, his arms curling across the table to cut another piece of leather. I never forgot the way he coughed, either, Mrs. Marshall; I saw what he hid in his handkerchief when he turned his face away to spit in it. And if you don't know anything about this, Mrs. Marshall, how do you think your father got to college? Ask him sometime, Mrs. Marshall, why there was nothing false or accommodating about him in those years at Columbia, when we worked on every committee and every mimeographed newssheet and magazine going. Ask him why we were willing to be kicked out of the seminary for our politics, Mrs. Marshall. Ask him why we swore to be rabbis and Socialists.

Ach, I could stand here all day in the hallway, talking to myself. I'll never get outside for my walk. Mrs. Kauffman is still in the kitchen, sharing her second cup of tea with the second cup of tea I never take.

"I'm going out, Mrs. Kauffman. For an hour or two. For a walk. I'll be back before I have to leave for afternoon services."

"All right, Rabbi Davis. If anybody calls, I'll tell them."

"Thanks, Mrs. Kauffman."

"Rabbi Davis."

"Yes, Mrs. Kauffman?"

"What did Rabbi Samuels' daughter want?"

Nosy old cow. Never satisfied. When I die she'll probably wail after me all the way to the cemetery, moaning about the last few questions she never got around to asking.

"She wanted to talk to me, Mrs. Kauffman. That's all. She simply wanted to talk to me. It happens sometimes, you know. People call up a rabbi, a spiritual adviser, because they want to talk to him. And usually, the rabbi doesn't then give an account of his conversation to his landlady. Now I'll admit that there are occasionally exceptional circumstances, Mrs. Kauffman, when a rabbi might overlook the demands of spiritual and professional integrity and confidence, and reveal to his landlady what was considered to be a private and personal conversation. But this situation does not strike me as one of those exceptions."

So go on, stare at me. If you didn't keep sticking your nose in where it didn't belong, I wouldn't have to keep shoving it out with my foot. How many years have I been banging you over the head to mind your own business?

"So goodbye, Mrs. Kauffman."

"Goodbye, Rabbi."

It's too late in the year to walk outside on a Sunday. If I didn't have to walk, if I could stay inside all afternoon and not let Mrs. Kauffman's pitter-patting get on my nerves, I'd stay inside and curse the newspaper articles that pretend to be measuring a change in our climate. It is getting slowly warmer, they say, due perhaps to the successive atomic explosions and the amount of radiation introduced into the atmosphere. I have a hunch that this is the beginning of an argument for the introduction of more atomic bomb explosions, since they turn the weather warmer. After a few gigantic introductions of radiation into the atmosphere, probably taking place over Russia, we will change our climate so much we'll have only summer all the time. Summer and cancer and the sweet smell of roasted Russian flesh circling in the atmosphere. I am probably a hopeless, senile old man, but my wrinkled flesh tells me that this Sunday's as cold as any winter Sunday was when I was a kid. And even if atomic heating could make us warmer, I think I'd prefer to struggle on through our natural raw winters. Except that nobody will come and ask me whether or not I prefer atomic heating. The choice is no longer mine. Or anybody else's except the generals in the Pentagon.

God knows I wish I didn't have to walk. Walking is for the country, not the city. Walking through these streets is like nothing, like death; like walking through stone canyons in some prehistoric graveyard. We have learned how to build with steel and concrete and glass so that we can throw our office blocks up so high that they cut off whatever light from a winter sun might grace this waste of a street where a blade of grass is stranger than a drunk curled into the gutter. Walking at street level in a city is almost like walking underground; only the men in the fortieth-floor office suites and the penthouses know what sun and sky and fresh air are. For us, down here on the street, the shadows from the skyscrapers start at morning, and only at noon, when the sun is directly overhead, does the sun filter down to warm our creaking old bones. But at noon the streets are so packed with people that if I wanted to stand on the pavement and stare up at the sunlight shining off the windows and the car roofs and the signboards, I would be swept along by the lunchtime mob into some bar or luncheonette or soda fountain, to wind up stuffing some tasteless sandwich down my mechanically performing gullet, while my jaws churned to the rhythm of the rock-and-roll spewing from the jukebox.

Every Sunday I walk in the cold or the rain and the wind, and I think the same things. Bitterness is all I got left. Bitterness, and understanding, which is no great asset, since I can't give it away. I used to write down some of the things I thought, but I stopped writing. What is the use of writing for some paper that a dozen people read? I used to say some of the things I thought from the pulpit, but long ago I stopped. What's the use of talking to people who don't understand what you're saying? So every Sunday I take my walk, I poke my way through the puddles and the cracked sidewalks and the garbage cans that are so rotten the bottoms are almost gone, and I think to myself, it's getting worse. Twenty-five years ago there was grass and trees here, twenty years ago these houses had windows. Fifteen years ago you could see sunlight on the pavements and the streets weren't cracked. So it's getting worse, I think to myself; millions of us, poor twisted wrecks growing closer to death in a hundred steel jungles, but I'm a big help, because I understand that it's getting worse.

Turn a corner and there is only another stretch of gray shadowed street, which stretches itself along cracked stained pavements, crumbling iron-railed steps, dirt-caked window-panes or cardboard panels nailed tight to keep out the wind. At the next corner, you can stop and think about which way to go, as if there was a choice, as if any of the four streets that stretch away from the corner hold something beside the same shabby brownstones, the three and four story wrecks with washing and mattresses and even furniture hanging out the windows. In Stuart, at least when I was a kid, you could stand at the main intersection and stare down any one of the four streets, and you could follow it past the diagonally parked cars and the square wooden façades of the feed stores and the new electric street lights suspended from shiny steel poles until the street lost its store fronts and ran past garden-trimmed houses into the farmland that circled the town. When the air was still in the late afternoon, and the sun was so hot on your skin it was like a heated glove pressing down on you, I used to walk with the sweat rolling off my face and neck, out past the edge of town, past the last white frame houses with the wide porches and the gliders in the front yard, into the fields. Here am I, I thought to myself, walking alone into the richest farm land in the world, walking alone for the simple reason that I was born a Jew, and who in this model town of twenty-two thousand white Protestants would walk with a Jew? No, no, of course there is no prejudice here, it is simply that everyone else has better things to do than to walk into the richest farm country in the world with a Jew. So I walked by myself, sometimes for miles, out into the soil that had just been turned and sown and now lay hot and waiting, the stench of manure rising like steam from the furrows, a black horse tossing its mane and rearing back on its hind legs, though no mare was anywhere in sight. I walked by myself and I said to myself, strange, that a Jewish boy, son of a Jewish bootmaker, should be walking through the richest farm country in the world. My father's name is Davitsky, I shouted, not Davis; he became Davis because the immigration official at Ellis Island was not patient enough to make out what my father was spelling in his slurred Austrian dialect. So Davitsky became Davis, and a Jew became a bootmaker in a white Protestant community in the middle of the richest farm country in the world, and his son walks like a disease through this clean, shining, all-American town. I understood, then, what my father had always told me, that this free country belongs to them, to the blond-haired, blue-eyed ones who came first, from England and Scotland and Holland and Sweden and Germany, to take the best land, form the first companies, fight the first wars, drive the first railways across the continent, and set their crazy pattern of conquest and competition on the land. I understood then that there were only two choices open in this land of the free and home of the brave; you could join the race, or you could refuse to run. If you joined the race, if you accepted the goals that the movies and the magazines and the newspapers and the billboards set before you, if you did everything that was required of you and even a little more, if you sacrificed your friends when it became necessary and convinced your wife that a little social whoring was not much of a sacrifice, if you cheated on your income tax and religiously cut your old friends as you moved above them, if you read the right opinions in the right magazines and assiduously mouthed them before your vice president's wife at precisely the right moment, you might find, as my father said, that the doorkeeper of the land of the free and the home of the brave gets a trifle anxious, and opens the door a crack, enough for you to slip in, change your job and your name and your home and your friends, and keep only the proper books on your shelves.

So fifty years ago I stood in a cornfield in Iowa and understood what my father had said, and in all those years what I have learned amounts to an elaboration on his text. There is no happiness in understanding. There is even more than an excuse for saying that he was happier than I am, working himself into the wood of his table without understanding how inevitable his defeat was. You can't beat progress, the branch manager told my father. And here I am, fifty years later, adding footnotes to the same words. None of my Sunday walks have ended in anything but despair. These sidewalks and these streets and these rotting buildings are my prison, these senile old men my corpses. And how many have I buried? The same sour-stained concrete, rotting wood and cracked glass surrounded my first synagogue in Akron, with the smoke from the rubber factories belching out over the city. In Birmingham it was the steel works, in Camden the soup and the chemicals, but in every city the little orthodox synagogue sinks into a slum of colored homes and factories. The congregations grow smaller and older, the young people drift away from a restricted life whose demands spell poverty, into the easier accommodations they already know, having been introduced by movies, newspapers, and the carefully cultivated objectivity of their schools. So I walk another Sunday afternoon to death through these streets, which are little different, in bleakness and amount of filth, from Akron streets or Birmingham streets or Camden streets, except that here the buildings are higher and the shadows, when the sun breaks through the smog, are longer; and sometimes, glancing upward through the thinning air space between the giant towers of steel, concrete, and glass, the sky is like some fantastic painting an absurd romanticist has topped the roof of this jungle with. I walk the afternoon to death through these streets, and I kick at a crumble of newspaper, and the thoughts I think are the words my father told me. I listen and I wonder what it has meant and what good it has done, that I have stayed faithful to my father's words when I have been able to live with no one but myself, and even Samuels has finally made and plumped up his bed.

Because I know exactly how Samuels finally brought himself to take that job and that home and that car. And it's not shock, or anger, or even hatred, that makes me swear never to write to him again. It's fear. It's fear because he's brought the conclusion I've always run from one step nearer my door, and I'm too old and too tired to fight it down again. If I could believe, even, that it's true, that I am a lonely, bitter, stubborn old fool, afraid to join, to share, to belong to anything; erecting my fears into moralities and my sensitivities into beliefs, then even if I didn't jump in headfirst like Samuels, at least I would have some sort of peace. It is very peaceful to give up, to admit all your heresies and to surrender your direction to the mercy of those who have never been mistaken. And we have learned so much from the inhumanities of our medieval predecessors that we no longer impose either penance or penalty, but embrace with open arms all those who realize that their refusal to join the community of Americans had nothing to do with integrity of conscience or brotherhood but only with their own—shall we say—psychological imbalances?

"Rabbi Davis."

Of course. What else should I expect, on a Sunday walk

when all I want to do is to try to work off some of the week's accumulated bitterness, but that I should meet my own *shamos*. It's too late to nod and walk past, he's got somebody with him.

"Oh. Hello."

"Rabbi Davis, this is my son, Carl. Carl, this is Rabbi Davis. My rabbi."

My rabbi. As if he owns me. I could say My *shamos*, and it would be closer to the truth. Especially after this morning's performance. Are you worrying, maybe, that I'm going to hold it against you? Even fire you, maybe?

"Pleased to meet you, Rabbi Davis."

Nod and shake his hand. A strong hand, calloused. A strong man. Big man, too.

"My son and I have just come in for a day, to see Dad. We're on our way to the subway. I tried to tell Dad he didn't have to come, because it's so cold outside—"

"He's right, you know. It's too cold to be walking in the streets, especially without a coat on."

"Rabbi, you should excuse me for saying it, but I'm all right without a coat. Six months already I've been walking around without a coat. The sweater is warm, and the jacket is warm. I don't need a coat."

So don't wear a coat. This morning your nerves were so shot you cried in my office, and now, three hours later, you don't even need a little friendly advice.

"It's colder now than it used to be, these winters. Sometimes I have to do some work outside, on a television antenna, and the wind's so strong and cold I can't work more than fifteen, twenty minutes without coming inside again."

"I know. I was thinking the same thing earlier, while I was walking. The papers all say that our winters are getting warmer, but I don't believe it. To me it feels like they're getting colder."

"Colder, warmer, what's the difference? I get up every morning at six, and I walk to the synagogue, to open the doors for the morning service. You think I worry about how cold it is? Every morning, rain or snow, I get up at six and I come to the synagogue."

Maybe he is worried. Maybe he thinks Zitomer talked to me afterward, explained to me about the outburst. Well he did, old man, but I don't intend to do anything about it. I never expected that any of my congregation were saints. I'm the last rabbi you have to worry about being guilty before.

"It's true. I can't remember a morning when you didn't get to the synagogue on time. I've been in five synagogues in five different cities, and you're the finest *shamos* I've ever known."

There. That ought to hold you. If you're worried, you can stop worrying.

"So, Rabbi Davis, this is my grandson."

"David, this is Rabbi Davis."

The boy's hand is hot.

"Pleased to meet you, Rabbi."

"Happy to meet you." But I'm supposed to say something else. I guess I'm supposed to make the old man feel good. "Well, you're a very big boy, David. How old are you?"

"Twelve years, seven months, and sixteen days. I forget how many hours."

Ho, ho. You've got a tongue in your mouth, eh?

"Well, you're very big for your age."

"I don't think so. All my friends are bigger than I am."

Of course. What do I know about the relative sizes of thirteen-year-olds, anyway? It's been a long time since I was thirteen. And how many thirteen-year-olds sit in my congregation?

"Oh. Well, maybe you have very big friends."

The boy shakes his head.

"I think I'm just little."

I look up at the sky, as if the next thing I should say is written there. A good boy, he is. Wouldn't give me anything. Probably thinks I'm a smelly old man. Well, thirteen-year-old, maybe you're right. Maybe I am.

"It's getting dark early these days," the father says.

"Yes," I nod. "It is. Be dark soon."

"We'd better be getting on. We've got to get to the bus terminal and then through the tunnel to the parking lot. I never bring the car into the city. Too much traffic."

"Well," I try. "It was nice meeting you."

The father and the boy nod.

"I'll see you at afternoon services," I say to the old man. "Unless you're still feeling bad. If you are, don't come. I can manage."

"No. No, I'm not feeling bad. I'm all right. I'll be there."

"What's this about feeling bad?" the son says. "What's wrong? What's the matter?"

So tell him, old man. Don't look at me. What am I supposed to do, lie for you? You can't even tell your own son that you're worried about something?

"It's nothing. Nothing, really. This morning, I didn't think your father was looking too good. I asked him what was wrong, and he said he had some stomach trouble. So I told him to go home, and to stay home the rest of the day, if he still felt bad."

"You didn't tell me about any stomach trouble," the son says.

"I got a lot of trouble I don't tell you about. You think I keep a diary of all my aches and pains, so I can tell you about them every two months? I'd need a whole Torah to write them all down."

"Well," I say. "I must be going. Goodbye."

"Goodbye," they all chorus. So. Walk to the corner and turn it without looking back. They are probably still standing there, the old man telling his son how ungrateful he is. Ah, well. It could have been worse. They didn't keep me talking more than five, ten minutes. But the old man is a case, certainly. What is it he has against the son? And what is it he's afraid of? Perhaps I'll head down toward the river, sit for a moment on one of the bulkheads. Fifteen years the old man's been *shamos*, and I don't know anything about him, except what Zitomer told me today. That he's afraid he won't go to heaven because of his sins. Christians, yet, I'm breeding, in my own congregation. All of us have sins, old man. You try harder to be decent to your son, instead of worrying about heaven.

Ach, the cement's too cold today. It sinks right through my clothes into my skin. I won't sit here long. The water's as dirty as ever. Scummy water lapping at the sides of scummy rotting coal barges. What would it be like to slip down into the blackness of that scummy water and just sink, sink downward? No, it's too cold. I'd probably freeze before I drowned. Better to try it in summertime, when the lights are blinking along the Brooklyn shore and the land breeze is cooler than the night heat of the water. Now it's too cold. Samuels is maybe staring at water, too, right now; staring out the picture window of his beachfront bungalow at the blue waves crashing their white froth against the rock shore. I read that somewhere; God knows what the Pacific really looks like. I don't. And I'll never see it to find out, either. Samuels sits and stares at the water and wonders whether he has made a mistake. And me? I'll never get close enough to a mistake to wonder. I'll spend whatever life is left in the rest of my days in the dirty backyards of this city, and the only water I'll ever see will be the scummy water of this stinking river. For hills, I'll travel across the ranges of apartment buildings, the television antenna wilds of Brooklyn and Queens, to bury some faceless old man in the living and dead cemeteries of Long Island.

So. Enough is enough. Not that I've reached the bottom of the despair that's in me. But it's enough for one Sunday afternoon. Mrs. Kauffman is waiting with my afternoon tea, and the second half of the *Times* is still unopened. Maybe I can even manage a chapter or two before it's time for services. And if one of the members were to face me in the congregation, point at me with a trembling finger, and say, Our rabbi spends his Sunday afternoon roaming through the city and pouring out his bitterness, what kind of an answer would I make him? Is there any answer? Does it make any difference to the refuse of this city if I add my lump of bitterness to all the debris?

Twelve

The old man chuckled as he worked his way up the subway steps. *Schwartzes,* he thought. Inside the good pocket of his jacket was the tight roll of Carl's three ten-dollar bills. *Schwartzes,* the old man thought, and chuckled again.

Outside in the street the air was raw, sliced through his jacket to send dry chills down to the aching hollows in his back. The soles of his shoes were so thin he felt the cold of the concrete on his feet. He walked as quickly as his back would let him, until he came to the little park where he met Rabinowitz almost every day. But the space near one of the park's three trees was empty. Rabinowitz was somewhere between his home and the park, turning the squeaky wheels of his chair with his misshapen hands to urge himself forward a few more protesting feet. The old man stared down the street from which Rabinowitz would come, deserted on a Sunday afternoon when only old Jews whose homes made even less sense were silly enough to walk the streets or meet in a windswept park.

The old man sat down on a bench, pulled his upturned jacket tighter around his neck. A little boy and his plump blond mother sat at the other end. The boy was feeding handfuls of plucked, uncrusted white bread to a crowd of scruffy neck-bobbing pigeons. The old man turned away, to tell the pigeons, the mother, and especially the boy that he was not interested, and huddled into himself.

But the boy was too young to notice or care, and joyed in feeding the pigeons on this cold Sunday afternoon. He groped into his brown paper bag and found a handful of bread to spare the old man.

"Here. You can have some too."

The lumps of bread fell into the old man's lap. He raised his eyes to the boy's face. The boy smiled. The old man decided to smile back. Farther along the bench, the young plump mother in the green corduroy coat smiled and nodded.

"It's all right. We've got enough. And Jimmie's been feeding the birds all morning. It's time somebody else got a chance."

The old man nodded. Clustered around a dotting of white crumbs were a dozen or more gray-and-white-flecked, top-heavy wobbling pigeons.

"Yes," the old man mumbled. "Thank you."

"Oh, you're welcome," the boy said. He walked back to his mother.

Beyond the pigeons and the wire-enclosed circle of dying plants and the second of the park's three trees, he saw Rabinowitz's wheel chair bump down the street, wheel slowly into the park and anchor next to the bare winter comfort of the first tree.

"Go ahead, mister. Feed them!"

"Jimmie! You let the man alone, now. You gave him the crumbs, it's his business when he wants to feed the pigeons."

The pigeons. The old man stared at the bread in his lap. I might as well feed them, he thought. At least it'll get all the bread off me, so I can get up and walk across to Rabinowitz.

He picked up some crumbs. The bread felt feathery and softly moist beneath his fingers. He threw a handful toward the stuttering mass of pigeons, not watching where it landed. Then he threw another handful. The birds moved closer, he saw how they waddled as they walked on their toothpick legs. Each one pecked at its crumb and tore off tiny pieces with its bill instead of gobbling up the whole morsel. When he had only a few crumbs left the old man noticed a smaller bluish-gray bird, alone, outside the scrabbling group. He threw a crumb. The pigeon gobbled it down in three or four swift pecks. He threw another. The pigeon waddled over, pecked it down. A third. The pigeon came closer. He could see it plainly. It was spotted and looked soiled under its wings and breast, not as fat as the other birds, its eyes a duller pinpoint of red. The pigeon bobbed beside his right shoe, almost touching his pants leg. He groped for another breadcrumb. There was none. All gone. The old man glanced at his empty lap, looked toward the boy who was watching the workmen on the new building at the far end of the park. He looked down at his lap again. The pigeon pecked at the old man's shoe. He looked down into its dull red eyes. Go away, he thought. There are no more crumbs. If I look long enough it will go away.

But the pigeon did not go away. It pecked at the old man's shoe till the old man thought he could feel the tiny pointed beak tapping against his foot. Then the pigeon turned and fixed its dull red eyes on the old man's face. It had a small ugly head and its red eyes blinked.

"Go away," the old man said. "Go away."

His foot lashed out and caught the pigeon in the neck, the sharp ridge of his shoe jarring just below the throat.

The pigeon staggered, flapped its wings feebly, toppled over, lay still.

"Mommy! He's killed the pidgy. That man kicked the pidgy and now it's dead. It's dead, Mommy!"

The pigeon lay on its side. It shuddered twice, then lay still.

"It's dead, it's dead, he's kilt the pidgy, Mommy, he's kilt it."

The boy started to cry.

The old man stared at the pigeon. It seemed much smaller on its side, still and peaceful, and the one eye he could see seemed no longer red.

"Oh Jimmie, Jimmie, be quiet now, angel. It'll be all right, the man didn't mean it. It's only a pigeon, please, Jimmie, Jimmie, don't cry!"

The old man pushed himself off the wooden bench, swayed on his feet, then shuffled toward the woman and her boy.

"Yes, I didn't mean to. I didn't—it was, it seemed so big, all of—"

The boy buried his face in his mother's lap. His mother stroked his hair and patted his shoulder, murmured words the old man could not hear.

"I'm sorry," the old man stammered.

The mother patted the boy's head, rocked him to quiet his sobbing.

The old man stood and watched, and when he finally realized that the mother would not look up, he turned and walked across the park to Rabinowitz, hearing the boy's sobs and the murmur of the mother's voice. When he had almost reached Rabinowitz the pigeon flapped its wings, righted itself, and waddled away; the mother stirred the boy and raised his tear-streaked face. The boy clapped his hands and shouted, but the old man was too far away to hear.

Thirteen

RABINOWITZ

Every morning, perhaps at nine o'clock, perhaps nine-ten, nine-fifteen, even nine-thirty, I unlock my door which has the bolt fitted low enough so I can reach it from my wheel chair, and I roll into the hall. I pull the door shut but I can't lock it, because the key is too high up and I don't have the money to get it moved lower. Jacobs won't have it moved for me, being a landlord is not a good business, he has too many expenses. But what do I have somebody would want to steal? Once I had the records, that's all. And now? Only the scrapbooks.

There is a thief in the house, they warned me when I moved in, keep your door locked. I can't, I said, and smiled so that they shouldn't feel sorry for me, because I can't reach the lock. Then call us, they said, call us whenever you go out, and we'll lock it for you, you can't go away and leave the door open in this house. There's a thief in this house.

So I thanked them, but I didn't call them to come lock the door when I went out. How can I make other people work for me, because I have legs that don't work so well? I am the world's only cripple? Everybody has his own troubles, and thank God I can manage with mine. There is so much misery in the world, I have to add my little load on people who already got too much?

So I didn't call them, and the fourth day, after I had wheeled out in the morning, with the door pulled shut behind me, somebody who knew I couldn't lock the door came in and helped himself to my records. I didn't have many, but he took what I had; the five Caruso records that I found wrapped up in tinfoil in the bottom of a pile of rags in the junk shop over on First Avenue, the dozen others that I bought one at a time, from junk shops where they sat, waiting, in dusty cardboard boxes marked "Old Records." I wheeled back in the early afternoon, and on the gramophone where I kept the records, there was only an empty space, with THANKS scrawled out in the dust I could never get rid of.

I cried. I cradled my head in my arms and rocked back and forth in the chair, and I cried like the littlest of babies. I cried past rage and past hurt, until there was only a sullen deadness in me, and then I cursed God for making me a cripple.

"You," I said. "You have made a rotten world, and I hope You like the stink of it. Making cripples isn't so bad, maybe You even got some sneaky reason why there have to be people like me, trapped in a chair so young they got to give up all thought of a normal world, but You had to go farther than that, You had to create a world where people steal from cripples. I hope You think it's funny. Your stinking world."

Then Jacobs came in and saw the tears all over my face.

"What's wrong, Rabinowitz? What happened?"

So I told him.

"No. Not your records. Not those records."

"Yes. All of them. Gone."

He stood for a long time and he stared at the THANKS scrawled out in dust on the gramophone lid.

"Rabinowitz, I'll get those records back. I don't even know how, but I'll get them back. If I have to break everybody in this house into two pieces, I'll get them back."

For a few days, I believed he would. The hurt for those records was so deep in me I thought that whoever took them would feel my pain, and return them. I even gave Jacobs a list of the records, and I sat in my chair and waited. But the records didn't come back, and slowly I realized that they never would, because I had cursed God, because I had doubted Him. And I saw that those records were another one of the crutches I was always making, to keep me from myself, to keep away from the insides that God had given me. What is music, I thought, that I have to hear it played to me from a machine, from little spinning pieces of plastic? How do you hear music, anyway? How did Beethoven hear music, from records? From a piano he couldn't even hear himself play? I need records to listen to music? So I played the music in my mind and I played all the operas I had ever heard, and when I didn't know the words or the melody I worked both out in my own head, in Yiddish if I didn't know the language. So slowly I saw that I could have music without records, and it was just as good, even better, because some of the music was mine, and when I thanked God I remembered the only other time I had cursed Him.

I was nineteen and still living in my father's house, though I knew that soon it would be time to go out and find a job for myself, and a room to live where I could learn how to do all the things for myself that my mother did for me. But still I lagged at home, and read, and thought, and listened to records and to the Saturday operas on the radio. Friends came to see me, and I listened, and they came again because they could talk and I could listen, and if any had asked me I would have told them that I listened because they taught me about life and what it was to live life on two sound legs, for by nineteen I was resigned to my life in a chair, which was still a life to live since it happened to be mine, but would not make sense to anybody else. So I listened, and when they asked me I told them what I thought, and many times I could say things that made sense, because I could look at the world they gave me with a clean mind, since only my mind walked through the world. And I spoke in a soft, gentle voice, because I was so choked with gratefulness that they should spare hours out of their walking day to come to me.

But when Naomi came it was hard for me to speak. I could only stare at her. Hours I spent, hunched forward in the chair, staring at her hands spread open before her, or bent like an old woman on the floor, her arms curled around her drawn-up knees. Sometimes she turned the big light off so the overhead bulb wouldn't burn into my eyes when I looked away, and in the small dim light from my old gooseneck desk lamp her hair had rivers of diamonds in it, and her eyes when she turned her head caught the faint gleams of light and twinkled like stars. She talked about men, about her father, about marriage, about what she wanted and what she was afraid of, and I could only stare and whisper to myself how lovely she was and how much I loved her.

One day she was talking about him. She had talked for a long while. I said a few things and then she talked a little more and felt better. She leaned her head against the blanket that covered my legs, and smiled. Then she reached up and took my hand, pressed it against her cheek, and kissed it.

"You are so good, Nathan. I don't know what I'd do if I didn't have a friend like you."

I stared down at her hair, that looked so much like rich brown honey stirred in fine smooth strands. I felt the warmth of her cheek against my hand, and the incredible softness of her lips on my palm, and for that moment I forgot.

"Did you ever think of me as more than a friend, Naomi? Could you?"

She stared up at me, and slowly she let go my hand, until it hung over the arm of my chair, grazing the rubber of the wheel. She said nothing, only stared at me, then got to her feet, and put her coat over her shoulders like a cape.

"Naomi," I said.

She turned at the door to look at me, and I saw she was crying. Then she opened the door and walked out. So I cursed God. All the hatred and anger and pain that I had stored up in me in the long process of learning what the rest of my life would be poured out of me, and I cursed God that I was born, that I hadn't died in my mother's belly instead of being born a cripple. I cursed God that my parents had fed and cared for me instead of letting me starve, the way they let crippled children starve in India. I cursed God that I was alive at all, that I would spend all my days lying on a bed or sitting in a chair, that I would never know a woman's love or lie next to a woman in bed after love. I cursed God because He made a world with people like me, dragging through life on useless legs.

Then I understood that Naomi would not come again, and I saw that it was just, because when she came I had talked to her for myself and not for her. I learned to forget about me when people came, to talk to them because I cared about them, and gradually I forgot about myself, until only those people who came mattered, for themselves and not for me. And I was glad when they came, sorry if they were sad, and happy if they could leave with joy inside them.

And now the only thing I keep that is outside myself is the scrapbook, with the cut and pasted pictures of all the opera stars I have ever heard, on records, or on the Saturday operas. I keep it open each day on my lap as I sit in the park, and I hope that someday, someone who loves opera will pass through the park, see my scrapbook, and start to talk. It will be a young man, and he will be amazed that an old Jew should sit in a park with an opera scrapbook open across his knees. When I talk about Caruso and Melba and Trotti he will be touched, and he will say to me, "How long since you been to an opera?"

I will look down at the ground, not daring to hope.

"Never."

"Never?" The young man will smile, will grow so excited that he may even clap me on the back. "Then you're going to one. Now. Today. With me!"

The large taxi will whisk us downtown to the palace of the Met, the young man and the taxi driver will lift me into my chair, and I will wheel through the whisper of silks and perfume, through the dress suits and fancy gowns, down the aisle to an orchestra seat. They will be doing *Carmen*, and I will sink into the soft red plush and watch the skirts of the gypsies swirl as the gold earrings in their black hair catch fire in the spotlights.

But I know that the young man will never come, nobody but old men like me ever come to that park. And I know that it is only my weakness that makes me sit in the park with the scrapbook open across my knees. Someday, perhaps, someone will steal into my room while I am sleeping, because I keep forgetting to bolt the door, and he will slip the scrapbook from the table and tiptoe out. Or perhaps I will be wheeling home and the scrapbook will slip from my fingers and fall to the sidewalk. I will try to reach it but I can't reach, my fingers will grope through air, a good foot away from the book. So I will wait beside the scrapbook for a half-hour, an hour. But nobody will come. It will get dark, and finally I will wheel away from the scrapbook on the pavement, knowing that when I return next morning it will be gone. Then perhaps I will curse God again, but the scrapbook will not come back, and after a time I will understand and not be sorry.

So I pull the door to behind me, and I wheel out the hall and down the boards that Jacobs has put down for me, and then I am in the street. I breathe the air deeply into my lungs, and wheel off for the park, only two corners away, with no streets to cross. It is a sad excuse for a city park; cracked cement, dirt, and a few brave blades of grass struggling up from the cracks. Somebody told me once that houses stood here, and they knocked down the houses to build a school, except they never built the school, nobody knows why. But they made a park instead, they planted a few trees, put down a few wooden benches, and set a wire trash basket almost in the middle of the cement square, with a large white sign that says in black letters:

YOU'RE YOUR CITY'S ARTIST
—HELP MAKE IT BEAUTIFUL
Deposit trash here

It is as cold today as the East Side always is in winter, with a raw wind that comes whipping in from the river, to sweep across the open spaces and whistle up the narrow alleys between tall buildings, but I have the small blanket for my legs, and the old man's coat to wrap around me. It is so warm that each time I feel it around my neck, I think that I should never have taken it from him. I stayed at home on the second raw cold day of winter, and the old man came to my room and told me that he had come to the park to talk, and I wasn't there.

"Yes. It's too cold for me without another blanket. Jacobs can only spare me one blanket, it's not enough."

He looked at me, I couldn't tell what he was thinking. Then he unbuttoned his heavy coat, struggled out of it, and set it on the bed.

"Here. Take this one. I don't need it. What do I need with a coat this heavy? It's so heavy I sweat every time I wear it. But for you it'll be good, you can wrap it around you like a blanket. So take it."

"No," I said. "I can't. I can't even think of it."

"Listen, take it, I'm telling you to take it. I don't need it, honest to God I don't need it. I've been thinking of giving it away to some old people's home, it's too heavy for me. Besides, I hate coats anyway, before I got the coat I went out in just a sweater under my jacket. I got plenty heavy sweaters, I don't want the coat. Take it, I'm telling you, take it."

He talked on and on. He told lies. He had an old coat before the one he was trying to give me, I remembered how loose it was and how the pockets bagged. I never saw him wear a sweater. But I listened, and I felt he wanted me to have the coat. So I thought that sometimes people need to give, and when they do you must take from them and not ask too many questions, and finally I took the coat without asking what I wanted to know. It is a good warm coat, I wear it even though I have looked under the label and seen the faint inkings of a name that isn't his. I wear it and I don't ask questions.

Wrapped in his coat, I listen to him as he sits on the wooden bench. I have listened about Feinstein and about Carl and the boy for so many long mornings. I watch the way his hands play with the worn patches on the knees of his trousers, and I say what I think, which isn't much. I watch him today as he comes shuffling across the park toward me, his head is bent against the wind, and I remember all the moth holes in the one sweater he is wearing underneath his jacket.

"Morning," he says, as if he can't bother with the good.

"Good morning," I say, and wait until he settles himself on the bench. "And how are you?"

"How am I? How am I ever? Pain gets less? Bones get younger? How should I be?"

"Is it worse?" I ask. "Is it getting any worse?"

He laughs. From the mouth and the throat only, he laughs; it whistles out of him like a cough forced up to clear the lungs.

"Worse, worse, you think I could tell if it's worse? To get worse, it has to be not so bad before. My pain is so bad always, you think I can tell when it gets worse?"

We talk about his pain and sometimes, God help me, I think his pain is not as bad as he makes it out to be. Then I tell myself I have never really known pain, that my legs have been dead since birth and the only pains I know came from my back, the evening my chair tipped over on the icy pavement and I tumbled out and struck the cold of the sidewalk, to lay until someone came to pick me up. So I listen, until he is finished with his pain.

"What's new?" I ask.

"What should be new? How much happens to old men, they should have news to tell each other? I killed a pigeon just now, that's news, if you want news. I was waiting for you on the other side of the park. After Carl and the boy took the subway, and I killed a pigeon."

"But it was an accident," I say. "You didn't mean to kill the pigeon?"

He stares at me, and I know he's thinking to say yes, because he likes to shock me, because he likes to make me think he's worse than he is.

"No," he says finally. "I didn't mean it. It was an accident."

"So," I say. "An accident's an accident. Forget about it. How's Carl and the boy?"

He shakes his head.

"Like they always are. They came to me today, and the boy sang the Blessings. Carl smiled like the boy was reciting the *Mishnah* backwards, he was so happy. Almost thirteen, and he knows a few blessings, the boy sings them to show me he comes from a Jewish home. As if I don't know better! What, I've forgotten what it means to grow up with parents who are still Jews? I'm supposed to fall on my face because Carl's boy goes to Hebrew school twice a week and learns a few blessings?"

"It's better than if he wasn't going at all," I say. "It's better than if he knew nothing."

"It's not better. Better he should be a *goy* and admit it, than pretend he is a Jew by sending his son to *shul* twice a week. Twice a week, that's all he goes. And he lays *tephillin* once a week. You know how many times a week he'll lay *tephillin* after he's *bar mitzvah*? I bet they bury those *tephillin* in some drawer where he never has to see them again."

"So he doesn't lay *tephillin*. So he doesn't go to *shul* every day. It's different here, being a Jew in America is different; just because he doesn't lay *tephillin* doesn't mean he's not a Jew."

But I know I shouldn't say it, that he won't understand. There is only one way to be a Jew, to follow all the laws and commandments. More than that, he doesn't want to know.

"You, too? You've been talking to Zitomer? It's an epidemic he's started, soon everybody in New York will be in two camps, screaming at each other what it means to be a Jew. Listen to me.

Zitomer's wrong, you understand, wrong! There's only one way to be a Jew, and Carl and the boy are *goyim! Goyim!*"

Today he screams. Usually he doesn't scream, he says the same things but he doesn't scream.

"Listen, I'm not Zitomer, you don't have to scream at me. What happened?"

His hands crawl into his pocket, he takes out some crumples of paper, and hands them to me. I smooth them out. Three ten-dollar bills.

"So?" I say.

"Carl. He gave them to me. Stuck them into my pocket and then ran through the turnstile. Told me I should go to a doctor."

Of course. And in spite of all the things you can do with that money, because it's Carl's, it spits in your face, all you can do is roll it in your pocket, and curse Carl because he couldn't be the son you wanted.

"So why not go to a doctor?"

"What good will a doctor do me?"

"You're so healthy you think you don't need one?"

"I'm so sick I don't think one will help."

"Why not try anyway?"

"With Carl's money? Use his money to go to a doctor? Could I go to one without his money? Thieves and robbers, all of them, if I lived four hundred years I still wouldn't have enough to be robbed by one. So if I can't go without Carl's money, I'm supposed to take it and see a doctor? Just use his money like it was anybody's? Say thank you, Carl, I don't think much of you as a son or a Jew, but I'm happy to use your money? You think I'm a whore, I just use whatever money I can get, from anybody?"

"Carl's not anybody, he's your son."

"It makes a big difference! He was my son when he ran away from me, why didn't he think of it then? He ran away like he was nobody, like he owed me nothing, like I was just a servant who brought him up, and when he went, I said to myself, all right, if he wants to act like a nobody, then he's nobody. I never had a son. All those years, when he wrote to me, sent me money, I ripped up his letters without opening them. Now I'm supposed to get down on my hands and knees because he gives me money? He can afford to give me money, he's got enough of it."

"He doesn't give you money just because he can afford to."

"You want to know why he does it? I'll tell you. He gives me money because he knows he was wrong, and he's trying to make up for it. He knows what he did to me was wrong, and he's trying to say I'm sorry."

"Then why don't you forgive him?"

"Forgive him? Forgive him? Why should I forgive him? Did he think of me when he ran away from me, I'm just supposed to forgive him?"

"Why not? Carry your feelings to the grave, that'll be better? You're an old man, he's got a son *bar mitzvah* already, it's time, it's more than time. He wants to be forgiven, so forgive him. Think of all the sons who never care whether or not their fathers forgive them. Carl cares. You don't even realize what kind of son you got. So forgive him."

He stares at me. Just stares. If you didn't hate Carl, you wouldn't have anything to live for. Sometimes, God help me, I feel like shouting in your face, who do you think you are, you sick old man? God gave you a decent upright son and you spit in his face. I never had the chance to have a son, but if I had one, you think I would treat him like you treat Carl? So Carl ran away to make his own life, so he didn't love you enough to stay, does that mean he doesn't love you at all? Does that mean you have to hate him forever? If I can't have love, you say, I'll have hate, I'll have revenge! How much love do you think a father deserves from a son? There aren't fathers who get no love at all? You should be satisfied with what you got, instead of turning it into hate. Carl comes to see you, and you poison his love with your hatred. God knows why he keeps coming.

But I don't say it. I bite my tongue and I clench my hands on the rubber wheels and I keep the words in my mind, where only God hears them. Because some men can only stand so much truth, and the old man is one of them. I sit, and I watch, and I feel the twists and tortures of his hatred and his love.

"Listen, Rabinowitz. I said it before and I'll say it again. You don't know anything about life. You've sat in that wheel chair almost since you were born, you never had a wife or a son or anybody or anything except those old records and that stupid scrapbook. So who are you to open your mouth and try to tell me what to do? I don't need your advice. It's not worth anything. What are you, anyway, a crazy old cripple wrapped up in my coat, your own clothes you don't even own. You sit in the park every day and from this wisdom comes to you, the cripple becomes a prophet who's got a right to tell me I should forgive my son? You forgive him! You want a son? I'll give you Carl. The boy, too. He's all yours. Next time he comes, I'll tell him to go to Rabinowitz, he'll forgive you. You'll see how fast he runs."

So now he goes. Too angry to say goodbye. My mouth, all I did was make him feel worse than when he came. Good for nothing, I am. Problems he had, his son he wanted to talk about, and did I help? Did I do anything but point more fingers at him?

"Wait."

But he doesn't even turn around.

"Buy a coat with the money. Go see a doctor."

He didn't even hear. And if he did? Sometimes I think, God help me, that there is nothing that can break the wall of his hatred. Whatever he does, wherever he goes, each day he carries it inside him, and feeds it with memories.

Aaach, it isn't fair, it isn't fair. Look at me and look at him. He has so much and it has all turned to sourness, to bitterness, inside him. I understand, and yet I don't. Perhaps only God understands.

Fourteen

The old man paused at the door to his room and tried to catch his breath. Someday, he thought, if my back don't get me first, those stairs will kill me. He leaned against the door frame until his breathing and his heart slowed, and then he opened the door and shuffled into his room.

Damn Rabinowitz, he thought. A nosy old cripple has the nerve to tell me how I should treat my son. It's my day to get lessons. First Feinstein, and now Rabinowitz. What does Rabinowitz know about anything? All his life he's spent in that chair, with legs that are so twisted he might as well be a tree trunk from the hip down.

The old man moved to the table, propped himself with his left hand resting against its scarred surface, and tugged open the small cupboard door. On the cupboard's one shelf sat a package of tea bags, a bag of sugar, a salt shaker, and some packets of soup mix. The old man took the box of tea bags down, shook it, then looked inside. Only two left, he thought. I have to get some more, from the supermarket. Chicken noodle. All the packages were chicken noodle. Litinsky had given him the packages as a free sample, two weeks before.

He filled the black earthenware pot with water, and lit the burner under it. Maybe Rabinowitz thinks I don't know why he's always making trouble for me. But I know. I knew long ago, but I never said anything. He wanted Naomi. She came to me one day, before we were married even, and she was crying. She told me. Could you ever think of me as any more than a friend? Rabinowitz asked her.

"I should have said yes. I should have said yes and stayed and married Rabinowitz, with his crippled legs and arms bent like an ape's."

"No," the old man said. He turned to the window and Naomi sat, perched upon the narrow ledge, swinging her stockinged feet into the room.

"But instead, I put on my coat, over my shoulders like a cape, and I walked out. I was crying, and I walked out of his room and closed the door. And then I came to you."

"Go away," the old man said. "Please."

"You were good to me that night. I talked, and you listened. I thought, you should forgive me for being so silly, I thought that you understood. I actually thought that I was talking to you, and you were hearing and understanding."

"Listen. Please go away now. Don't make me scream again. Go away, and I promise, I'll talk to you after lunch. Just now I was thinking to myself, who am I going to talk to after lunch? So I'll talk to you. I promise. We'll talk about anything you want. Rabinowitz, your father, anything. But please, go now."

The water bubbled in the black earthenware pot. The old man took the package of chicken-noodle soup mix in his hands and very slowly poured the powder and noodles and spices of the soup into the bubbling water. He poured until the package was empty, and shook the package to make sure that no loose grains were trapped inside. Then he crumpled the package into a tight wadded ball and let it fall into the pail that sat beneath the sink. He took a spoon from the drainboard and began to stir the soup until the powder and the spices began to dissolve into the yellowish water. He stirred faster, until there were no lumps of powder floating around the circles caused by the motion of his spoon. After he had turned the flame of the burner low enough so that the soup should simmer and not boil, he looked carefully over his shoulder at the window. The ledge was empty. Naomi was gone.

The old man nodded. He was afraid to wonder why she had gone for fear she might return. So he sat down at the kitchen table and began to go through his pockets. There was nothing in his pockets except the synagogue keys and the hankerchief and the few pieces of change that he had carefully taken with him in the morning, but he sat down at the kitchen table and began to go through his pockets. After he had set the keys and the change and the handkerchief on the table, he reached into his one good jacket pocket and brought out the crumpled roll of Carl's three ten-dollar bills. He smoothed them out against the scarred enamel surface of the kitchen table, and stared down at them.

So, he thought. And what am I supposed to do with you? He closed his eyes and saw again Carl's quick movement through the turnstile and down the steps to the subway platform. Always, he thought. Always he runs away from me. Even when he gives me money he runs away from me. He opened his eyes. So what should I do with my son's money? I should buy a coat maybe, like he says? I should go to a doctor? Even if the money was mine, if I found it on the streets, I wouldn't go to a doctor with it. What good's a doctor to me, a doctor's going to keep me alive longer? A coat I might even buy, but a doctor? Never.

But I could pay Levin. Once and for all I could pay Levin, and the stone wouldn't be around my neck any more. He pulled open the drawer of the kitchen table and groped till he found the pile of receipts and the little tablet. He set them on the table. Seven dollars fifty cents I still owe Levin. God knows how many years I've been paying for my tombstone, to still owe Levin seven dollars fifty cents. But I could pay it all off. I could pay him off and still have over twenty dollars left. I could pay him off and never have to worry about what happens if I die before the last few payments are made. I could pay him off and then I'd never have to walk down there any more on a Wednesday afternoon, to push five dimes over the counter and wait while he enters it in his book and writes my receipt and hands it over.

The old man dropped the receipts and the tablet back into the drawer, and forced the drawer shut. Then he dropped his keys, and his change, and his handkerchief, back into his pants pockets. He left the money on the table, and pushed himself out of the chair. The soup was thicker in the earthenware pot. He stirred it for the last time, turned off the burner, and set his chipped soup bowl on the table. Then he wrapped a towel around the handle of the soup pot and poured the soup into the bowl.

He set the soup pot back on the stove and reached into the oven for the cracker box. Only a few crackers rattled as he shook the box. Everything's running out today, he thought. First tea, and now crackers. Before he prized out two crackers he glanced over his shoulder to make certain Naomi had not returned. He started to close the box lid, hesitated, then pulled out another cracker, closed the box, and let the oven door slam shut.

Steam circled lazily upward from the soup bowl. Too hot to eat, the old man thought. He stirred it slowly, blowing down on it between the slow sweeps of his spoon. Should I really talk to Naomi after lunch? he thought. She never has anything new to say. The same old stories, the same old accusations. It might be nice, for a change, to talk to Smetyanov. Except Smetyanov would probably say something about the silver. Smetyanov always says something about the silver.

"I didn't mean to steal the silver," the old man said to the steaming soup. "But how can a Jew start his life in a strange city, with nothing in his pocket? I wasn't like Smetyanov. I didn't have a family to come to, somebody to find me a job or give me a place to stay. Nothing I had. What else could I do?"

The soup was only beginning to cool. The old man stirred it more quickly. Fifty dollars I got for that silver set. Solid silver, an heirloom, and fifty dollars was all I got for it. It was just enough, thank God. Who knows what I would have done without it?

The old man stared at Carl's thirty dollars, still spread out on the table. "Maybe," he said, "I could talk to Levinson. I haven't talked to Levinson for a long time." Levinson had worked next to him for ten years at the cutting tables of the Acme Dress Company, and the old man had known all of Levinson's secrets, for Levinson had been stealing bits of material from the cutting tables, and had introduced the old man to his system. But the old man never had anything to say to Levinson, these days. Even when Levinson praised the old man for the daring and cleverness of his many thefts, the old man felt no pleasure.

"Levinson has been dead for too many years," the old man said. "Soon I will have to stop talking to Levinson."

The soup had stopped steaming. The old man tasted a spoonful. It was still hot, but it tasted stale and flat. The old man spooned the stale flat soup into his mouth and cursed Litinsky, who had given him the samples two weeks ago.

"What good is package soup if it doesn't keep?" the old man said. "What kind of soup you trying to sell, it goes stale if you don't eat it right away? Who wants to buy soup in a package anyway, if they got to worry about its going stale? You go round to all your customers they should hurry up and eat their soup, before it spoils?"

Litinsky stared down at the floor. "I'm sorry," he said.

"Sorry! Anybody can be sorry. Sorry doesn't help the taste of my soup. And look," the old man said, pushing himself to his feet and shuffling to the cupboard, "you call this a sample? This package that's so small I'm lucky if I can wet my teeth on it?" He yanked open the cupboard door and waved one of the soup-mix packages at Litinsky. "For midgets," he said. "Samples for midgets."

"If you don't want them," Litinsky said, "I can take them back. I got—"

"What's the matter, you don't have enough samples?" the old man shouted. "You can't even leave your father's best friend, who's practically starving on your doorstep, a half-dozen samples of cheap soup? Your father wouldn't have offered me six lousy samples. A whole box he would have given me—two, even. He would have made me take them. Oh, your father, now there was a decent man. A man who never forgot his friends when they needed something."

The old man shuffled back to his chair and stood behind it, folding his arms across the chair's top and leaning down toward the soup. He stared into the watery noodle-strewn yellow of the soup, and when he looked up, Litinsky was gone.

"Good riddance," he said, unwrapped his arms from the chair, and sat down to eat the rest of his soup.

"So, you couldn't even wait for me for lunch?"

The old man reached out to cover the three crackers he had set out on the table, but Naomi's laughter tinkled through the room before his hand could shield them.

"Don't bother," she called from the window. "You think I don't know you've been stealing from the supermarket? Even when I was alive, I knew you were stealing."

"It's not true. I never stole while you were alive."

"Oh, listen. Listen to him. The honest man upholds his innocence. So you never stole when I was alive, hey? You never took money from the customers that you cheated in my father's butcher shop, you never shortchanged and overweighed and then pocketed the fifteen cents, the quarter? You never brought yards of material home every Friday afternoon from Acme, rolled inside your jacket and slipped into the pouch that I sewed for you?"

"All right. So maybe I did steal, a little." The old man stirred his soup and tried to shut out Naomi's laughter. "But I was stealing for you. Who else was I stealing for? It was for you."

"Yes, I know. It was for me. Because I sat home all day and wrote long lists of what I wanted before I could be happy. I sent you out to steal from my own father because I was so unhappy without all the things you couldn't buy me. Did I buy clothes from the money you got for the material you stole, or did you? Did I buy a new suit, and two new shirts, or did you?"

"But I asked you! I asked you, didn't I? I pleaded with you. Naomi, please, I'd say, go and get some new clothes. It'll make me feel good, seeing you in something new. Go and buy something. But you wouldn't."

"And you're surprised? You're surprised I wouldn't use stolen money and buy myself some clothes? I could have made it a lot better for you, couldn't I, putting clothes on my back with the money you stole? But I wouldn't."

"All right," the old man said. "So I stole. Now go away until after my soup." He bent to the soup and began to spoon it into his mouth. His hand shook, and some of the soup spilled over the rim of the spoon and coated his lips and the flesh around his lips.

"And did you steal my silver for me?" Smetyanov asked. "Did you do it for me?"

"And stick Marfa on me, for me?" Shmuel Yaakov asked.

The old man bent his head to the soup bowl.

"Go away," he ground out. "Go away."

Naomi laughed. Smetyanov laughed. Shmuel Yaakov laughed. Then the box of crackers in the oven began to laugh. The oven door banged open and the box of crackers laughed and danced and sang on the open iron grillwork of the oven shelf. "Thief, thief," the crackers called to each other inside the laughing spinning box, which suddenly fell from the open grillwork of the oven shelf and spilled the crackers like gold coins across the cracked linoleum floor.

Naomi laughed louder, and Smetyanov and Shmuel Yaakov's heartier laughter sounded behind her. The old man pounded his fist down on the enamel surface of the kitchen table.

"Go away until after my soup," he screamed.

The laughter continued. The old man pounded the table again, and the soup bowl tipped over the side of the table and poured some of the yellowish watery paste down into the old man's lap.

"Aiii!" the old man screamed as the hot liquid scalded into his flesh. He struggled to his feet, and his legs bumped the bowl and sent it completely off the edge of the table. The rest of the soup spilled against the old man's knee and calf, and the soup bowl slithered to the floor and shattered. Some of the larger chips flew almost to the window, and for a long moment the empty room was heavy with the echo of the old man's scream and the crash of the soup bowl.

Fifteen

LEVIN

On a Sunday I get a chance to stand and stare. The breeze from the river furls and sways the fluffy white curtains on my window and door. They laugh, sometimes, though they never laugh to my face; it is funny, they think, that a tombstone cutter should have lace curtains on the window and door of his shop. But a tombstone cutter is still a man, and a man can have curtains wherever he chooses. Besides, they never laugh to my face.

So I stand, on Sundays, and I stare past my curtains out my one store window that is as clean and clear as any fancy Fifth Avenue shop, although the three stones that I set in the window thirty-three years ago, when I stood in the middle of this floor with my citizenship papers still in my hand and I thought, three stones will I set in the window, with only *Shema Yisroel* carved on each, those three stones I have never changed. But a window is kept clean, just as the names on a stone must be cut with patience and care.

I stand at my wall desk, an old wooden hulk with a rolltop, the first piece of furniture I moved into the shop. My account books are spread open on the desk, but the books need little checking, because I am more than careful with each entry, and so I have time to look away from my neat columns of figures and stare through my window into the peacefulness of the street.

There is no desk chair. There is no chair in the office. A stonecutter stands when he cuts or carves his stone, and if a stonecutter can stand for thirty-three years, weekday and Sunday, stand as the tempered chisel bites into the smooth hard stone, or the buffing wheel rounds out an edge or smoothes away a scar, then a stonecutter can stand while he checks his books in the early afternoon of a quiet Sunday. Perhaps some stonecutters sit as they check their books. I have heard of some cutters who hire young girls to sit at a flat-topped desk, to keep the books and records. I have even heard that there are some cutters who work from a bench, who sit as they cut stone. I would like to see the stones they cut.

I keep my books better than any young girl could. A young girl would be soft, would listen to excuses, would not demand that a stone be paid for. What could she know about the way a stone is made, about the cold sure work of hours that finally comes to mark a man's resting place? What is a stone to her but something to make money from? She would give credit, she would not write letters that must be written. Like Yarmolinsky. I look down at Yarmolinsky's column of figures, finally closed out and paid in full. I was right about Yarmolinsky, there was no other way to do it. Yarmolinsky died before the payments on his stone were completed, and his burial society refused to pay his debt. But I had Yarmolinsky's next of kin. Too many years ago I learned to make sure I had the next of kin before I cut the first notch in the stone. So I wrote to Yarmolinsky's next of kin, and when they refused to finish the payments I worked out how much of the stone Yarmolinsky had paid for, and shipped it to the cemetery with the last four letters of his name and the final date missing. The stone came back. What else could they do with a stone that said

YARMOLI   1887—   ?

With the stone was the money for its completion, and when I sent a bill for shipping expenses, that, too, was paid. So I carved the last four letters and the final date, and sent the stone back to the cemetery, where it rests peacefully on top of a Yarmolinsky who doesn't have to know how cheap his next of kin tried to be.

The door handle creaks, then the hinges squeal as somebody pushes into the store. He comes across the wooden floor with very light hesitant footsteps. On a weekday I would be at the counter before he reached it, but today I don't even bother to turn around. No customer comes on Sunday. This is one of the loafers, one of the *kibbitzers*. Blumberg, Rosenthal, Shapiro, come to fool away some heavy hours in my shop. Well, not today, you good-for-nothing loafer. Not in my shop. You go find somebody else to horse around with. I got all the friends I want, and I didn't choose them in any hurry, either. I found them one at a time. Men like me, who know what hard work is, and how to keep their mouths shut. If we bend over a chessboard for five hours, and the only sound is our teaspoons scraping the glass when we stir our tea, you think that's bad? I don't. I finish a game. I clear my throat, I stand up to go. Becker nods his head and I lay a hand on his shoulder.

"A good game," I say.

He nods.

"Tomorrow?"

"Yes," he says.

And I go. There is too much talk in the world. It leads to nothing but trouble. With your friends, you don't need any talk. Only in business you need it, and even in business, sometimes, you can do better keeping quiet.

"Levin."

So. It is not Blumberg or Rosenthal. I take my time about turning around, because this is my Sunday and no customers come to the store. The old man stands at the counter, fingering his worn black purse.

"I came to pay you," he says. "I didn't have anything to do, and I thought, maybe I'll take a walk. So I walked down this way, and when I saw you were in your shop I thought, why not pay Levin today instead of Wednesday?"

That's what you say. But why don't you look at me like a *mensch* when you say it? And why is your hand shaking so much any minute you'll drop that purse on the floor, and I'll have to open the counter door to pick it up for you? What are those stains on your sweater that look like you threw up on yourself; your eyes are red, from crying or from rubbing them for hours?

"Well, I'll tell you. I don't usually take money on Sundays. I keep my cashbox locked over the weekend and I leave the key home every Sunday. I just come in to check the books and look around the shop. I never expect any customers on Sunday."

How's that, eh? Lie for lie. If you just walked in here because you saw me from the street, you can walk out again and come back on Wednesday. All of a sudden, something's wrong with Wednesdays? Every week for ten years you've been coming in on a Wednesday to pay for that stone that sits in my workshop waiting for you to complete the date on it, and now all of a sudden you're tired of Wednesdays?

"You can take my fifty cents and leave it in the desk until tomorrow, when you bring the cashbox. Fifty cents isn't such a lot, you have to worry about leaving it loose. Since I'm here, why shouldn't I pay now instead of Wednesday? Maybe I'll have something to do next Wednesday, I won't be able to come."

"For ten years, every Wednesday you come. Now you got balls to go to on Wednesdays, you have to come in the middle of my Sunday and push your fifty cents on me?"

He lays the purse on the counter, fumbles open the latch, and lays five dimes one by one on the counter. But he still doesn't look at me. He lays those dimes out and he stares at them like they'll run away. What's he afraid of? He stole the money or something, he's afraid if he doesn't pay me quick they'll catch him and he'll have to give it back?

"Look," he says. "I'm a customer, I got a right to pay when I want. You going to take my money or not? You don't take it now I'm not coming especially on Wednesday, just to bring it to you."

So that's it. That's his game. He's trying to slide out of paying the rest of it. Next thing you know he'll skip a week and try to swear he's paid me, or he'll yell that I didn't want his money because he came on the wrong day.

"All right, all right, stop grumbling, I'll get you a receipt."

But you won't get away with it. Not with me. The only way to prove you paid me is to show me a receipt, and you can only get that if I give it to you. And just to make sure, I'll date the receipt for Wednesday, and I'll enter it in the book for Wednesday's date.

Wait a minute. I better check his entry. Let's see, I got the name and the address, the synagogue and the burial society. Name of a pregnant pig! I never got his next of kin. A fool I am becoming in my old age. His next of kin I never got. And how many times have I stood at the counter and listened to him complain about his son? Without even thinking, without even checking to see if I had the son's name and address?

"Here's your receipt. I dated it for Wednesday."

"Thank you," he says. He picks up his purse, slides it into his pocket, and turns to go.

"Wait a minute."

He turns back.

"I just checked my books. I never listed your next of kin."

"So," he says, staring at the floor.

"So," I say. "So I need your next of kin. So give it to me."

The floor must have pictures carved into the wood, he stares at it so hard.

"Do you have to get my next of kin?"

"Yes. I got to have it. It's almost a law, I got to have it. I never cut a stone without the next of kin is written in my books."

So still he won't look up. What's wrong with him? If he didn't have anyone and was ashamed to admit it, I could understand. But he has a son, what's such a big trouble about giving your son's name and address? It's a suffering, to tell somebody where your son lives?

"Look, I don't have all day. I was working on my books when you came in, like I do every Sunday, and I want to get back to them. Give me your next of kin so I can write it in the book and be done with it."

With his head bent like that, how am I supposed to hear what he's saying?

"What? You think I can hear you, when you talk to the floor?"

"I don't want you to put a next of kin down. I don't want to have one."

"What? What are you talking about, you don't want a next of kin? It's not up to you whether you want one or not. You got one. You got a son. He's your next of kin. So just give me his name and address."

"No. I can't. I don't have a son."

So. Either he's gone out of his head, and just thinks he doesn't have a son, or else his son died, and that's why he's acting so crazy. Either way is no good for me, seven dollars he still owes me, nobody will give that to me if I don't get it out of him. Suppose they cart him away to the asylum, what do I do then? Even if the son has a wife who's not dead, I can't write to her if I got no address. And suppose the old man kicks the bucket? He looks like he's not far away now! He's liable to die without anybody even knowing he's got a stone. They'll bury him in the charity field and I'll be stuck with a three-quarter cut stone I can't use and a seven-dollar debt I can't collect. A charity I'll be running yet!

The best thing to do is to scare him. Maybe his son isn't dead, maybe he's just playing games with me. So I bang my hand on the counter.

"What kind of a thing is that for a Jew to say? 'I don't have a son!' You do have a son, you talk about him all the time. Now you give me his name and address. It's a law. I got a right to have it! What happens to me if you drop dead tomorrow, who do I collect seven dollars from? You think I'm running a charity? Or a game of chance?"

What's he fumbling in his pocket for? Money, he's bringing out a bill. It's ten dollars. He lays it on the counter like it was a dishrag. So he's going to pay the whole thing off? Why did he bother to give me the fifty cents if he's got ten dollars in his pocket? He's crazy! Where did he get ten dollars, all of a sudden? Maybe he stole it? But what do I care? They can't get it back from me. Long as he pays up and I get rid of him, I don't care whose money he's paying with.

Make up your mind, will you? Crazy old man. Now he's putting the money back in his pocket. He pushes it very carefully into his jacket pocket, and then he looks at me like he just tore out a part of his heart.

"Here is my son's address," he says, and in a very soft voice he dictates his son's name and where he lives.

I write the address in the book and when I finish I set the pen on the counter. He's still standing at the counter, but I don't want to look at him. Go away, I got work to do.

"I guess I will go now. Goodbye," he says.

"Goodbye. I'll see you a week from Wednesday."

I hear him walking toward the door, and the creak of the handle as the door opens.

"No. I will come back next Sunday!"

The hinges creak, then the door closes, and if I listen very carefully, I can hear his footsteps moving away on the pavement. A madman. A real madman. Good thing I got his son's address out of him. Walks all the way down here on a Sunday, just to pay fifty cents that's due on Wednesday, like he was afraid Wednesday would never come. With ten dollars sitting in his pocket.

Aaach. It's a way to spend a Sunday, crazy old man? You got nothing better to do? Me, I like it here. Between working on the books I can look past the white curtains on my window and door, into the quiet of the street.

Sixteen

The old man pushed open the outer door of the supermarket and shoved through the turnstile. The metal bar swung back faster than the old man could scuttle through the passage, and whacked him solidly in the ribs. Swine, the old man cursed. Pig of a Levin. Someday I'll get even with him. I'll fix him. Swine. Just wait, he thought, and looked around the store. He wanted to find the manager and the grocery clerks, but he did not pause in the empty space between the bottle-return counter and the rows of shopping carts jammed one inside the other. It would be stupid, he thought, to call attention to myself. He rolled the thirty dollars in his pocket and shuffled into the fruit and juice aisle.

A stand at the end of the aisle held a sale on tuna fish. A contest blank clamored silently for examination. The old man glanced at the tuna fish special, turned, came back to the display, picked up a can, weighed it in his hand. Only women moved through the next aisle. The produce men were working near the windows, the bakery clerk was talking to a customer.

But he may be pretending, that clerk! Where was he when I came in? The old man could not remember, he had scurried into the fruit and juice aisle too quickly. Next time I should come in more slowly, I should look around. Maybe keep a list in my pocket, pull it out to see what I had to buy. I could even bring a pencil with me, after I passed through the turnstile I could lean against one of the carts, chew on my pencil, add something to the list. But I would have to use the bottle-return counter to write on. So? Even better. Because of the way the floor slopes, I could see everything from the bottle counter. I could stare at the list, take out the pencil, chew on it, then move slowly to the counter and make some changes. Cross out something, look up and down each aisle like I forgot something important, mumble to the bottle boy "I wonder what it was," then shake my head. If he answered, perhaps I could talk to him for a few minutes.

The old man was still holding the tuna fish can, wondering if his new plan would help him to locate the manager and the grocery clerks more easily. It would give me much more time. But maybe it would not be so smart to talk to the bottle boy. I never liked his looks. He was the one who stared through the window the time I took the giant-size box of crackers. The old man chuckled as he remembered his image in the cracked mirror of his apartment, the great bulge of the cracker box, which had refused to be covered by the folds of his loose jacket. That cashier, he thought. How stupid *goyim* were. That cashier was a *schwartze!* Of course! What else could you expect from *schwartzes?*

But that bottle boy, did he suspect something? When I looked back into the store from the street, with that giant cracker box sticking out from my jacket, the bottle boy was staring at me through the store window. So maybe he saw something? The bulge, perhaps, when I went out the door? Maybe he talked to the cashier and she told him I only bought a box of tea. No. It would not be smart to stop at the bottle counter, why should I pull out a list when I'm only buying a box of tea? The bottle boy was tall and thin, with blond hair and the tail end of pimples. He looks like a Polack. Sharp eyes! All thin Polacks have those sharp, beady eyes that stare at you like you were a *ganif*.

Well, the old man thought as he replaced the can of tuna fish on the neatly stacked spiral that twined its way up to the smiling bathing beauty kissing the giant-size cardboard can, I am a thief. But the Polack does not know that yet. And he never will. He's not smart enough, no Polack is. Even Levinson, careful old Levinson who had cut patterns next to him at the Acme

Dress Company, had made fun of Acme's little Polack watchman. Never guessed we were the ones sneaking out material and patterns, week after week. But Levinson was too careful, too scared and never smart enough. And he couldn't laugh as I laughed when the little Polack watchman was finally fired. Kahn warned him that the thefts must be stopped, Levinson said. He is supposed to search everybody, Kahn told him it must be somebody inside, they're losing too much money, everybody has to be searched. Levinson loafed so much he always overheard Kahn the foreman's conversations.

Don't worry, the old man had laughed. He won't search us. He won't have enough nerve, to stare us in the face and tell us he has to search us. No *goy* has that much nerve.

That afternoon, Levinson and he were stopped at the door, Levinson with nothing and he with a length of material tucked inside the loose folds of his jacket. The little watchman shuffled his feet and stammered something about searching everybody. The old man laughed, harshly, then tapped the little watchman on the shoulder.

Listen, Warnskey. The watchman's real name was twice as long and impossible to prounounce, so the old man called him Warnskey, slurring the *w* and dragging out the *y* to make it sound Jewish. For twenty years I been stealing from this company. I think it's a little late they should begin searching me now. You tell Kahn I wouldn't let you search me, I was afraid you'd see the holes in my suit. Levinson laughed as they both moved past the watchman and out of the plant.

But Levinson stopped. He didn't have enough nerve. He wasn't smart enough. After they fired Warnskey and put in the new bookkeeping system he got scared. But I figured a way to beat them. A woman's cart, stuffed with cans and boxes, brushed the old man's elbow. He realized how much time he had spent at the tuna fish display, tore a contest blank from the pad in the cardboard hand of the smiling bathing beauty, and shuffled into the next aisle.

Why I like Queen Mist Tuna, in twenty-five words or less. Maybe I should tell them. Maybe I should write them how to steal from a supermarket. In twenty-five words. Was the woman in the red coat staring at him or at the soup? Maybe she had seen him at the tuna fish? You could not trust the customers any more than the workers. He folded the contest slip and tucked it carefully into his pants pocket, into the left pocket which was ripped across the bottom. Maybe it will slip out later in the store. Then I will not have to carry it home, but anyone watching will think it was an accident. The manager was in the office, talking on the phone and gesturing to the office girl; the bakery clerk had started to stock his counter. The produce men were heaping vegetables at the window, but he saw only two grocery helpers. Where were the other two? And the grocery manager? There were always five working on Sunday afternoons. He looked at the clock over the meat and fish counter. Nobody is out to dinner yet. And it was too late for lunch. Then they are in the back, in the warehouse. Three of them are in the back.

He glanced down the meat and fish counter. There were enough women waiting to keep both butchers and the fish man busy. Naomi's father had been a butcher. What a rotten job, being an honest butcher! Naomi fought when I quit, but I was right! It's a job for a fool. Only Zitomer would have been honest enough for a butcher's helper: his fingers also would have weighed nothing. Naomi's father would love Zitomer, both of them could slave happily day after day. Yes and yes and yes to one fat woman after another, hands raised in plain sight far above the scales. One dollar ninety-four, Mrs. Bernstein. Yes, I'll trim the fat. Save the bone? It's a crime, just to wait on these fat old sows, but did he understand? All he talked about was his business, his years in the neighborhood, the trust of his customers. So you can see, he said, day after day, his hands patting his fat belly, why I don't stand for any crooked business, no sliding prices, no thumbs or crayons on the scales. I want to make money, sure, but I've been here a long time, I have the respect and trust of my customers. That's worth more.

Paradise. Medals he'll get, an honest butcher. Best thing I ever did was to quit him. What a fool of a father-in-law. Naomi didn't like it, but I cared? No, I didn't care. All those stupid women! In the end, he had lost his temper with Naomi. I'm smarter than that, he had shouted at her. I'm too smart to spend my life being an honest butcher to fat women.

The old man felt he was in the tea aisle before he looked at the shelves. He shuffled slowly toward the coffee and tea, glancing sideways—they could come from the warehouse anytime! There were no boxes piled in the aisle, so no one had been working on the shelves who was now taking a short break. If someone does come out, he will be pushing a truckload of groceries and I will hear his truck and see him before he sees me. The old man knew the sounds of both the two-wheeled hand truck and the larger four-wheeled cart the grocerymen used. He looked back at the shelves, trying to shut his ears to the women's chatter so that he would be alert for the whine of the wheels.

He saw the tea he always bought. This will be the first time I have not paid for you, he whispered to the tea. Usually he bought a small box of tea and stole the crackers. But after lunch, after he had picked up the pieces of the soup bowl and wiped the floor, he had promised himself not to steal the crackers any more. At least I ought to take a larger size box of tea, he thought, as long as I'm buying the crackers. He plucked the large size box of the tea he used and the same size of a tea he had never used from the shelves, and weighed the boxes in his hand, turning them, examining them, considering. Then he edged close to the shelf, replaced the box of tea he did not want, and slipped the other package inside his jacket, into the large pouch he had sewn in the lining. He turned from the counter, letting the folds of the jacket hang loose about him, thankful he once had sense enough to buy an extra-large jacket. He glanced up and down the aisle. None of the women were watching, the cashiers were working their machines. The meat counter was still crowded, both butchers were at the scales. He squirmed inside his jacket, to let it hang still more loosely about him, smoothed the front to hide the outline of the tea box, turned, and shuffled out of the aisle.

He dodged the carts and the women moving toward the meats and frozen food at the far corner of the store, decided to buy only a box of cough drops which he could use if his cough returned, and turned up an aisle toward the cashiers and the candy stands at the front of the store. But he picked the wrong aisle. He saw the crackers before he could turn back. He remembered the crackers laughing and dancing inside the oven shelf, and closed his eyes, prayed silently through moving lips for the world to hold, for the lights to stay bright, for the people to go on with their shopping, for all the dead whose memories he had used to fill his evenings not to come flooding into his mind. And when he opened his eyes, the crackers sat, innocent in their red and blue box, on the shelf. Good, the old man thought. But what will happen tonight—when I'm alone in the apartment? They don't listen to me any more! I should have let the dead stay dead. Maybe there is something sinful in using their memories to fill my evenings. But I did them no harm. I talked to them the way we used to talk when they were alive. I won't think about it. I just won't let it happen again, that's all. I'm still strong enough and smart enough to beat them. He took a box of crackers from the shelf, slipped it inside his jacket, and moved away.

All the cashiers were crowded. The old man picked his box of cough drops from the candy counter in front of the last cash register, chose a line that looked as if it might move quickly, and shuffled into it. The woman in front of him, with two huge baskets of groceries and a small boy with a candy bar smearing his mouth, turned.

"Is that all you have?"

The old man did not trust himself to speak. He nodded.

"Why don't you go ahead of me? Charley, move the baskets so this man can go ahead of us. All he has is the cough drops."

She spoke loudly, the old man felt heads turning, eyes staring. The boy grumbled something before he moved the carts. Perhaps I can slip away, the old man thought. To another line. But it would not be smart. The woman would say something. Maybe she was already suspicious. I don't like the way she smiled.

As he nodded his thanks and moved ahead of her he wondered where the manager was, whether the woman had already told him, whether the cashier knew. The woman in front of him was putting her last few cans on the counter, and as the register rang the total and then fell silent, he could feel everyone watching him, wondering about his lone box of cough drops.

The cashier was putting the cans and boxes into the dark green paper bags. The old man felt the need to say something, to explain why he was buying only the cough drops, but who could he say it to? He did not trust the woman who had offered him her place. He tried to look around the store, to find the manager and the grocery clerks, but the weight of the crackers and the tea pulled on his jacket. He wished he had not taken the crackers, wished he had kept his promise to take only the tea and never touch the crackers again. It is the crackers' fault, the bulge is too big with them. He felt the crackers beginning to stir and laugh inside the package and he shivered; any moment Naomi and Shmuel Yaakov and Smetyanov would burst through the window, would come rolling merrily into the store and laughingly reveal him as the thief, the *ganif!* He tried to squirm so that the jacket hung looser, dreading the moment when the crackers would begin to laugh and sing, to yell "Stolen, stolen," as they had yelled at lunchtime in the oven. Again he saw them sprawled across the oven shelf and the floor, glistening like gold coins in the darkened room.

"Is that all, sir?"

He looked up. The little colored cashier was staring at him. He put the cough drops on the counter.

"Yes," he mumbled, "yes, that's all—I was here before but I—I forgot to get—"

He stopped. He had forgotten to take out the money. He turned away from her as he dug into his jacket pocket to find the quarter. He hunched forward, trying to hold the jacket tight against him as he searched. Twice he grasped the quarter, twice it slipped from his fumbling fingers as he tried to pull it from his pocket.

"I—it's right here," he mumbled to the girl, not daring to meet her eyes. The crackers were laughing in his ears and the floor was shaking. Finally he found the quarter. The register rang as the girl opened the drawer and handed him the change. "Thank you, sir," she said.

Both hands were shaking now as he moved to the door. He did not like the tone in her voice when she said Thank you, but it didn't matter. She didn't know. The little *schwartze* with the stupid moon face hadn't even guessed, he had almost shoved the tea and crackers under her nose and still she hadn't even seen. God, she was stupid. They were all stupid, *goyim* and *schwartzes* alike. I made a mistake, took an unwise chance, and I still fooled them. I can always fool them!

"Wait!"

He had almost reached the door when he heard the voice. The bottle boy, the Polack with the pimples. He had been watching everything. He had seen.

The old man could not turn. He stood, trembling at the door. Inside his mind, Naomi and Smetyanov and Shmuel Yaakov were shrieking with laughter. The crackers began to stir. He stood, waiting for the boy to pull open his jacket, waiting for the boy to call the manager. Tears formed in his eyes.

The boy was at his elbow.

"Here, you dropped this."

The old man turned slowly. Through his tears he saw the folded slip in the boy's hand, the contest slip he had tucked into his torn pocket.

"Here," the boy said.

The old man reached out to take the slip.

"Thank you."

"Is anything wrong?" the boy said. "Are you all right?"

The old man nodded. He wanted to wipe his eyes with the sleeve of his jacket, but he was afraid, he let the tears run down his face.

"Shall I get the manager? Are you sick?"

The old man shook his head.

"No. No, thank you."

He forced himself to move to the door and push it open with his shoulders. Then he was outside; the cold wind whipped his tear-streaked face. He backed against the wall of the store and wiped his face with his sleeve. That stupid Polack! I fooled him, too. I can fool all of them forever.

He pushed himself away from the wall and shuffled across the street. It was slowly getting dark, and he felt the weight of the tea and crackers on his jacket as he pulled it tighter around him. He wished he had not taken the crackers as he heard them stirring with his walk. It was still light enough to get to the synagogue in time for afternoon and evening prayers. But after evening service, it would be dark and nowhere else to go but home, to the empty apartment. He heard Naomi begin to laugh and shuffled more slowly into the dying afternoon.

Seventeen

The rabbi reached the synagogue with his afternoon cup of tea still warm in his stomach. The synagogue door was locked. The rabbi set one foot on the cracked stone step that ran the length of the seamed wooden doorway and forced the metal ring, crusted with flaking black rust, through its short arc. It thudded dully against the door, and the rabbi pressed his ear against the cold wood of the door to hear the thud ring hollowly inside the synagogue.

So, the rabbi thought. He's not here, my *shamos*. He did decide to stay home. Maybe he's more worried than I thought. Or maybe he's really sick. More probably he had another argument with his son, before the son and that little boy who didn't like me took the subway for the Port Authority building. And now he's so upset he decided to stay home, and he's resting on his narrow bed. Probably all the blankets have moth holes in them.

A cold blast of air whipped around the unprotected corner, caught the brim of Rabbi Davis's high old black hat, and forced it back from his forehead. He groped in his pants pocket with his right hand, found his ring of keys, selected the large brass key for the front door, and, the other hand tugging down at the brim of his high black hat, inserted the key into the lock, and twisted it a quarter turn to the right. The door groaned.

The rabbi set his shoulder against it, forced it open, and slipped inside.

The rabbi had known the insides of five synagogues. He had learned the touch and the smell and the look of all the dark places, had offered up thousands of prayers into the mysterious flickering shadowed air, had stared for hours at the stuttering light of the *Ner Tamid* above the Ark of the Covenant. And still his first moment inside the doors of this last of his five synagogues always awakened some not quite dead feeling of hush, of reverence, of ancient and unexplainable sacredness in him. Perhaps it was the sudden move from the cold gray deadness of the afternoon city, into air thick with memories of holiday incense, the fir smell of *lulav* and the *shabbos* linger of grape from the *Kiddush* wine. The rabbi knew that a part of the smell was rotting boards and the hoards of too many families of mice, and an odor from coats and suits that had covered torn shirts and stained underwear too long. But still the first moment inside the quiet twilight of the synagogue, before the door creaked shut and its final thud reminded the rabbi that there was a service to be prepared for, transfixed him in a momentary pause, a peace that spoke in almost forgotten tongues of mystery and reverence.

But the moment passes, the rabbi thought. It comes for an instant, and then it passes. Maybe that first instant is what is left of the Jew in me, what is left in all of us after five thousand years of wandering. Five seconds' worth of mystery and reverence. And a lifetime full of bitterness. How much, I wonder, does my congregation still retain, of that silence, that pause in the bowels, that is neither deadness nor fear? How much is left in them, of that feeling that hushed so many millions of our ancestors, when the cantor fell on his knees before the Ark and uttered the unmentionable unpronounceable secret name of God? How much is left in them of anything I could dignify by the name of feeling, poor barren hulks of human beings? Their sons and daughters have graduated to Queens and the Bronx and Jamaica, and sometimes even the commuter communities stretching out toward the tip of Long Island. Their grandchildren sit in classrooms with *goyim* and *schwartzes* and try to decide which college they should attend. And yet the old ones cling to each other, here on this little island they have defined out of the chaos of the city. They cling to each other, and to the dead rhythms they have performed since the city shuffled them off the cattle boat from Europe, and interred them.

And me, I can blame them? I can say to them, You were wrong, you were foolish, you were afraid! It was a mistake to try to rebuild the old country on the doorstep of this new world? You should have done something else? You should have become Americans? You should have, as they say, integrated yourself into the greater American community? Where is that? They had a choice, I could say that to them? They had anything in front of them that even hinted that somehow, in this gigantic sprawl of a country, a group of people had taken their sweat and their minds and their integrity and built a community a person could live in? Not a community for Jews, even, a community for anybody? What they tried to build, here on the East Side, was so wrong, even though they failed?

So, the rabbi thought. Enough is enough. Though God knows what I can do to tap the feelings inside me. He switched on the four light controls in the panel set against the molding rimming the doorway, and the four dirty glass globes glazed their soft yellow light down into the synagogue. The rabbi walked slowly down the faded carpet of the right-hand aisle and mounted the five steps that wound up to the main platform, that held the Ark, the chairs and the large table covered with a maroon velvet cloth embossed with a gold Star of David. He stood behind the table and bent himself against its rim, running his hands along the folds of the coverlet that hung down at the sides. He closed his eyes and tried to search backward in his memory, to the first time he had hunched himself over a reading table and stared down at the softened faces of his congregation. Somewhere, when I was still a student, he thought. A high holiday sermon I gave. Elmira? Scranton? But it was too long ago. It was too long ago, and there were too many faceless congregations twinkling in softened light in the recesses of his memory. Probably, he thought, I can't even remember the look of my own first congregation in Akron. He shut his eyes again, and tried to remember. And could not.

Too long, the rabbi thought. Too many years, too many

members, too few people. And how many, he wondered, how many of those I can't remember can remember me? How many of them remember me as a person named Rabbi Davis?

He opened his eyes.

"I want to tell you something," he said to the empty congregation. "Or maybe I want to tell me something. Anyway, I want to say it aloud, and the fact that none of you are here to listen to me is maybe a better thing, since I have said nothing, and wanted to say nothing, in all the sermons I have preached, for too many years. I have said none of the things I might have wanted to say because I understood too well there was none of you to understand them, and there is no worse feeling than talking of something you want to say to a congregation that does not and cannot understand. And so I stopped caring, and said nothing. Or worse than nothing, I said the words that were expected of me, said them with no thought and no care and no passion. And I would do the same tomorrow, were it time for my sermon. Because you are sheep, and you cannot understand, and it is not merciful to unduly trouble your slumbers."

The rabbi stopped, licked his dry lips, and loosened his hold on the cloth that hung down from the sides of the table.

"But today," he began again, "today you are here only in my mind, all the congregations of my past, in spite of the fact that you have no faces and the yellow lamplight shines dimly off the indistinguishable crowns of your foreheads. So I will tell you something. I will tell you a lot of somethings that make you meaningful to me, and perhaps, were you here, might make you meaningful to yourselves. I will start at the beginning, or, rather, I will pretend that there is a beginning to start from, since that pretense will allow me to start. So I say, beginning. Beginning. My beginning was different from yours, because I was born in this country and you were not. But perhaps all beginnings are alike, in that they share a hope. How can a child be born without a joy and a hope? Another life! That is one kind of beginning. There is another kind, the beginning of the idea of what a man's life can mean. The point at which a man begins to see that he has the chance to take his life up in his hands, and perhaps, to make something meaningful of it. That beginning we call choice. My choice came to me in Stuart, Iowa; yours came to you across the old continent of Europe. For you, the choice began with a word, a rumor, a snatch of a story from a wandering laborer's lips. Somewhere across the sea there was a country called America, where men were free and land was free and a man's religion was his own business, where grass was greener than money and brooks ran choked with fish. And throughout the old country, from huddled wood and straw workers' huts scattered like cubs around the great shining mother of the manor house, from basement room or attic in crumbling houses walled into ghetto tightness, from field, canal, ditch, mine, crossroads, store, prayer bench, factory line, prison, shipyard, library, and forest; the word, the choice, inflamed you, nagged at you. You thought, you worried, you prayed, you pleaded. And finally, one day when all the arguments were rehearsed and there was nothing new to say, you balanced all the fears and dangers against the hope that somehow, life might be different. You stared at the life that your fathers had fashioned for you, there in the dog kennels of Europe, and no matter how you rearranged the letters, America spelled out choice, a choice that a man could make, to take his life up in his own hands, and perhaps, create something meaningful from it.

"The hope won. The choice was taken. You bought your tickets and you packed everything you owned into trunks, valises, suitcases, boxes, cardboard cartons. Blankets, even, huge rolled blankets crammed with pots and pans and rolling pins clanking like a St. Nicholas' pack's answer to a tinker's Christmas prayer! You sobbed goodbye to those who chose the surety and let the hope default, staring for the last time at a village, a town, a city, you would of certainty never see again, and turned your face westward, toward America.

"To Hamburg, Riga, Bremen, Brest, Antwerp, Danzig, you came. Even to Southampton and Liverpool. You poured into every rotten dock of any city where the meanest scow set her signals west. You waited for your ship to sail in filthy rooms in waterfront hotels, surrounded by the litter of travel: abandoned baggage, lost children, separated families. Nightmare days of agonized waiting; trapped, tongueless, in a foreign land, at the mercy of every thief and swindler who spoke your tongue and called you brother.

"And when your ship arrived, did it dull some of your

hopes? When you poured into the rotten hold that smelled of vomit and mold and even of corpses, did you begin to doubt? Packed worse than animals in the hold as the scow scudded and wallowed through the waves and swells so huge the Atlantic might have been God's waters on the day before light, sharing scurvy and pellagra and other itches and irritations you never learned the name for, did you begin to question that hope? My father breathed the air you breathed, and too many nights I sat on the arm of his chair and listened to the tales he told about the slave ship that brought him across the Atlantic. He was a simple man, my father, but he understood that someone was making money out of the blood he vomited up from his guts, the mornings he could struggle up to the deck and breathe some fresh air as he retched over the side. Bought captains, bribed inspectors, shipowners who sent condemned tubs across and back again and again and again. Eighty per cent survival a fair crossing. All fees paid in advance. No refunds. No money down. Hurry, hurry, hurry, grab your ticket to the land of the free and the home of the brave.

"But you lived, somehow. You survived. My father survived. You held the dead and the dying in your arms and one day after you had given up all hope of arrival, sunlight was shining on a city of stone and glass and strange buildings that poked their concrete noses toward the sky. You passed through the long incomprehensible ritual of immigration, were pinched and pulled and squeezed and questioned through hours and days and sometimes weeks, until finally they handed you the paper and ferried you across the harbor, past the green lady holding the torch above her head, and set you down in New York City.

"And here," the rabbi said, "here in the cobblestone streets of this city, is where the hope ended. Here in this city is where the choice became no choice at all. You came for freedom, and there is no freedom here. You came for equality, but here only money buys you the right to be treated as an equal. You came because life was easy here, because the streets were paved with gold, but what you found was a life lived so fast and so violently that each man is his brother's enemy. You came to this land because you thought there was a choice here, that a man could take up his life in his hands, and perhaps, make something meaningful from it. But no one takes up his life in his hands in this country; no one creates anything meaningful. What they create here is money; to make a life meaningful means to become successful. The people who built this land, who took their lives in their hands because they wanted the choice of something meaningful to flow from that taking, those people are dead. And those that came after them, that came too late to be called 'pioneers,' found it so hard to grind out a simple living that they had no time to imagine the taking of their lives up in their hands. You came to a land where no choice existed, so you found your niche. You stayed on the East Side where there were countrymen who spoke your language, friends to find you a room, a job. You built your synagogues and your burial societies, you pushed your carts through the streets, you overstocked your shops and subdivided your rooms into apartments. You worked as hard as you had to work, to buy the food and pay the rent and put a little away for the hospital and the funeral and the children."

The door creaked open, and the rabbi peered down through the yellowing twilight of the empty synagogue and saw the old man standing by the door. So, the rabbi thought. He's come after all. He's only late, instead of being sick. So I should stop talking. God knows what he'll do with the words I'll give him.

But the words had made their own life inside the rabbi, and there was more he wanted to say. He waved the old man to a seat, half determined to explain, afterward, that he was practicing a sermon or rehearsing a speech, and cleared his throat.

"And so we are left, existing. The smell and the softness of the synagogue, that makes me pause each time I come inside, are part of a memory, an echo of a life we left behind and yet did not leave behind, a sliver of reminiscence poised between the dying customs of the old country and the vacuum of customs in the new. The prayers we recite each morning, afternoon, and evening, may have meant something once, when your father explained as you bent your mind to learn the strange figures of the alphabet that crawled from right to left across the page. But now it is forgotten, that meaning; the whole ritual of gesture and response, of voice and motion, chant and quaver, is etched indissolubly into all the fissures of the mind, to be repeated night after night, day after day, without thought, without feeling, without comprehension. Nothing is left from the life whose patterns you once moved inside, there in that little space allowed you in the dog kennels of Europe, but a series of rules and rituals, imposed on an alien land. And nothing is offered you, by the land you came to, but a grudging plot of land. To die in. All of us, me, you—Horowitz with his side shuffle, Shapiro's rolling shoulders, Kopplewitz's dance that looks like palsy, we are what is left of five thousand years of choice and suffering. We are the pathetic reminder of that night on the desert, when God showed Abraham the multitude of stars, and made his covenant. We are what is left."

The rabbi's voice caught in his throat, and he stopped, suddenly, realizing he had no more to say. He had been prepared for more, but now that he had stopped he realized that there was no more. He groped backward from the table until his knees felt the wood of his chair, and he sat down and rested his head in his hands.

God knows, he thought to himself, where I found so much feeling left in me, to say all that. God knows why I bothered. Maybe I will make a new Sunday ritual for myself, instead of taking a walk I'll come to the synagogue and preach a sermon to the empty congregation.

Above the buzzing of the echoes of his own voice in his ears, he heard the soft step of someone shuffling up the carpet to the pulpit. The old man, the rabbi thought. Now he will have something to say. Perhaps he thought I was talking to him.

The rabbi looked up. The old man stood at the bottom of the five steps that wound upward to the main platform.

"Rabbi Davis?" the old man said.

"Yes."

"I'm sorry I came in while you were talking."

"How could you help it?"

"I thought, maybe I should have stayed outside. I didn't disturb you?"

"No, you didn't disturb me. What was there I should be disturbed about, making a speech to an empty congregation? Speeches should be made to people, not pews."

The rabbi pushed himself out of the chair and went to the small cupboard where his prayer shawl and skullcap were kept. He eased off his heavy coat and folded it into the cupboard, traded his hat for his skullcap, and wound the prayer shawl around his shoulders. He adjusted the fringe of the prayer shawl about his neck and turned back to the old man.

"Don't be troubled by what I said. I was trying to put into words something that I have been thinking about, that's all. So when I came here and the synagogue was empty, I thought maybe I would try to put the words into a speech."

Why do I bother to explain, the rabbi thought. Will he understand? Does he care?

"But you," the rabbi said. "How do you feel? Are you better? I meant it when I said you didn't have to come unless you felt good enough."

The old man nodded. "No," he said. "I'm all right. I'm fine. It was nothing, what happened to me this morning. It was just nerves. I don't understand it myself."

"Don't worry about it. Just forget it, that's all. Happens to all of us."

The old man turned and shuffled down the aisle, then turned back toward the pulpit.

"Rabbi Davis?"

"Yes?"

"Zitomer—after I left—Zitomer didn't say anything to you? About me? About what I told him that night?"

The rabbi stood and stared through the yellowing twilight, down into the aisle where the old man stood.

"No," the rabbi said finally. "He didn't say anything about you."

The old man nodded. "You see," he said, "once I told Zitomer about what bothers me at night, about the things I have done wrong and the people I did wrong to. I told Zitomer how they wouldn't leave me alone, those people, and I asked him what to do. So I thought, Rabbi Davis, that if he told you about what I said, you could tell me what to do. Because I can't stand it any more," the old man shouted suddenly. "They're driving me out of my head."

The rabbi listened to the old man's echo sound through the

synagogue. So, he thought, and what am I supposed to say? He worked his way down the five steps that wound from the pulpit, and walked down the aisle to the old man.

"You're tired," the rabbi said. "You're tired, and you're not feeling well, and you're probably catching a cold from walking around with no coat on. Now come," and he put an arm around the old man's shoulder, "sit down here and let me talk to you for a little while."

Eighteen

Annabel Williams nudged open the door to the old man's room and set down her floor mop and the bucket with her rags and scrub brush. Then she peered nearsightedly over the wire-frame glasses that always slipped down below eye level to rest owlishly on her nose.

"Don't even look like nobody lives here. Empty old room. Smells bad. Windows ain't been opened."

Slow footsteps clumped up the uncarpeted stairs.

"Ain't no use cleaning this room, Mister Feinstein. It's clean enough now, after I get done he won't know the difference."

"Just as good he doesn't know the difference," Feinstein said. "He'd only grumble. An old mule, he is, always grumbling. Do anything the least little bit different, and a civil war you got on your hands. But you go ahead and clean the room, Annie." He patted her shoulder, thin and bony underneath the faded cotton smock. "It'll be a favor for him even if he doesn't notice. Only if you move something, put it back in the same place. Even a chair in a different place is enough to start him off. He'll have a fit about it. He'll come down and talk my ear off for hours."

Annabel shook her head.

"I don't see no sense to it, no sense at all. If he doesn't care about the room, and you don't even want him to know about it, why do I have to bother cleaning it? No sense to it. Just plain silly."

"Well," Feinstein laughed. "After all, Annie, when we get old we got a right, every once in a while, to be a little silly."

He patted Annie's shoulder again and turned to go down-stairs. Annie was right and he knew it, there was no reason for her to clean the old man's flat, except that he paid her three dollars for a day's work, had run out of work for her to do in his own apartment and had watched her leave an hour early the last three Sundays. Who would have thought it wasn't a good day's work, cleaning his apartment? It was fun, maybe, to watch Annie leave an hour early, to watch thirty, forty cents out of his three dollars, wasted? Every week? Feinstein had met Annie at Kaufman's shop, when he was on his collecting rounds. Kaufman had grudgingly invited him in back for a cup of tea, hoping to weasel out of giving Feinstein's charity the five dollars he was written down for. Annie was on her knees, scrubbing away at the square of soiled linoleum under the leaky kitchen sink, humming tunelessly but cheerfully to herself.

Oh ho, Feinstein thought, so Kaufman can afford a maid, hey, and doubled Kaufman's subscription in his mind. But it turned out she only asked three dollars for a good day's work, and Feinstein was tempted, because he had never hired a maid, and though he did the absolutely necessary cleaning and washing himself, still, it was a nuisance, and the apartment was always dirty. But a maid! How many of Feinstein's friends or even his classy relatives in the Bronx had a maid? For only three dollars a week! A real bargain, Feinstein thought. But writing down and adding again and again his budget, his bank balance, he debated for three weeks before he went back to Kaufman's and tried to bargain for a cheaper rate.

"Nossir, Mister Feinstein. I'm sorry, but I don't do nobody's work for less'n three dollars. No sense to it. I jest can't afford to work for less'n three dollars a day. Only reason I can work so cheap is 'cause I got nobody to keep but me. But it ain't worth me going out for less'n three dollars."

So after a little more argument, so she shouldn't think he was giving in too easy, Feinstein agreed. Sunday, it turned out, was the only day she could give him, but Feinstein did not mind, to him Sunday was just another day. My maid comes on Sunday, he whispered to himself, and it was pleasing in his ears, he could hardly wait to tell his friends.

The first few Sundays were fun, almost exciting. Annie, as he called her instead of Annabel, which sounded godless and pagan and would not roll off his tongue without confusion, found much more work to do than he had ever imagined. It seemed that her ideas about cleaning were far different from his, and he was really a filthy old man, which amused and delighted him. The carpet was taken up and all the dirt he had swept under it brushed away, the woodwork and the baseboards washed and polished, the furniture, what little there was of it, waxed, the kitchen floor scrubbed, the porcelain sink and the soot-caked stove scoured. The cleaning went on and on, each Sunday a new discovery was rescued, cleansed, transformed for Feinstein's enchanted eyes. But slowly the novelty wore off, the battle against the dirt was stabilized, until there was finally nothing new to reclaim from dirtdom and only a routine job of cleaning, a weekly ritual, which left Annie with time on her hands. So Feinstein began to worry. Then he began to think up new jobs. The silverware should be polished. But there was so little, it took her no time. The candlesticks. A half-hour's work. He tried wearing more clothes, soiling them faster, putting them in the wash sooner so she would have more laundry. But he had worn his clothes with laundry bills on his mind for so many years that it was impossible to break his habits. A shirt still lasted him a week, his socks five days and his underwear four. He managed, by blowing his nose almost every hour, to use up one handkerchief a day, but how big are handkerchiefs? Nothing would do; after all his plans, Annie still finished up and went home an hour early. So finally, Feinstein decided to have Annie do the old man's apartment. It was really a waste of time, because Feinstein knew he would get nothing out of the old man for it, and he guessed that the old man would probably grumble anyway, if he found out. But at least it was better than letting Annie go home early, with all those free hours that Feinstein was paying her for wasted on her son and her daughter-in-law. What else can you do, Feinstein thought. So let her clean his apartment. I'll do him a favor for nothing, even if he doesn't deserve it. It'll be a blessing on my head.

"Yessir, Mister Feinstein," Annabel mumbled as Feinstein clumped down the stairs, "I'll clean it careful as I can, but still seems like a waste." But I don't care, she thought, cleaning ain't no trouble to me, and so long as I'm getting paid for it, I guess it don't much matter whether I clean clean apartments or dirty ones.

She emptied her scrub bucket and set to work, adding and re-adding the small, neat, painfully formed figures of her bank account as she cleaned. Every week she brought home twenty-one dollars, from seven full days' work cleaning apartments at three dollars a day. She gave five dollars to her son, not because he asked it for her little cubbyhole at the back of his basement flat, but because she wanted to. And food, when she was careful, which she had been for the last twenty years, never cost her more than three dollars a week. So unless she wanted a new dress or a scarf or a pair of heavy woolen stockings, or her old black shoes needed heels or one of her little grandchildren wanted something that her son and daughter-in-law couldn't afford to buy, Annabel deposited thirteen dollars every week at the same window of the Chemical Corn Exchange's Harlem branch. She kept her bankbook beneath her clean underwear in the top drawer of the old scarred bureau she had bought at the Salvation Army warehouse, and beside it she kept her five-cent notebook with her own careful figures, which she checked each week with the bank's. Not that she thought the bank would make a mistake, but because it satisfied her more to keep track of her money in her own hand.

Week after week, except when Christmas came or presents were needed or somebody got sick, and occasionally when the weather got so bad she treated herself to a taxi, Annabel had deposited her thirteen dollars in the bank, until now, ten years after her second husband, a coal delivery man, passed away, she had paid off all his debts and helped to finance her daughter-in-law's operation and her son's new teeth, and had still managed to save over five thousand dollars. She wrote it out in her head, five thousand three hundred and forty-seven dollars and sixty-three cents. She wrote it out a few times, taking her time because it was a long number and pleasing to write. Five thousand three hundred and forty-seven dollars and sixty-three cents. Such a lot of money. Soon it would be time to stop working and say goodbye to her son and daughter-in-law and grandchildren and get all the money out of the bank and take a bus down to Tallapoosa, Georgia, where there was a fine tidy farm with a white farmhouse only about a quarter of a mile from where she was born. With the money she could buy the house and the farm and hire some nice young folks to run it and do the cooking and housework, so she could sit at her front porch in an old oaken rocker, rocking back and forth and smiling at the fields in the Georgia sunshine.

Yessir, Annabel thought, pretty soon there'll be enough money, an' I'll jest say goodbye to New York and go on home for good. She did not know quite how much money she would need, but she guessed that farms were expensive these days, especially tidy little farms with white frame houses and oaken rockers on the front porch. And the farm would cost her more because she was colored, and white men didn't like to sell farms to colored people, so they would give her trouble. But long ago her father had told her that enough money solved almost all the trouble white folks could cause, and Annabel figured to save up enough to give the white man all he asked, with no fuss raised. She had lived among white folks for many years, and because she did not like trouble she found giving them what they wanted the simplest way to get along. Some of the younger folks said she was just making things worse for all the colored people, but if they wanted to argue and stir up trouble, that was their business. Others said she let herself get cheated when she didn't have to be, but Annabel figured that the little extra bit they might have cheated from her was worth the trouble she saved.

The old man finally reached the door to his apartment building, and started up the stairs. Annabel was scrubbing the floor in the corner by the old man's bed when she heard his slow footsteps on the stairs, but when the old man shuffled into the room she was surprised, because he was so much older and smaller than Mister Feinstein. He looked tired and cold. Bad weather out, Annabel thought. He's too old to be out, on a bad day like today. Ain't even got a coat!

The old man went to the little wooden table by the sink, and Annabel stopped scrubbing, still on her knees in the corner. He fumbled inside his jacket, brought out some boxes and set them on the table. Annabel turned back to her scrubbing and bumped the bucket with her brush.

The old man started. Turned.

There now, Annabel thought, I went and scared him. Course I did, I done forgot he don't even know I'm supposed to be here. She smiled at the old man.

But the old man only stared, his mouth open and his hand palm up, fingers spread, as if he was pushing her away.

"Aiii, Aiiii!" he moaned.

Annabel smiled again and wondered what to say.

The old man backed up against the radiator.

"What—what you doing here?"

Annabel shook her head.

"I'm jest Mister Feinstein's cleaning lady. Ain't no need to fuss. Mister Feinstein, he asked me to clean up your apartment."

Annabel struggled to her feet. The old man was still crouched against the radiator.

"Get out."

His whisper was so low Annabel wasn't sure she heard. She walked closer.

"No!" the old man screamed. "Stay back. Stay away from me. Get out!"

So Annabel just stood, her wet hands hanging at her sides.

"Get out! Get out!"

"I ain't even cleaned but a little bit of your apartment yet. If you're worrying about paying me, Mister Feinstein takes care of that, I'm jest—"

"GET OUT!"

Well I never, Annabel thought. Poor old man. Been living alone up here so long he's teched in the head. Lucky thing I done what Cousin Sarah told me and moved in with my son. I mighta wound up like him.

"All right," she said. "No sense to it, though, seein's how I'm already working, and you could have your whole apartment done up for nothing. But if you want me to go, I'm going." She turned to gather her rags and brush and bucket. Mister

Feinstein wasn't half kidding about him. He's more'n an old mule. He's crazy!

"GET OUT!" the old man screamed again. "Get out from my apartment, you *schwartze!* I'll call the police, arrested I'll have you. Get out!"

Lord. Lord. Poor, crazy old man.

"I'm going," she said over her shoulder. "Jest gimme time to get my things collected, and I'll be right clear outa your way."

A dish crashed against the wall over her head and smashed into pieces.

"Now! Right now! Get out!"

Annabel got up with her bucket in her hand and brushed the chips of pottery from her smock and the rag she kept tightly wound about her gray hair. Mighta hit me with that dish, she thought. He's sure a mean old man.

"You be careful now," she said. "Some day you gonna hurt somebody."

She tucked the broom under her arm and stepped carefully around the bed toward the door. As she moved to the middle of the room the old man grabbed the packages from the table and hid them behind his back. Annabel walked out the door and started down the steps.

"And stay out, *schwartze.* Don't ever come back!"

The door slammed shut behind her, the latch clicked.

Nossir, Annabel thought, don't you worry, no matter what Mister Feinstein says, I ain't never gonna come back. Crazy old man. At the bottom she hesitated, then tried the door to Feinstein's flat. It was locked. She knocked. No answer.

Musta gone out, she thought. Well, I guess it's about time I was heading home anyway. She unwound the rag from her head and stuffed it into her smock pocket, set the bucket down in the hallway, and unpinned the handkerchief with Feinstein's three dollars from her waist. Her red coat with the rabbit-fur collar that had long ago turned from white to grayish-black hung on its usual nail in the hall closet. Annabel slipped into it and folded the three dollars flat in her right palm, then slipped her red woolen mittens on. She picked up her bucket, emptied it into the drain by the door, tucked her mop under her arm, and started for home.

Nineteen

The bus from the Port Authority Terminal sets them down on the Jersey side of the river, beside the huge parking lot. Carl produces his ticket at the attendant's shack, pays for his three hours, and shepherds David toward the car. Carl unlocks his door, slides in, stretches across the seat to click open the lock so that David can get in. He turns the key in the ignition switch and pumps the gas pedal. The starter whirrs. The engine coughs once, twice, then subsides.

"Come on," Carl says.

He turns the key off, turns it on again. His foot comes down steadily on the pedal. The engine catches, hums gently into life. Carl eases off the emergency brake, adjusts his rear-view mirror, and nurses the car out of the lot.

A long, curving ramp, and then a straight road to the Turnpike entrance. "Afternoon," the guard says, and hands Carl his ticket.

Carl nods. He inserts the ticket between the sun visor and the upholstery of the car's roof, and rolls the window up as he pulls away. He takes it slow on the access road, but the Turnpike south is almost empty. He glances at the lone car coming up in the outside lane, then swings into the Turnpike. Thirty fast miles to home. Carl settles himself into the seat.

Beside him, curved against the seat-back, his legs propped against the floorboard underneath the heater, David carefully picks his nose. The thumb and index finger of his left hand serve as collectors; the index finger of his right hand as searcher. Carl has been silent for almost all of the grinding subway trip across Manhattan, so the index finger of David's right hand has plumbed both nostrils, and a sizable collection of grayish-black snot, of varying consistency, rests on the ball of his left thumb. David stares through the windshield into the winter afternoon, at the smooth gray-black of the asphalt as the road unfolds before him. He turns to glance at his father, and watches, for a moment, the set lines of his father's face, intent on the curve of the road.

"Be dark soon," David says.

Carl nods.

"We get home before it's dark?"

Carl nods again. "Probably."

David shifts in the seat, still staring at his father's face. "Mom be angry?"

Carl shrugs, and his eyebrows arch upward and furrow his forehead as he mugs his puzzlement. "I wonder. She wasn't angry when we left."

David nods.

"But she's been by herself the whole afternoon, waiting for us to come home. And it's not a nice day for waiting."

"Yeah," David says, and pokes at the loose corner of the floorboard with the tip of his shoe. "Maybe she'll be angry when we get home. Or maybe cold and quiet, like this morning. I think I'll go up and read after dinner. Or I could write a letter to Gran'pop."

Carl glances down briefly, then looks back over the wheel, through the windshield at the slowly curving road. "You tired?"

"No," David answers. "I was thinking. About Gran'pop."

Carl's mouth tightens into a frown as he stares over the wheel at the road, but David does not see his gloved hands tightening on the wheel. The car swings into the arc of the curve, and Carl waits until the car has caught the swing and then presses down on the gas pedal and whips the car racing through the final portion of the bend. He lets the wheel swing back to find its own level before he speaks.

"What about him?"

"I don't know," David says. "He's always so angry—and mean. Why does he always get mad about you and Philly?"

"Takes a long time to explain," Carl says.

"So? We got at least a half-hour before we're home."

Carl edges his wrist away from the rims of his shirt, jacket, and coat sleeves, checks his watch. "Yeah. I guess we do." He squirms again in the seat, to settle himself more comfortably behind the wheel. He checks the rear-view mirror and lifts his foot momentarily from the gas pedal, stretches it, wiggles, eases it back.

"It's maybe hard to understand. You saw Gran'pop. You can tell a little of how he thinks. Well, imagine living with him. Maybe if I went to a *yeshiva* it wouldn't have been so bad; when everybody else is doing the same things you're doing, then you don't miss anything, you don't want anything else. But Gran'-pop couldn't send me to *yeshiva*, because he didn't have enough money. So I went to public school. I went to public school in short pants and a *yarmilka*, and *payas* that curled down past my ears. And I got laughed at. There were some other Jewish boys who came to school looking same as me, and we all got laughed at. We got laughed at, insulted, chased, and beaten up. Once a gang ruined a pair of my pants. Another time they ripped a good shirt right off the back of one of my friends. Well, I didn't understand. I didn't understand why we had to get beat up, and all Gran'pop could tell me was that it was because they were *goyim*, and *goyim* were like that. Gran'pop used to spit in front of every church he passed, and pray to God to please hurry and destroy all the churches. But I didn't spit. I had to come straight home from school and go to synagogue, and after services I had to study, first my Hebrew lessons, and then my school lessons. Every morning I had to get up at five-thirty, to go to synagogue before I went to school. And all the other Jewish boys had to do the same, so like I say, it wouldn't have been so bad if the *goyim* hadn't been around. Because the *goyim* didn't go right home after school. They hung around on the street corners, outside the drugstore and the candy store. They played ball in the playground, in the empty lots. They ran through the streets in gangs, shouting curses at each other. They fired at each other with guns, and died rolling in the gutters. On Saturdays, and sometimes on week nights, they went to the movies. They played on the docks, and in the summer they swam off the docks and the barges that tied up along the waterfront.

"Well, I wanted to be like them," Carl says. "I wanted to do all the things they did. I wanted to buy long pretzel sticks and fat thick twisty ones; I wanted to buy licorice babies and fudge squares and drink from dirty bottles of chocolate soda. I wanted to stay out late in the streets, and play hide-and-seek with the girls, and understand the giggles that came floating up from the back alleys and dark corners. But what was I supposed to say to Gran'pop? You think there was any way he'd understand? All he knew was the old country, and in the old country a Jewish boy didn't play hide-and-seek after dark. A Jewish boy didn't go to the movies or go swimming off the docks. A Jewish boy went to school and worked hard, and came home and prayed hard and studied hard and worked hard at his chores and then went to bed. That's all. How could I tell my father I wanted to do what the *goyim* did? *Goyim* were worse than animals, worse than pigs even! In high school, I had some *goyim* for friends. I even went out once with a *shikse*."

God, it seems so long ago, Carl thinks. I have to think about it to remember what a lousy stinking time that was. High school was a hell, a real hell! Not the things I couldn't do, not even the quarrels so much. But the sneaking! Christ, I hated the sneaking! Stay after school to work on the paper, and then lie to Dad about why I wasn't in synagogue. Or play a basketball game in the schoolyard and then go inside to wash my face and hands, straighten my clothes, and comb my hair before I went home. And the lies I told to get a free evening. When I took Mary Ann out, I worked for weeks to set up the lies so that he couldn't trap me. And then she wondered why I was nervous. Why are you so quiet, she kept asking me. I felt like telling her. Because if my father works hard enough, he'll find out that I'm not helping Marshall Zucker's cousin to translate Second Samuel, and then I'll have to tell him that I went out with you. And he won't care that your hair is coal-black, and so fine that it floats on your shoulders, that you have the bluest eyes I've ever seen. He will care only that your last name is Watson, because it means you're a *shikse!* And then I'll get it!

He never got me, that time. Sometimes, though, I had the feeling he knew what I was doing; but as long as he didn't face me with it, it wasn't really true. Because how much did I really fool him? By the end of high school, I wasn't going to synagogue in the mornings at all; and only once or twice a week in the evenings, just to keep him happy. And all the times he caught me lying? You're no good, he'd scream at me. A liar? I had to work my hands to the bone to bring up a sneak and a liar? Better if you went out and beat somebody up, like a stupid *goy*, than to sneak around and tell lies about it. *Oy Gott*, he'd say, and he'd bang his clenched hands against his forehead. That a son of mine should be a sneak and a liar.

I'd stand there. What could I say? What sense would it make? I'd stand there and I'd try to tell myself that I wasn't rotten, that I wasn't the worst kid who ever lived, that if I cared anything at all about my father, I couldn't treat him the way I did. You're an animal, he'd scream. You're worse. Even an animal, even a horse, cares more about his parents than you do about me. Not even an animal could treat me the way you do. You don't care for anybody in the world but yourself. You don't think about anybody but yourself!

So finally I decided he was right, and I stopped listening. I did what I wanted to do, and if he caught me, I stood there and listened to his screaming. You don't love me, he'd yell, and I'd nod my head. That's right, I'd say. I don't love you. Now can I go? Are you done screaming at me yet? And when I finally saved up enough money to get to Philly and get started on my own, all I told him was that I was leaving. Don't come back, he shouted. You go away from me, you're on your own. For good. You don't have a father, once you go. I don't have a son. So go, he shouted, and the hell with you!

The dark green signboard, lit now because the afternoon is slowly darkening, announces only a mile to Exit 9. Carl checks the rear-view mirror, switches on his right-turn indicator, and edges into the right lane. "So," he says. "We're almost home."

David nods. "Yeah."

"I didn't explain very much. Maybe you have to live with somebody like Gran'pop to understand."

David wriggles his handkerchief out of his pocket, and carefully oozes the snot collection on his left thumb onto the cloth of the handkerchief. He folds the handkerchief over the mass and squeezes until he can feel the slip of the cloth as it slides over the snot. Then he slides the handkerchief back into his pocket.

"But when I left for Philly," Carl says, "I walked out on him, on everything he cared about, on what he wanted me to be. Almost like I stopped being his son, stopped being a Jew, even, when I went to Philly."

He swings the car to the right, off the main road up onto the ramp that curves around to the ticket booth, slows to a dead stop by the ticket booth, and hands over the ticket and the money. He watches as the guard processes the ticket through a machine he can never quite see, then hands him back his change.

"Thank you," says the guard.

"Thank you," Carl says, revs his engine, and eases up on the exit road. Christ, he thinks, I'll never get free of him. All I have to do is dream about him, and my whole day gets soured. I don't know, I don't know at all, some people must have normal parents, who treat them like simple human beings, so they grow up happy and contented and reasonably unworried. Some people must have decent parents, but I'll be damned if I can see who they are. Or how they did it. All I know is that sometimes I think I'd be a hell of a lot better off if Dad had died when I left for Philly. At least I wouldn't have had to live all these years with a real father in New York and an even worse one in my head.

The car turns into Belmont Avenue, and slows before the house. Carl glances at the upstairs window, and sees that the Venetian blinds are still three-quarters open. Damn dream, he thinks, started everything.

He slips the key out of the ignition, opens the door, climbs out, stretches. The cold pulls at his cramped muscles, burns along the overheated flesh of his neck. David still sits curved against the seat-back, his feet propped against the floorboard.

"Come on," Carl says. "You look too tired, your mother'll be sure you should have stayed home and rested."

David opens the door and gets out, waits while Carl locks his side and then moves around the car to lock David's door.

"I'll kill all my yawns," David says. "I'll stay wide awake through dinner."

Carl grins and pats David's backside.

"Home sweet home."

They turn to go up the steps.

Twenty

The new box of tea stood on the shelf, the crackers were tucked away into the stove. The old man sat on his bed, head cradled in his hands stretched from joined palms at his chin to fingers along the worn sides of his face, and stared out the window. A cold early evening's winter dark obscured whatever gull might have swooped lazily down the street, sailing through the tiny channel the twin rows of buildings granted with graceful humble flap of white-lined wing; obscured whatever pigeons massed, roosting, on the telephone wire that traced its black length of cable above the street. The old man sat on his bed and stared out his window into the blackness of the early evening, at the window across the street where light shone through the rips in the green shade, pulled all the way down to veil whatever life the woman with the red bandanna and her acrobatic cat had managed to build for themselves.

Through the thin glass the old man heard the flap of wings and soft cries of birds settling into the eaves and crannies of neighboring roofs, and thought again of the pigeon's dull red eye, staring up at him an instant before his foot sliced its neck. I didn't mean to. It was so fast, it happened in a second. It's such a little thing, a bird's life. One kick, and it's gone.

So, he thought. And for a person, it's so different? Walk across a street just once without looking, and where are you? The morgue! One day on Canal Street the old man had come out of a newspaper shop and seen an aged colored man weaving into the street. Stupid *schwartze*, he thought. Drunkard. He thinks that traffic'll look out for him. The colored man shook his head, apparently dazed at finding himself trapped in the middle of a teeming street; cars, cabs, and buses brushed past him. He ran. He swerved between the first two cars and for a second the old man thought he had a chance to reach the sidewalk. But a piercing squeal of brakes just failed to cover the colored man's wail as the side of a skidding cab sliced into him. The old man turned away as the body arced into the air. Other screams echoed in his ear, and then the thud of something soft and heavy splatting against concrete. The old man did not turn. Stupid *schwartze*, he thought, serves him right for getting so drunk.

And even not drunk, it still happens. Like that. Like snapping a finger, or lighting a candle, your life can end.

The old man heard the soft cooing of the nesting birds again. I wish I hadn't killed that pigeon. Once, Shmuel Yaakov had told him a story, as they sat on a bluff high above the Dnieper, the sheep grazing peacefully in an almost bare meadow behind them. There was a boy, Shmuel Yaakov said, streaking the corner of his nose with the dirt from his huge black mittens as he rubbed his face, there was a boy who lived all alone on a farm. Oh, he had parents, but they didn't pay much attention to him, because they had to run the farm, and he had no brothers or sisters or little cousins or friends to run and play with. So the boy made friends with all the animals, especially the cat and the dog. And one day, the cat, who was old and fat and felt she never got enough to eat, said to the boy, Why not take your slingshot and try to shoot down some birds? It would be great fun. The boy stroked the cat's thick fur and thought. No, he said, I like the birds. Why should I shoot them down? Because, the cat answered, they are a nuisance to your father, always eating his seed, they are a nuisance to your mother, always yammering and making noise, and they are a nuisance to you, always nesting in trees which must be cut down. The boy thought for a bit, and had to admit to himself that the cat spoke true.

Still, he said, it is not enough of a reason to take my slingshot and shoot down the birds. But the cat was persistent, for in her mind was a wonderful picture of dozens of birds, tumbled from their nests by a well-aimed stone, lying stunned on the ground, begging to be devoured. So she purred and coaxed and pleaded, and finally the boy agreed. At first it was hard. The birds looked so gay and peaceful, preening on their branches and prattling to each other, that he could not bring himself to aim his stone at them. Then you are not very brave, the cat sneered. What kind of a soldier will you make, if you cannot even bring yourself to down a few birds? So the boy fired his stone, and the birds scattered. Except for the one that plummeted downward through leaves and branches, to land with a thud at the base of the tree. The cat was on it in a flash. Excellent, she said, through a mouth stuffed with flesh, feathers and blood. You are indeed an excellent shot. The boy stared at the cat gorging herself on the bird he had shot, and his heart was inflamed with anger. Quickly he found three more stones in his pocket and set off deeper into the woods, and every time he fired another bird dropped through the air. Each day the boy and the cat went out to hunt in the woods, and each day the cat returned with the blood of a bird on her mouth. The birds tried to set up a warning system against the boy and the cat, but the poor pigeons could never fly high enough to escape the boy's slingshot, and as the days passed, the stones sent more and more pigeons tumbling to the ground. The birds held a great council, and sent a swallow to beg the dog to help. The dog could only shake his head. I can do nothing, he said. The cat was never my friend, and the boy will no longer listen to me. There is only hatred in his heart. The swallow returned to the council, and the birds made their decision. The next day, when the boy and the cat went out into the woods, no calls echoed through the branches, no birds graced the trees. The boy and the cat pushed deeper into the forest, until the cat lifted her head. Listen, she purred, I hear birds calling. The boy stopped, held his breath, and listened. Very faintly, from far, far away, he heard the soft cooing of many pigeons. The boy and cat stared at each other, and each felt the beginnings of a strange uneasiness that was almost fear. Perhaps we should turn back, the cat thought, and then felt the empty place in her stomach where a bird would not sit that night. Perhaps we should turn back, the boy thought, and then felt the hard weight of the stones in his pocket, and the hatred in his heart. So they plunged on, and followed the sound of the cooing until they burst into a clearing which was almost a perfect circle. And in the middle was one small, stunted tree, on which sat more pigeons than the cat and the boy had ever seen, all cooing. The cat and the boy looked at each other, unable to believe their eyes, and slowly began to creep toward the tree. The boy's slingshot was out, and a round smooth stone was curled into the rubber launcher, in case the pigeons should take alarm and rise into the air. But the pigeons sat, as if they had never seen boy or cat before, as if they lived in the primeval garden and had never been warned that everything which does not fly is dangerous and must be flown from. The boy and the cat were almost underneath the tree when suddenly there was a long piercing cry, the cry not of a pigeon but of a hawk, a hunting hawk which has sighted its prey and circles with weighted wings before it folds them to drop like an arrow from the sky. The air was full of wings, so many that the sky was almost black, and the boy and the cat watched as bird after bird wheeled down from the sky and ringed themselves around the tree. There were birds the boy and the cat had only seen from great distances in the sky, huge gnarled eagles with twisted beaks and great wings that stretched longer than a man's outstretched arms, killer hawks with beaks like knives and claws that had carried off lambs and pigs. The circle grew thicker around the boy and the cat, until there was only a small cleared space at the base of the tree. Suddenly there was silence, a deadly brooding silence, and the boy and the cat stared, seeing not an inch of clear space to run through, to escape into the woods, seeing only the beaks and claws of the huge birds that blocked their paths. Then the same piercing cry split the air, and the cat whined a piteous meow. There was a stirring of thousands of feathers, short sharp pigeon cries that merged into one angry snarl, and like a swarm of bees the pigeons left the tree and descended on the boy and the cat. The cat curled herself up into a ball and shrieked and wailed until one of the pigeons' beaks finally pierced her brain. The boy fought, silently flailing his fists and kicking with his feet, and many pigeons tumbled to the ground. Once the boy made a break and almost got free, but two eagles swooped for the fleshy parts of his legs, and a huge hawk dug its claws into his hair and beat the air with its wings until the boy's feet slipped out from under him, and he fell to the ground. The pigeons closed in, and after a time all cries and movement stopped. The pigeons rose and circled back to the tree. There was a fresh stirring of wings and a dozen gray vultures swooped over the body. A swallow was sent back to tell the dog, who led his master and mistress to the clearing and the one lone tree. Nothing whatsoever was left of the cat, but beside the tree the mother and father found a slingshot and seven smooth stones.

I shuddered, the old man thought, when Shmuel Yaakov finished the story and we stared out at the clouds rolling across the bluffs upriver, and I shuddered again just now, thinking about it. But I only killed one pigeon, and I didn't do it on purpose. So perhaps I will be safe from the birds. But the others, will I be safe from them? Will they go away when I tell them to? He pushed himself off his bed and began his dinner, wondering if he would be able to get through one meal without Smetyanov and Shmuel Yaakov and Naomi.

The soup bowl and the dinner plate were washed and put away. The old man sat over his steaming glass of tea, scraping the sides with his teaspoon. No one had disturbed his meal. The light that shone through the torn shade of the window across the street had flicked out and then come on again; the wind had howled past the windows and sent sharp cold gusts of air through the cracks in the window frames into the room, but Naomi's laughter had not come dancing down the hall, Shmuel Yaakov's stubby figure had not stood by his table. The old man stirred his tea and thought again of Zitomer, stirring another glass of tea in the front room of his store. But he isn't alone, in that small front room. He sits on a rickety chair and stares down at a chessboard, maybe, and Dawidowsky on the other side scratches his head and rubs his hand along his trousers before he moves one of the pieces. Or maybe he is having an argument with the man with the twisted back, about Israel, or all the other hundred and one things I didn't understand. Or maybe he just sits and watches all of them spending their hours in his store, and he thinks to himself, it's a little thing I started, but it's better than being alone. Because he doesn't have to worry about being alone any more, the old man thought. He doesn't have to come back to his room and sit in fear that ghosts out of his head will come back to spend the night with him.

The old man shifted in his chair, so that he could see out the window. The light was on behind the drawn green shade in the window across the street, and bars and crescents of golden light poked through the rips and tears in the shade. I could have gone to Zitomer's, the old man thought. Zitomer asked me to come, and I could have gone. Maybe it wouldn't have mattered much, that I didn't understand what they were talking about. I could have gone and sat on one of the chairs, and warmed my hands around a glass of tea. And listened. Maybe even a game of checkers I could have played. Once I was good at checkers.

But now it's too late. After this morning, it's too late. I wouldn't blame Zitomer if he never talked to me again. Liar, I called him. Liar. In front of Rabbi Davis, I called him a liar.

The old man bent his head until it almost touched the table, and folded his hands on the back of his neck. I was so afraid, he thought. As soon as Zitomer started to talk, I was so afraid. And yet, afterwards, in the afternoon, when I talked to Rabbi Davis in the synagogue, it didn't matter to me, that he knew. I didn't care that he knew what I was so afraid that Zitomer would tell him. Maybe, the old man thought, maybe I didn't care because Rabbi Davis didn't care. He didn't care at all. To him it made no difference. All of us have mistakes that worry us, he said. Mistakes! Can you call giving a girl a child and then running away a mistake, I said. Can you call stealing a set of silver from the man who pays your passage to America a mistake? So he shrugs his shoulders, the rabbi. You were younger then, he says. You feel different about it, now. You wouldn't do it now, would you? I didn't answer. What could I say? Would you, he says again. I shake my head. Of course, he says. The very fact that you're still worried about it shows that you're penitent, that you're sorry.

So what could I say? Could I say to him, Rabbi, the reason I'm worried about those mistakes, like you call them, is because all the people that I made the mistakes against come and spend my evenings and my nights with me? Could I say to him, Rabbi,

I forgot all about Marfa until she walked into my room one night while I was eating my soup? Penitent! Who was penitent? I couldn't even remember what Smetyanov looked like until I saw him sitting on my radiator cover!

You're genuinely sorry for all those mistakes, Rabbi Davis says. Stop worrying about them. God is merciful. God forgives. You've done the best you could, most of the time. All of us have. So stop worrying about the mistakes you made. Everybody makes mistakes.

Mistakes! What could I tell him? Could I tell him that before I came to synagogue for afternoon services, I made another one of my mistakes at the supermarket? That all the time I was talking to him, the crackers and the tea were rattling and whispering inside my coat? Why, the old man thought, why did I have to take that box of crackers?

"Because you're a thief. Because you're a thief, and you always were a thief."

The old man closed his eyes and rested his head against the cold enamel surface of the table. "No. Go away. Go away. I can't talk to you again, ever."

"Certainly," Smetyanov said. "I'll go away. Immediately. Didn't I always do everything you wanted? When you first showed up at my farm, your boots dangling around your ankles, and your coat so covered with mud I thought you were the manure collector, didn't I let you talk me into hiring you, even though I knew the farm needed only one hand? And when you wanted to get away from Marfa's father and Shmuel Yaakov before Marfa gave birth to your child, didn't I finally agree to pay your passage? Didn't I even refuse to believe that you stole the silver set, until my cousin found it in a pawn shop over on Delancey Street, and the owner described you so perfectly I couldn't doubt it any more?"

"A mistake," the old man mumbled. "A mistake. Everybody makes mistakes."

"Oh, yes," Shmuel Yaakov laughed. "Everybody makes mistakes, all of us understand about mistakes. When Marfa's father asked you if you had given her the child, and you swore that you had never touched her, that it was me who slept with her in the hayloft, that was a mistake, was it?"

"And when you said you loved me, that night in the sweet

hay, that was a slip of the tongue?" Marfa whispered. "That was a mistake?"

"Me, you never made that mistake with. Me, you never told you loved," Naomi laughed. "But tell us, go ahead. Tell us what Rabbi Davis said, but make it sound like you believe it. Tell us that you think the tea and crackers got into your coat by mistake. Tell us that all those parcels from Acme Dress got into your coat by mistake."

The old man raised his head. Naomi perched on the radiator cover, and ringed around the table sat Smetyanov, Shmuel Yaakov, and Marfa.

"What do you want?" the old man said. "What do you want from me? How many nights are you going to do this to me? Why don't you leave me alone?"

"But we're company," Naomi said. "You're ungrateful. You used to bring us here every night, and talk to us for hours. You remember, don't you? You used to say to yourself that there couldn't be any harm in bringing back the dead to fill up an empty evening."

"That was before—before—" The old man stopped.

"Before what?" Smetyanov chuckled. "Before what?"

"Yes, before what?" Naomi shouted.

"Shut up!" The old man's scream echoed off the walls and the one window. He pushed up from his chair and stumbled toward the bed. His slipper caught on a square of torn linoleum and slid off his foot, so he hobbled, on one slippered foot, to the bed. A splinter from one of the floorboards sliced through the thin layer of his sock into a calloused corner of his big toe, drawing only a little blood. He reached the bed and sank down onto it, wrapped the blankets around him, and buried his head beneath the pillow.

"It's no good. You can't run away from us."

"Be quiet," the old man begged. "Be quiet. God is merciful."

"God is merciful," Shmuel Yaakov parroted. "God is merciful. But how merciful will God be to someone who has never shown any mercy?"

"Mercy?" Naomi shouted. "Mercy? Never mind mercy, simple kindness would be enough! All the years I lived with you, did you touch me the way a man touches a woman? Did you ever talk to me the way a man should talk with the woman who shares his life? I was just a thing that brought you a dowry and a job, a thing that kept your house and cooked your meals."

"I cared for you. I cared for you."

"Yes, you cared for me. Did you ever tell me? Did you ever show me? You didn't even go with me to the hospital, the night Carl was born!"

Carl. The money was still in his pocket. The old man squirmed onto his side and groped inside his good jacket pocket until he found the tight roll of Carl's three ten-dollar bills. He eased them out of his pocket and spread them open against the pillow.

"And what will you say," Marfa whispered, "to the God that is merciful, about Carl? What will you say about the way you've treated Carl? What will you say?"

The old man twisted himself on the bed and buried his face back into the softness of the pillow. "Carl had it coming to him," he whispered. "Everything I did to Carl serves him right. He left me. He's not even a Jew. For Carl, I got nothing to say. Serves him right."

"Merciful?" Smetyanov mocked. "Listen to what God is supposed to be merciful to."

Breathe deeply, the old man thought. Breathe deeply, and keep your eyes tightly closed, and think of nothing. Then they will go away. Breathe deeply.

"Merciful," Naomi chanted to the rise and fall of his breathing. "Merciful."

"Merciful," Shmuel Yaakov added. "Merciful."

"God is merciful," the old man mumbled. "Oh God, please, forgive me. Oh please, God, forgive me!"

"Merciful, merciful!" they shouted, and the old man heard the thud of their feet against the floorboards, and felt the bed shake as they danced across the room. He dug his face still deeper into the pillow, and felt the first few wet tears against his cheeks. He folded his hands over his ears, but still he heard the chorus of their voices, and the bed tossed and shook to their dancing.

"Oh God, stop them, stop them!" His nose was choked with his tears and the clamminess of the pillow. He raised his chin. Their voices shrieked into his ears. He clapped his hands tighter against his ears, until the voices pierced like a thousand bird cries. The air was heavy with the smell of blood and the flap of wings, and the dull red eye of the pigeon gleamed in the black space behind the old man's eyes.

"No! I didn't mean to kill the pigeon. I only touched it. I didn't mean it."

The crackers laughed and danced in the oven. The wind snapped against the windowpanes. Across the street, the cat of the woman with the red bandanna snarled and spat at the birds circling the old man's bed. Above the bird cries, the old man heard their endless chanting.

"Stop it! Stop it, stop it, stop it!"

His face was buried in his hands and the pillow was wet from his weeping when the door creaked open. A cold whoosh of air, then firm hands on his shoulders.

"Quiet, quiet now," Feinstein said. "From all the way downstairs I heard you. I couldn't believe my ears, that an old man like you could have so much breath left. Such screams! My God, I couldn't believe my ears."

The old man opened his eyes. The room was empty. There was only a buzzing in his ears, and the mucus from his blocked nose in his throat. He rolled onto his back and stared up at Feinstein. Underneath his head, he felt the crackling of Carl's three ten-dollar bills, and he reached a hand behind his neck and crumpled them into his pocket. Gradually his tears slowed, and he could stop gasping for breath. Feinstein handed him a handkerchief, but he pushed it away and wiped his face on the sleeve of his jacket.

"Thank you," he whispered to Feinstein as his face touched the sleeve of his jacket. "Thank you for coming."

But he whispered so softly into the sleeve of his jacket that Feinstein did not hear.

Twenty-one

The tea steam rose to wreath the old man's face. Feinstein watched the old man's chin and then his nose waver and finally curve behind the fragile column of steam that trailed up toward the ceiling. He watched the old man's face until the chin and the nose reformed as the cold evening air of the room condensed the steam. He followed the path of the old man's stare and saw that the old man's eyes were focused on some pinpoint far out the window in the nighttime sky.

Maybe he's mad, Feinstein thought. Maybe he's off in the head. When you're old, you shouldn't live alone. I said it before and I'll say it again. When you're old, you shouldn't live alone. He stays all day in this little box of a room, and twice a day he pushes himself down the stairs to the synagogue. What does he have, he should keep himself from going crazy? Books he has? Friends, maybe? Even the paper he doesn't read! And when somebody does come to see him, what happens? Is he happy? Does he care? If I treated my Irving the way he treats his son, it would serve me right if Irving never came to see me.

How much luck I have, to have a son like Irving. God knows, I wasn't so bad a father. But still. To have a son like Irving. And a grandson like my Brucie.

"Listen," Feinstein said, and edged his chair closer to the table. "Did I tell you about my grandson Brucie?"

The old man made a small motion with his right hand, which rested palm down on the enamel tabletop. His eyes were still focused far outside the room.

"Yes, I told you," Feinstein nodded. "I told you about him too many times. Maybe it's true, like Irving says, I'm too proud for a grandfather. Irving says that my Molly told him I talk about Brucie all the time. So what, I said. It's a sin for a grandfather to talk about his grandchild a little? Especially when he's got a grandchild like Brucie?"

Feinstein licked his lips and stared at the old man, and waited. But the old man was staring out the window. So, Feinstein thought. I should save my breath. Why I even waste time coming up those stairs, God only knows. Maybe you're not crazy, but one thing I know. Wherever you are right now, it's not in this room. I could be talking in Chinese, for all you care. I should save my breath. You never listen to me, anyway. Even when you come downstairs for a glass of tea, you never listen to me.

"But," Feinstein said, "because I started the story, I'll finish it. Even if you're not listening, I'll finish it. I was telling you, Irving told me this new story about Brucie. One afternoon, Irving tells me, Brucie comes in from a ball game, from playing ball with the other boys on the street. He walks in the front door, like a little *mensch* he walks in, and he starts up the stairs. Irving is in the front room, and he hears Brucie start up the stairs. So he shouts out, 'Brucie? Where're you going?'

"He hears Brucie stop on the stairs. 'To take a piss,' Brucie shouts back."

Feinstein rubs his right hand back and forth across the sleeve of his left arm and chuckles.

"To take a piss. Imagine, eight years old. To take a piss. So naturally, Irving is a little worried. Not shocked, understand, because Irving isn't that kind of father, he should get shocked. He's not old-fashioned, my Irving; he understands things. Dad, he always says to me, one of the things I was always glad about was that you weren't old-fashioned. And I'm not going to be old-fashioned, either. So he's only a little worried by what Brucie says. So he thinks about it, and he waits till Brucie comes downstairs before he calls him in. After all, Irving thinks to himself, he's heard it on the streets. He doesn't see anything wrong in it. Anybody could pick it up off the streets. There's no harm in it. So he calls Brucie in, and he explains very carefully that if Brucie wants to be a polite and well-mannered little boy, the kind of little boy everybody likes, it's better to say going to the bathroom. He explains it a few times, until Brucie says that he understands."

Feinstein raised his tea glass, and sipped. It was still hot, but soon it would be lukewarm. The old man's tea glass still sat, full, on the enamel-topped table. Feinstein set his own glass down on the table and wiped his mouth with a corner of his handkerchief.

"So a few days later, Irving is entertaining some friends. Some of his business friends, partners and executives and all. Brucie is playing with his trains in the breakfast room, but after a while he gets up and walks through the sitting room toward the stairs. Now Irving knows where he's going, but he wants to see if Brucie remembers. So he says, 'Brucie, where're you going?' Brucie stops and turns around and stares at Irving. 'Upstairs, Daddy,' he says. 'To the bathroom. To take a piss.'"

Feinstein clapped his right hand on to his knee and cackled, the breath hissing through his false teeth. He laughed until his stomach began to strain under his belt, and then he subsided.

"Brucie's always pulling things like that," he choked out. "A real roughneck, he is. A real American boy! The other day, Irving tells me, Brucie came in from the lot—there's an empty lot on the corner that all the boys play in—Brucie came in from the lot all covered in white paint. White paint!"

Feinstein stopped. The old man was nodding his head. Sitting slumped in the chair, with his eyes still focused out the window, the old man was nodding his head.

"It was a giant," Feinstein probed, "a giant bigger than Goliath. With twenty arms and flowerpots for legs. He lives in the lot and he paints all the little boys white. All the little Jewish boys. He's a *goyishe* giant."

The old man kept nodding.

"With purple teeth. And a tongue made out of thousands of *mezuzahs*, all wired together. Instead of hair under his arms, he grows spinach, and when he catches little *goyishe* boys he makes them eat the spinach, so they grow up to be *goyishe* giants with twenty arms and flowerpots for legs."

The old man nodded.

It's no use, Feinstein thought. I could tell you lies so big the moon would collapse into the room, you still wouldn't hear. What can I do with you? To a home somebody should take you, you're so crazy. At least a doctor you should see. But even if I paid for you, would you go to one? Would you let one come here? Doctors can't help me, you're always screaming. I should call Carl, maybe, tell him how crazy you are. In case he doesn't know already. But do I know where to call him? If I asked you, would you give me the number?

Feinstein shook his head and reached again for the tea glass. It's no use, he thought. Nobody can do anything for you. God knows why I get myself so upset in the first place. It doesn't do me any good, running up four flights of stairs. Next time I'll let you scream. Maybe it won't help you, but it'll keep me from getting so upset my stomach's rotten for hours. For hours I'll have trouble, all because of you.

The old man reached into his pocket. Feinstein watched. The old man brought a roll of bills out of his pocket and spread them on the enamel-topped table. Three tens, Feinstein saw, as the old man spread them out.

"So," Feinstein said. "Congratulations, you're rich. You robbed a bank, maybe?"

The old man shook his head. "Carl. Carl gave them to me. This afternoon."

"So, good. I told you it wasn't your money he was after. Thirty dollars isn't chicken feed, you know. It's a lot of money for Carl."

"He should have kept it. He should have kept it and never given it to me."

Not again, Feinstein thought. Once a day is enough, I'm not going to fight with you again. He curled his fingers around the tea glass and scraped its bottom against the enamel of the tabletop.

"He should have kept it."

Feinstein stared into the glass and saw how the lighter-colored water had begun to float to the top, leaving the darker, thicker tea to settle at the bottom. All of the sugar sinks to the bottom, too, Feinstein thought. And if there was lemon to put in, the lemon would be at the bottom, too.

"He should have kept it."

Certainly, Feinstein thought as he twisted the tea glass and watched the water swirl, he should have kept it. He should have kept it, and you should have moved in with somebody else, and I should have rented my top floor to an old shoemaker who plays chess, and all of us would have been happy.

"So what should I do with the money?"

The money? Carl's money that he should have kept, instead of giving it to you? Oh, burn it. Throw it away. Throw it into the gutter. No, somebody might pick it up. That would be a shame. Somebody getting some good out of Carl's thirty dollars. Throw it in the sewer. Or even better, give it to some dog and watch the dog tear it up. Stupid dog, tearing up money. Maybe its owner will whip it when it trots home with torn pieces of ten-dollar bills in its mouth.

"I asked Rabbi Davis," the old man said, "what I should do with the money. He said I should keep it. I told him I didn't want it, I didn't want to touch it. I told him Carl didn't have a right to give me money. He said Carl was my son, and sons have a right to give money to their fathers. I said Carl stopped being my son when he ran away from me. He said if I felt that way, I should give the money to charity. I said was it right, to give dirty money to charity? He said the money wasn't dirty. I said it was dirty to me. He said if I give the money to charity, it won't be dirty to them. So I think," the old man said, pushing himself out of his chair, "that I will go and see Zitomer."

Feinstein set his tea glass down on the table with a bang.

"Listen. I heard everything you said. I understand about the money, I understand what Rabbi Davis said. But what does anything have to do with Zitomer? What's Zitomer, all of a sudden?"

"Nothing. I just feel like going to see Zitomer."

"Now?"

The old man nodded.

"It's after ten o'clock. On a Sunday night. And it's not summer outside, the streets are cold. When the wind blows, it blows right through you. It takes over a half-hour to get to Zitomer's. And another half-hour to get back. Or you maybe taking a taxi?"

"You don't have to give me weather reports. I went to synagogue at six o'clock this morning, not you. I go out more in one day than you do in a week."

"You got a spyglass, you can sit on your bed up here and see how many times a week I go out? And you're a hero, because you go to synagogue twice a day? Listen, maybe I sit downstairs in my apartment twenty-four hours a day, seven days a week. I don't have fits. I don't scream loud enough to bring the house down. I don't make my neighbors come running up four flights of stairs to see what's wrong with me."

"You didn't have to come," the old man said. "I didn't ask you. Nobody asked you. Next time, stay downstairs."

"Next time I will," Feinstein said. The old man rolled the three ten-dollar bills into his pocket and turned his jacket collar up against his neck. He shuffled to the door, then looked back at Feinstein. Feinstein stared down at his tea glass. The old man opened the door, stepped out into the hallway, and closed the door.

Feinstein listened to the slow footsteps descend the stair. God, he thought, thank God I don't have to worry about growing old the way he did. Thank God, at least I'm normal. The old man's almost full tea glass sat on the enamel-topped table. A millionaire he is, Feinstein thought, with Carl's thirty dollars, he can afford to leave a whole glass of tea standing. A millionaire, and a crazy old man. He reached across the table for the tea glass. The sides were still warm. So, he thought, raised the tea glass to his lips, and drank. What's the use in wasting good tea?

Twenty-two

The stairs were dark. The old man stumbled onto the last landing and set his shoulder against the door. He felt the wind against the stubble of his cheeks as he leaned against the door and caught his breath. A trembling started in his fingers resting on the doorknob, and traveled up his arms. He stretched his fingers limply against the knob and shivered the trembling to a narrow cold ridge between his shoulders. Still against the door, he closed his eyes and let his face rest against the wood.

The wind moaned through an inch thickness of rough wood. The old man swayed, dimly sensed his feet moving to prop himself more firmly against the door. He stumbled backward on the steps and sat, dizziness swimming upward from the pit of his stomach. The landing was dark, no light crept in from underneath the door. The old man closed his eyes again, and rested his head in his hands.

I shouldn't go, the old man thought. I shouldn't go. I'm tired. And it's a long way. And it's cold. And it's late. I needed Feinstein to tell me that, like I didn't know already.

"But if you don't get up," Smetyanov whispered, "Feinstein will come down the steps to his own apartment, and find you sitting here. And what will you say to him?"

The old man pushed himself to his feet and stumbled to the door. He set his shoulders against it, turned the knob, and forced himself into the street. The wind whipped against him, curling the upturned collar of his jacket. The old man plunged his hands deep into his pockets, hunched his shoulders more tightly into himself, and started off for Zitomer's.

"A *mishiginer* you are," Naomi said. "You're not a chicken any more; it's too cold at night to be taking trips."

"It's not a trip. And besides, it's my business. Leave me alone."

"Hoo-hoo. Listen to him. It's my business, he says. So let us hear then, what kind of business you got with Zitomer to make you *shlep* all the way down to see him at ten o'clock on a Sunday night?"

I shouldn't listen to them. I shouldn't answer them. Just shut my ears and try not to hear them. And if I hear them, pretend I didn't hear them.

He turned the corner. From the river, a dredger sent up its long, mournful wail. The swish and throb of overhead traffic on the FDR Drive carried down to him as he shuffled along the block, and he began to count, to himself, the haloed crescents of street-lamp light as he stepped into their pools and then out again.

One, he thought. Then how many steps until the next? How should I count steps; should I count every step or every other step? Every step is too much trouble; better every other step. So. Start again. One for the street lamp. Then one, two, three, four. The old man counted to sixteen before he came to another puddle of street-lamp light. Then he counted seventeen between that lamp and the next. Funny, the old man thought, maybe I missed a count. He managed to reach twelve before he came to Second Avenue, where there was a street lamp on the corner which the old man didn't count. He glanced up and down the Avenue. The street lamps stretched in a long, graceful arc of dotting lights.

It's a nice night, the old man thought. Peaceful. He started across. A few blocks away he saw the one yellow eye of a street sweeper probing toward the corner. A truck pounded into the Avenue from a side street, and the old man watched the truck's headlights pick him up. The truck shifted gears, picked up speed, ground past, and the old man continued across the street.

I forgot how many numbers I was up to at the corner. But I can start from here. One, he counted. Two, three, four. The street narrowed as it ran west from Second Avenue, and the old man moved closer to the darker mass of the building walls. A light flickered off in a window above his head. A car door slammed shut. Far ahead of him, a short sharp skit-skat of heels sounded on the pavement. It's too cold, the old man thought. It's too cold to be walking. The wind reached up the legs of his loose trousers to chill the flabby flesh of his thighs. But I'll be there soon. Not too many more blocks, and I'll be at Zitomer's.

"But why?" Naomi whispered. "I don't understand. Why Zitomer's? You think Zitomer's already forgotten what you called him, this morning in the rabbi's office?"

"I don't think he's forgotten. How could he forget?" the old man mumbled. "It's every day somebody calls him a liar in front of his own rabbi? I don't think he's forgotten. But at least, I can tell him I'm sorry. At least I can do that much. Maybe it's true, that I never told anybody I was sorry before, but at least I can tell Zitomer I'm sorry."

Another light, the old man thought. That makes four. But here I turn the corner again. A dog padded into an alley next to a store, and the old man watched the light flicking off his tail. The dog disappeared into the alley, and the old man shuffled around the corner.

"I still don't understand. What good will it do, to tell Zitomer that you're sorry? Zitomer doesn't hold it against you, anyway." Naomi chuckled. "Listen, Zitomer is the one man who has a good idea how rotten you are. Zitomer wasn't surprised when you called him a liar. He's the one man who probably expected it."

"I can still tell him I'm sorry," the old man mumbled. Five, six, seven, eight. "I can still tell him I'm sorry." Eleven, twelve, thirteen, fourteen, fifteen. Fifteen this time. Maybe they don't space out their street lights very good?

"So what? I keep asking you, so what? And what kind of an

answer do you give me? No answer at all! After sixty years of lying and cheating and stealing, all of a sudden you think you're doing something big, by going to Zitomer and telling him you're sorry? He doesn't need you. He doesn't need you to tell him you're sorry. He doesn't have any worries about what happens to his nights."

"Be quiet. Be quiet and go away. It's not my room, now, you got no right bothering me on the streets. So go away. It's a nice night, I can see the moon over that factory roof, and if I listen, I can hear the trucks all the way over on West Street, loading up before they start their deliveries. So be quiet. Let me enjoy the night. How often do I go out for a walk, this late at night?"

"As often as you've told somebody you're sorry for something you've done. Never. So listen," Shmuel Yaakov said, "why don't you stop pretending about Zitomer's? You don't have any reason to go to Zitomer's. Why are you going? This fairy tale about saying you're sorry is very nice, but since when have you cared about being sorry?"

"I'm starting now. I'm turning over a new leaf."

"Huh, ho! A new leaf, yet. At sixty-eight, he's turning over a new leaf. Why not a set of New Year's resolutions, like the *goyim?* Honesty is the best policy. I will never tell a lie. How many cherry trees you chopped down this year?"

The old man stopped underneath a street lamp.

"Listen. I told you to go away. I told you once. I'm telling you again. Go away. Don't bother me. I'm going to Zitomer's."

One, the old man counted to himself, stepping a little more quickly out of the pool of street lamp light and down the street. Two, three, four. A cat crawled along the top of a fence across the street, then curled and sprang at the top of a garbage can. The lid was loose, and as the cat hit the lid, it shifted and slithered off the can to the ground. The cat yowled and screeched as she scrambled up from beneath the lid.

"Aiii!" the old man gasped. Shivers coursed up his arms again, and his back trembled, until he could force the quivering into a tight line that ran between his shoulder blades.

"It's only a cat. What's a cat to be afraid of?"

"I'm not afraid," the old man said. "Go away."

"Unhospitable," Smetyanov mourned. "Unhospitable. Drags us out on a cold night, then tells us to go away."

"I didn't ask you to come. If you're cold, it's your own fault. Go away."

"And for such a fool's errand, to walk halfway across town to tell Zitomer that he's sorry. As if anybody cares whether he's sorry or not."

"Go away!" the old man screamed. "Go away, go away, go away!"

A light snapped on in a window above his head. A shade rolled upward. Somebody struggled with a window and then forced it open.

"What's going on down there? What's going on? You don't go away, I'll call the police! You hear me? The police! I'm not standing for any more of you messing around this block!"

The old man stood trembling in the building's shadow, and waited for the window to close, the shade to lower, the light to switch off. Finally he edged away from the wall and tried to tiptoe down the block. But his body shook so badly he had to move back to the wall and support himself against the houses as he moved along. He moved carefully past a ground-floor window, bracing himself against the wall, and collided with the low step of the house next door. His foot swung up from the step and sent a milk bottle rolling off the step to crash and splinter against the sidewalk. He forced himself over the step and, half stumbling, half running, he hurried down the street. He reached the corner with shouts and threats and curses ringing in his ears, and sank down to rest on a low stoop beneath another street lamp.

"Oh, God," he sighed. His chest was heaving, and his foot ached where it had jammed against the step. "Oh, God." A bitter rasping fluid formed in his throat, and he hawked until a globule of spittle formed at the back of his tongue. He spat. The trailing end of the spittle dragged down to rest on the front of his jacket. The old man raised his arm to wipe it off, then let it fall. It's not much farther, he thought. It's not much farther, to Zitomer's.

He pushed himself to his feet and stumbled through the last few blocks. "Oh, God," he kept whispering. "Oh, God, please."

"Please, what?" Smetyanov asked once, but the old man didn't answer. He kept whispering, "Oh, God, please," until he rounded the last corner and saw the light from Zitomer's store window.

Then he's up, the old man thought. But what's he doing in the front at this hour? The old man shuffled closer to the window. Zitomer had piled the chairs and tables in one corner and was unfolding and stacking the shelves that he had piled against the wall. The old man stared for a few moments, as Zitomer bent to grasp a shelf, slip the hinges off, and then separate the two boards. Finally the old man rapped at the window. Zitomer looked up, nodded, wiped his hands on his trousers, and walked to the door.

He slipped the latch and opened the door. "So it's you. Come in, come in. How do you feel, after this morning?"

"Better. That's what I came to talk to you about."

"So come in. Here, I'll take one of the chairs off, so you can sit. You should pardon how this place looks. All night I'll be up, anyway, trying to clear it out."

The old man sat on the chair that Zitomer had reached down and placed for him, and Zitomer returned to the pile of shelves.

"Why are you doing all this? What's happened?"

"Hah. A lot. Too much is happening, that's the trouble. But you were there this morning, weren't you? You heard what Rabbi Davis told me, that the members would do something if I didn't stay away. Well, it was nice of him to warn me, but it was just a little too late. Kopplewitz came to see me this afternoon. He's standing at the door, one foot in, one foot out. Come in, Kopplewitz, I say. The store won't bite you. No, no, he says. I can stand here and tell you what I've come for. Then he clears his throat, like he's about to make a speech. Zitomer, he says to me, maybe I shouldn't have come, maybe I'm wrong, I don't know. But I'll tell you, Zitomer. Although I don't believe what you're telling the members, that I don't believe at all. But you, Zitomer, you I believe, you're an honest man. And an honest man shouldn't go to jail."

"Jail?" the old man said.

Zitomer slapped down at a stubborn hinge. "That's what I said. Jail, Kopplewitz, I said. Kopplewitz nodded. Jail. All the rest of them, Zitomer, Horowitz and Kaplan and the rest. They hate you, Zitomer. I heard Kaplan swear that if you ever set foot in his store again, he'd have you arrested. Kopplewitz, I say, Kaplan's already said that to me. You didn't come here to tell me how Kaplan feels? Kopplewitz shakes his head. Zitomer, he says, Kaplan called a meeting. All the members came. I came too, he says. And they got a plan. Tomorrow morning, Zitomer, Kaplan is going to the police station, and Horowitz is calling up the fire inspector. Kaplan is going to tell the police that you're running a club on a commercial premises, that you're serving refreshments without a restaurant license, and that you've been having meetings of Communists and subversives. Horowitz is going to tell the fire inspector that you're running a fire hazard, that you've been packing twenty, thirty people into a little store front, that you don't have any extinguishers, that there's only one entrance and exit, that you've got piles of wood all over the place."

Zitomer straightened, set the separate planks of a long shelf on the pile of planking rimming the front window, then turned to look at the old man.

"So how do you like that? The police and the fire department on my neck. I just stood there and stared at Kopplewitz. Finally he says, so I thought I should tell you, Zitomer, and before I even have a chance to say thank you, he walks away. I came back into the store. What can I do, I thought to myself. What can I do? They will send me to jail. The rest of the afternoon, I couldn't think. I just sat, with my head in my hands. Finally, about seven, Dawidowsky comes in, and I tell him about it. Thank God for Dawidowsky. What a head he's got! Where I'd be right now without Dawidowsky, I wouldn't want to think. I tell Dawidowsky the whole thing. First of all, he says, you should stop worrying. It's not that bad. The police and the fire department have a lot to do; there's a chance they won't even pay any attention to a couple of cranky old Jews making a complaint. But even if they do, you don't have much to worry about. You don't need any kind of a license to have people come, and sit in your store. And as long as you're not selling food, you don't need a restaurant license. You're not selling any food, you're making tea for some old men. They don't buy it, you give it to them. So you got nothing to worry about.

The other thing is the Communists. With the way things are these days, the police may listen to that. But still, it's no crime. They may give you a little trouble, but they can't take you to jail for letting a Communist or two come in and have tea with you. No, they can't get you for that.

"So by now," Zitomer said, "I was beginning to feel better. But, Dawidowsky tells me, where they can get you is on the fire laws. I think there's a law about how many people can inhabit a room with only one exit. And I think, if more than so many people use a room, you have to keep an extinguisher in it. And one bad thing, Dawidowsky says, is all this wood. If an inspector comes around, if he wanted to, he could get you for maintaining a fire hazard.

"Can I go to jail for that, I ask him. He shakes his head. I don't think so, he says. But they can fine you. If they want to. They can fine you pretty heavy if they want to. So I start worrying all over again. Money I haven't got, to pay any fines. What am I going to do? Listen, Dawidowsky said. Take all the shelves, and all the display wood, and get them out of the store. Get them out by Monday morning, and clean up the floor good. So at least, if the inspector comes, it won't look so bad. It'll still be small, and you won't have an extinguisher; but at least there won't be any wood around, you won't be a fire hazard. And maybe he won't even come. Maybe, when he comes, all he'll tell you is to get an extinguisher.

"So," Zitomer said, "that's what I'm doing. Tomorrow morning, early, I'll call up somebody to come and take away the shelves. I'll wash down the floor, and wash the tables and chairs before I put them down again. I'll fix the place up as good as I can, and I'll pray that the inspector doesn't come. And if he comes, I'll pray that he won't fine me. And if he fines me, I'll pray that it won't be very much. And if it's too much, I'll pray, because then I don't know what I'll do."

The old man sat in his chair and watched Zitomer bend over his shelves. "I'm sorry," he said.

"Listen, it's not your fault. What's to be sorry about? They warned me, didn't they? All of them warned me. They told me if I didn't let them alone, I'd be sorry. So I didn't leave them alone, so now I'm sorry. But I'll tell you something," Zitomer said, and turned to point his screwdriver at the old man, "I feel worse for them than I do for me. I don't even feel sorry for them. I feel disgusted. I feel angry. I feel so bad about them, it scares me. Because before, I didn't feel bad toward them. I thought they were wrong, I thought they were stubborn, I thought they were afraid, even stupid. But I didn't feel bad toward them. Once in a while, maybe, I pitied them, but I didn't feel bad toward them. Well now," Zitomer said, waving the screwdriver, "now I feel bad toward them. Now I got all kinds of bad feelings inside me; disgust I feel, anger, even. It's their fault! Why did they have to go so far to get back at me? I'm not a Jew? Even a member of their own congregation I'm not? The police! The fire department! I feel bad toward them."

The old man sat in his chair and tried to imagine the way a fire inspector would look at the store, but he had never known a fire inspector, so finally he stopped trying. Then he wondered what he would have said if Horowitz and Kaplan had asked him to the meeting. And finally, he remembered what he had come to Zitomer's to do.

But he sat silent for a long time, until Zitomer rose from the pile of shelves and came and took a chair to sit on. "I'm tired. I been pulling shelves apart for two hours now. God knows how long it'll take me."

"Zitomer," the old man said, and would not look up. "Zitomer, I came about this morning. To say I was sorry."

The old man stared at the floor and scraped his shoe against a caked spot of gum or cloth between the boards. The room was very quiet.

"You don't have to say anything," Zitomer said. "You didn't have to come. There's nothing to be sorry for."

The old man shook his head. "I called you a liar. In front of the rabbi, I called you a liar."

"So? It's not a sin, to call a man a liar. Listen," Zitomer said, "I was the one who was wrong, not you. I was the one who started to talk about things that you told me in private, about things I didn't have any right to mention. I was the one who was wrong. I thought about it all morning. I was wrong. I lost my head in the argument, because I thought the rabbi was so wrong, so I said the first thing that came to me. But I was wrong to say it. I'm sorry."

The old man looked up from the floor. "Zitomer, they

won't leave me alone! They come all the time, in my room! They even followed me here!"

"You mean the voices?" Zitomer said.

"The voices. And the people. Naomi, Shmuel Yaakov, Smetyanov, Marfa. They come whenever they want to already. And they don't go when I tell them to. I scream at them, I cry, I pray; it doesn't make any difference!"

Zitomer shook his head. "It doesn't sound good. Maybe you should see a doctor?"

"A doctor! What good's a doctor to me?"

"I don't know. Maybe he could tell you what to do."

They both sat, their elbows propping them forward on their thighs.

"Sometimes," the old man whispered, "I feel like stepping out in front of a car, just to get it over with. They're making my life a hell."

Zitomer got up from his chair, crossed the room to the old man, and put a hand on his shoulder.

"Listen, you can't think like that. You can't. That's a real sin, to think that your life is worth so little you can throw it away. Listen, I'm not trying to say that you're not suffering. Believe me, I'm not trying to say that. But you can't give up hope. You can't give up faith. Look. I don't know what to tell you about those voices. I just don't know enough, what can I say? But Rabbi Davis, Rabbi Davis might help."

The old man shook his head. "I talked to Rabbi Davis. This afternoon. He says I shouldn't worry about all the things I did when I was younger. He says everybody makes mistakes. He says God is merciful." The old man buried his face in his hands. "Mistakes," he mumbled. "Mistakes."

Zitomer's hand patted his shoulder. "So he's right. Everybody does make mistakes. And God is merciful. He's right, you should stop worrying."

"Who's worrying? I don't even have time to think any more! They come any time they want to, I don't ask them to come. They just come! And they don't go away when I tell them to!"

Zitomer took his hand from the old man's shoulder and walked slowly toward the back of the store. At the wall, he turned and looked at the old man. Then he walked back to his chair and eased himself into it.

"What can I tell you? About voices, I don't know anything at all. About mistakes; listen, I got plenty. Every day something comes back to me; I remember somebody I treated wrong. And it bothers me, I just can't forget about it. It's true they don't come and talk to me, the people I hurt, but it bothers me all the same. But what can I do? If I worry about what I did wrong every single minute of every day, it wouldn't help me. I couldn't go back and do everything all over again, so I could make sure to do it right. So I try not to worry. Because I still got some years in front of me, and it's important I do as much good as I can, from now on. Instead of worrying about what I did wrong to people before, I try to think about how I can help people now. Because I think Rabbi Davis is right. God is merciful. Maybe he'll understand more than we do, about the things we did that hurt other people. But at least, it's up to him. There's nothing we can do about it."

"I knew that before I came here," the old man said.

"So what can I tell you? I'm no doctor, and I'm no voice specialist. I'm a candy-store owner. And sometimes I think I got an idea how people could live better with each other. So what can I tell you? You got to have faith, that's all I know. Listen, there are millions and millions of us, we can't all be bad people. We got to keep trying to help each other, and we got to have faith. Look at me. My own fellow members are trying to get me arrested, and I'm scared. Scared I'll wind up in jail, scared I'll get fined. But most of all, I'm scared because I can't forgive them. Because I feel bad toward them. Because I can't feel good inside, about what they've done. But I will," Zitomer said, and banged his hand against his knees. "I will. So help me God, in a day or two it won't bother me, what they've done. Just a day or two, I need."

The old man closed his eyes, and when he opened them, Zitomer was back at the pile of shelves. The old man pushed himself to his feet and shuffled across the room to Zitomer. "I must have gone to sleep."

Zitomer looked up. "You did. I was going to wake you, and then I thought, no, I'll let him sleep. But listen, it's late now, it's too late to go home. Why don't you go in the back and sleep in my bed? I'll be up all night with these shelves, anyway. And if I get tired, I can come in and sleep in the armchair. I spent too many nights that way, sleeping in the armchair because I was too lazy to get into bed."

"No. No, I think I'll go home. It's better if I go home."

"You sure? The bed's waiting. I won't use it. And it's clean," Zitomer chuckled.

"No," the old man said. "I'll go home."

"So. It's up to you. But it's cold outside."

Zitomer set the screwdriver on the top shelf and walked with the old man to the door.

"Wait. I forgot. In case you have to pay a fine," the old man said, groping into his good jacket pocket. "Take this. Just in case."

He brought out the crumpled roll of Carl's three ten-dollar bills and handed them to Zitomer. Zitomer unfolded them and stared down at them. Then he handed them back to the old man.

"I can't take it. Thirty dollars. It's too much money."

"Take it. What difference does it make, how much? If they don't fine you, use it for the store. Fix it up."

"I can't. Don't you understand, I can't take it. Thirty dollars is a small fortune; how can I take thirty dollars from you?"

"Because I'm giving it to you. Because I don't want it. Because what difference does it make how much it is, I'm giving it to you. Here, take it. I don't want it."

Zitomer shook his head. "I can't. It's too much. It's not right. I wouldn't feel right."

"Please," the old man said, and he held the bills in the palm of his hand, and extended them to Zitomer. "Please, take the money. I don't want it. It's my son's money. He gave it to me. I don't want it. I can't touch it. If you don't take it, I'll throw it away. I swear I will. I'll throw it away."

Zitomer stood at the door and scratched his head.

"No. I can't. Maybe it's silly, but I can't. If he gave you the money, he didn't give it to you so you could give it to me. I can't take it. I'm not trying to tell you what to do with your son's money, but I know I can't take it. I don't know why, but I can't. It's not right. You should keep the money. You should use it the way he wants you to use it. I can't take it."

The two of them stood in the doorway, and finally the old

man pushed the three crumpled ten-dollar bills back into his pocket. He shuffled out of the doorway onto the sidewalk.

"So," he whispered. "Goodbye."

"Goodbye," Zitomer said, and the old man turned and walked away.

Twenty-three

Carl leans over the washbowl and lets the hot water run over his hands and wrists. The heat courses up his wrists into his arms, and he bends lower over the bowl, curving his arms in under the water. He stares into the mirror guarded by the twin fluorescent lights and thinks that his eyes are a little bloodshot, and maybe there is another line pushing outward from the corner of his mouth.

Dinner went all right, Carl thinks. Millie didn't have much to say, but she didn't look too jumpy, either. Maybe she had a good afternoon.

Good. Carl shuts off the hot water tap and reaches for his towel. He rubs the nap slowly up and down his arms, feeling the weight at the back of his neck spread into a warmth that travels down his shoulders. He throws his head back and then moves it from side to side, almost touching his shoulders.

Christ, he thinks, but I'm tired. Good thing I'm getting to bed before eleven. Dad tires me out more than a day's work.

He folds the towel onto the rack beneath the sink, switches off the fluorescent lights, and takes a last, quick look at himself in the mirror. Good night, he thinks to his face, walks to the door, switches off the overhead light, and steps out into the hall.

A light shines beneath David's door. Carl opens the door softly. David is propped against the headboard, with two pillows folded behind him so that his back is supported as he reads. The bedlamp is almost directly over his head.

"What're you reading?"

David holds up the book so Carl can see the front cover.

The Naked and the Dead, Carl reads. "How many times you read that book?"

David shrugs his shoulders. "I don't know. Three, maybe. Or four. What's the difference?"

"None. I guess. Seems like a lot of times to read one book."

"I like it. Besides, it gets better each time."

"I guess it's a good book then," Carl says. "But it's late, David. It's almost ten-thirty. Time you were asleep. School tomorrow."

"Yeah, I know. Just lemme finish this one chapter. I only got," and David turns the pages, "three—four—five pages to go. That's not long. Five minutes. Then I'll stop and put the light out. Promise."

Carl looks at his son. "Why can't you ever put the book down when I tell you to? Why do we always have to bargain?"

"Oh, Dad."

"All right. Five minutes. Finish the chapter and then put the light out. But don't dawdle over it. And make sure you get right to sleep. Mother says it's harder and harder to wake you in the mornings."

"I will, Dad. Honest. I'll just finish the chapter, that's all."

Carl moves closer to the bed, bends to kiss his son good night, squeezes his shoulder, and moves back again to the door. "Get a good night's sleep. I'll see you tomorrow night."

"Dad," David says, as Carl is about to open the door. "Mom never said anything about Gran'pop."

"I know."

"That mean she's angry?"

"I don't think so," Carl says. "No, I don't think so."

"You going to tell her? About the money?"

"Yes."

The boy stares at his father for a few seconds more, then picks up the book again. "Good night, Dad."

"Good night, David." Carl opens the door, steps out into the hall, and closes it softly.

In his own bedroom the bedlight is also on, but Millie is curled beneath the covers. Carl sets out his wallet, keys, and handkerchief in their precise and usual order on the bureau, runs his hands over his trousers' creases before he slips the trousers onto their hanger. He trades shirt and underwear for pajamas, checks to make sure the clock is set for 7:30, and pulls back the covers on his side of the bed. He clicks off the bedlight and climbs in beside Millie.

"Mmmmhh," Millie mumbles. "David asleep yet?"

"He's just finishing a chapter. He'll turn the light off in another five, ten minutes."

"The Naked and the Dead?"

"Uh huh." Carl squirms under the covers, settling himself on his back.

"How many times has he read that book now?"

"That's what I asked him. He said three. Maybe four. He said it's a good book."

"Sometimes," Millie yawns, "I wonder whether it's right, for him to read books like that. Maybe we should be more strict about what he reads."

"Maybe. But you think it'd work? He can get what he wants in a library without showing it to us. And besides, with all the paperbacks out today, he could save up and buy whatever he wants. We couldn't stop him. We probably wouldn't even know about it."

Millie nods and snuggles under her pillow. "I guess you're right."

Carl lies on his back and stares through the darkness of the room at the Venetian blinds, which Millie has closed again, so that only thin slivers of light from the street lamp across the street slice into the room. Carl lies on his back and goes over his jobs for the next day, and when he has worked himself into Tuesday afternoon, he turns his head toward Millie.

"We had a bad time at Dad's today."

Millie doesn't answer. Carl sees that her head is fairly far under the pillow, and wonders if she has heard. He is about to nudge her when she moves her arm out from under the pillow.

"What happened?" she mumbles.

"A lot. He's feeling pretty bad, so he was upset. I tried to tell him he should go to a doctor, so we argued about that. He used to have a good heavy winter coat, but he's given it away, he says. I tried to tell him it was too cold to walk around only in a sweater and a jacket, so we argued about that. He picked on David a little, and then he got angry at me again. And on the way to the subway we met his rabbi, and we had another argument in front of him."

"What'd he pick on David about?"

"Oh, the usual thing. Wanted to know how often David went to synagogue, whether he laid *tephillin* and all. I said it wasn't fair to ask David, so then he jumped on me. Said it was my fault. Said I was bringing David up to be a *goy*. Said he warned me all this would happen when I left him."

"Same old stuff."

"Yeah. Same old stuff."

A car turns into Belmont Avenue and comes up the block toward the house. Carl watches the headlights play against the blinds, and then the car moves past, and the hum of its engine grows fainter as it moves down the street.

"Does it ever worry you, the way we're bringing David up? You think maybe we're doing something wrong? You think he's not Jewish enough?"

"Oh, Carl, he's Jewish enough, for God's sake. It's bad enough you have to go to see the old man, you don't have to take him seriously."

She's probably right, Carl thinks. Besides, what more could we do with David? He goes to Hebrew school twice a week, and sometimes services on Saturday. We're supposed to make him go more? Or make him get up a half-hour earlier, so he can lay *tephillin*? He's not even thirteen yet.

No, it's silly. We're probably lucky he enjoys Hebrew school. Maybe he'll even keep going after he's *bar mitzvah*. Things are just too different from when Dad was young. It's impossible for him to understand.

Carl turns on his side and closes his eyes. He breathes very deeply, and lets the breath ease slowly out of him. He is almost asleep before he remembers about the money.

"Millie," he calls, softly. "Millie?"

"Uuuuhhmm?"

"I gave Dad some money. So maybe he'd go to a doctor. Or buy a coat. I slipped it into his pocket on the subway platform.

And I went through the turnstile before he had a chance to give it back to me. I was ashamed," Carl says. "It was almost like playing a joke on him. But I wanted him to have the money, and I didn't know how else to do it."

"Waste of money."

"Thirty dollars. I gave him thirty dollars."

"Too much. A waste. He won't use it. Just a waste of money," Millie mumbles.

Carl sighs. "Maybe," he says. "But I couldn't do anything else. I had to give it to him. He needs a doctor and he needs a coat. And God knows what else. Maybe it'll be harder for him not to go to the doctor, with the money sitting in his pocket."

"Uuhhh-hhmmm," Millie says. Carl closes his eyes again. I wish he would spend that money. It wouldn't do him much good, maybe, but I wish he would spend the money. He begins to drift downward into sleep, and wonders briefly whether he will dream again about the old man. Then his toes disappear, and his calves, knees, and thighs. His arms and shoulders are weightless, and finally his stomach curls into a feathery little ball, and Carl is asleep.

Twenty-four

It was after midnight when the old man finally forced open the outer door and stumbled onto the landing. He had tried four times to force his shoulder against the door hard enough so that the door would creak open and ease him inside. But each time the wood bit into his shoulder, and the door refused to budge. Now he stumbled onto the landing and bumped against the bottom stair, fell forward until his hands rested against the steps. He swayed, supported by the arch of his hands and legs, his head lolling in slow half-circles. From his mouth came a thin stream of sound, like a kitten mewing.

The door creaked shut behind him. The old man pushed upward with his arms until he stood on his feet. He swung slowly toward the wall, managed to mount the bottom step, and half lurched, half propelled himself upward, clinging with both hands to the wooden rail of the banister.

He reached the first landing, shuffled across the few feet of flat space, and mounted the second flight of steps. His left pants leg caught on a nail protruding from one of the banister rungs. The old man reached down to try to slip the cloth free. His hand shook as he groped to find the trapped cloth, and he sank down until his knees pressed into the jutting ridges of the steps. He found the nail, but could not slip the cloth free. The nailhead was twisted into the cloth, and the old man's trembling fingers could not work the cloth up and over the nailhead.

He stood up. He grabbed the rail with his left hand and slowly lifted his left leg, so that the cloth would slip up over the nail and come free. He felt a slight pressure, then heard a ripping sound as the cloth caught on the nailhead and tore free. He shook his head and continued up the stairs.

He opened the door to his room and shuffled in. Without bothering to switch on the light, he eased his shoulders back and began to slip off his jacket. His shoulders were stiff with the effort of straining inward to keep a little warmth in his chest during the long walk home from Zitomer's. He felt the sore twinges and the throb as he eased his shoulders back. He slid the jacket off and let it drop onto the kitchen chair. He shuffled to the bed, sat down, and began to slip off his shoes and socks. He could not untie the knot in his left shoelace, so he slipped the shoe off with the knot still tied.

He groped with his left hand for the belt of his trousers, then gave up and sank onto the bed. He rolled and twisted until he was underneath the quilt, and pushed his nose beneath the pillow. He tried to shut his mouth, to stop the thin stream of sound still issuing from his lips. He clamped his teeth together and sucked his lips inward. The room was quiet. Then, from far away, he heard the soft shrieking of Naomi's laughter. Smetyanov's bass rolled softly into his head. The old man moaned and twisted his head beneath the pillow. The laughter grew louder. He shifted on the bed. His left hand was knotted under his stomach, and slow fingers of pain began to move down from his shoulders. He worked his right arm out from under the pillow, and let his right hand fall limply over the side of the bed. He opened his hand, so that Carl's three crumpled ten-dollar bills unfolded themselves from his cramped palm and slipped to the floor. Above the beating of his heart, he heard the steady throb of Naomi's laughter. He heard it for many hours. Toward morning, the old man fell asleep.